The Complete Psychotechnic League

Volume 3

**Baen Books
by Poul Anderson**

The Technic Civilization Saga
The Van Rijn Method
David Falkayn: Star Trader
Rise of the Terran Empire
Young Flandry
Captain Flandry: Defender of the Terran Empire
Sir Dominic Flandry: The Last Knight of Terra
Flandry's Legacy

The Psychotechnic League
The Complete Psychotechnic League, Volume 1
The Complete Psychotechnic League, Volume 2
The Complete Psychotechnic League, Volume 3

The High Crusade

To Outlive Eternity and Other Stories

Time Patrol

To purchase these and all Baen Book titles in e-book format,
please go to www.baen.com.

The Complete Psychotechnic League

Volume 3

POUL ANDERSON

Interstitial Material by Sandra Miesel

BAEN

The Complete Psychotechnic League: Volume 3

"The Acolytes" originally appeared in *Worlds Beyond*, 1951. Reprinted by permission of the Poul Anderson estate.

"The Green Thumb" originally appeared in *Science Fiction Quarterly*, 1953. Reprinted by permission of the Poul Anderson estate.

"Virgin Planet" originally appeared in *Venture*, 1957. Reprinted by permission of the Poul Anderson estate.

"Teucan" originally appeared in *Cosmos Science Fiction and Fantasy*, 1954. Reprinted by permission of the Poul Anderson estate.

"The Pirate" originally appeared in *Analog*, 1968. Reprinted by permission of the Poul Anderson estate.

"Entity" originally appeared in *Astounding*, 1949. Reprinted by permission of the Poul Anderson estate.

"Symmetry" originally appeared as "The Stranger was Himself" in *Fantastic Universe*, 1954. Reprinted by permission of the Poul Anderson estate.

"The Chapter Ends" originally appeared in *Dynamic Science Fiction*, 1953. Reprinted by permission of the Poul Anderson estate.

Baen Publishing Enterprises
P.O. Box 1403
Riverdale, NY 10471
www.baen.com

ISBN: 978-1-4814-8337-7

Cover art Kurt Miller

First Baen printing, July 2018

Distributed by Simon & Schuster
1230 Avenue of the Americas
New York, NY 10020

Printed in the United States of America

10 9 8 7 6 5 4 3 2 1

Contents

Contents

Forward

by Sandra Miesel

With the development of a faster-than-light hyperdrive in 2784, the eight century-long saga of Earthlings in space entered a bold new phase. Previously, slower-than-light craft had crept from star to star, each journey requiring decades, even generations, of travel to complete. But now at last, the whole galaxy lay open to our kind.

Yamatsu's classic history Starward! *may be consulted for details but let us pause here to commend those twentieth century pioneers who first pierced our homeworld's sky. Achieving spaceflight has been called "a tragic era's proudest boast." That our remote ancestors, crushed by three world wars, could still spare enough energy from vital reclamation projects to launch spaceships demonstrates the resilience of the human spirit.*

Moreover, space research was the one great twentieth century innovation that kept its initial promise. Neither the preliminary form of global government established in 1965 nor any succeeding regime was able to guarantee peace and justice. Psychodynamics, the ambitious science by which humanity sought to remake itself, not only failed to attain this goal, its techniques were grossly misused by the Psychotechnic Institute. From age to age, our species has remained indomitable but imperfectible.

Naturally, the pace of extraterrestrial expansion slowed or quickened in response to overall social trends. As our previous volumes have shown,

1

that first idealistic surge of colonization gave way to frustration and then to conflict. In the twenty-second century, anti-scientific Humanism challenged the pro-scientific values of the New Enlightenment, only to be suppressed in its turn following the bloody Revolt of 2170. Afterwards, a precarious balance among factions was maintained well into the twenty-third century.

Given the chronic material and spiritual malaise afflicting the Solar Union, is it any wonder that the stars came to have the same frontier significance that the New World once had for the weary peoples of the Old. Both visionaries and malcontents sought an absolutely fresh start under some other sun. Indeed, the launch of the first Centauri-bound craft in 2126 was as much an experiment in sociodynamics as in astronautics.

Although starflight could not avert that systemwide plunge into ruin known as the Second Dark Ages, it gave the forces of renewal a potent rallying symbol. Just as in the aftermath of World War III, dire sacrifices were made to get Earthlings spaceborne again.

By the twenty-seventh century, improved STL ships ranged the stars once more. Stellar colonies again took root and seeded other colonies in their turn. Some of the communities thus planted grew in curious patterns far removed from the original norm of Solar civilization. The hyperdrive breakthrough meant an end to colonial isolation as well as quicker dispersal of new settlers.

Enthusiastic emigrants did not immediately recognize that transit time and distance scales made their cherished transatlantic analogy imperfect. Whether achieved slower or faster than lightspeed, the very process of interstellar travel itself would change the travelers.

One thing that did not change was humanity's dream of finding a New Eden among the stars. But sometimes colonists assumed too quickly that their dream had come true.

The Acolytes

THE VERY FIRST DAY he was there, Aunt Edith said to him, "Now, Peter, be sure not to leave the grounds alone."

"Why not?" he asked, suddenly wondering if this was going to be as much fun as he had thought. It had been a sort of disappointing trip from Sol, days and days locked inside the metal walls of the spaceship. And the steward had taken his mother seriously and watched him so carefully that it had been just like being back in school. And now this—

"It's just a matter of common sense, Pete," said Uncle Gunnar. "We don't know enough about this planet yet. You could get into trouble. Sure, we'll go everywhere you want, but not alone. Together. No space explorer who rushes off by himself on a new world and gets in a scrape that his friends have to pull him out of is a hero. He's just a bloody fool. You've got more brains than that. First chance I get, I'll show you through the woods—and I'll take my gun along."

That made it different. Wilson Pete was suddenly glad all over to be here—here, on a frontier planet, on his uncle's farm. And Uncle Gunnar was an old explorer himself. He'd been all over the Galaxy before he settled down on Nerthus. He was a huge man, with bright blue eyes in a tanned strong face. His hair and beard were red as fire. And he knew enough to call a fellow "Pete" instead of that sissy "Peter." When you're going on eleven, you like to be talked to man to man.

"Sure," said Pete. "Sure, I'm old enough to know that."

"Fine," said Uncle Gunnar. "After all, this is a pretty big place we've

3

got. You'll have quite a bit to see before you want to explore the woods or the hills. How about a look around now?"

"Oh, that can wait," said Aunt Edith. "You must be tired from your trip, Peter. Don't you want to take a nap first?"

"I'm not tired," said Pete. "It was an easy trip."

He had been a little tired when the spaceship landed at Stellamont, the only city on Nerthus. It was a small place, too, just a cluster of buildings stuck on a broad green plain, not much to look at. But Uncle Gunnar had been there to meet him. They'd gone into the noisy dimness of the *Spaceman's Haven* where he'd had a glass of ambrosite while Uncle Gunnar had a beer, and he'd met a dozen men he only remembered dimly, the men who were pioneering out among the stars. Then they'd gone to the aircar and flown to the farm.

It had been a long ride through a lonely sky, hundreds of kilometers of emptiness rolling beneath them. Not really emptiness—there were the hills and forests and lakes, a seacoast glimpsed from afar, broad valleys with long shadows sliding across them. But no men. Wind and sunlight and murmuring rivers, but no men.

Nerthus was almost disappointingly Earthlike, no moving mountains or columns of fire or glittering alien cities, just the wild green land slipping away beneath a humming aircar. But Uncle Gunnar made it sound interesting enough as he talked.

"There's tomorrow in this world, it belongs to the future," he said. "Man has only been here a few years, there aren't many of us yet, but more are coming in every month. It's going to be one of the great planets of the Galaxy, and we're in on the beginning."

"Aren't there any natives?" asked Pete.

"Not a one. Nerthus is one of the few planets where a man can live without artificial help and have the place all to himself to boot." Uncle Gunnar sighed. "But sometimes I wish there were natives. It'd make matters a lot easier for us."

"How so?" asked Pete. "They couldn't work any better'n your machines, could they?"

"No, though Cosmos knows I could do with a little extra help. Edith and Tobur and I have all we can do to manage a farm the size of ours. But it's a question mainly of ecology. Nerthus may be like Earth basically, and even in rather fine details of biology and chemistry, but still there are some two billion years of independent evolution on the two worlds. Naturally there are differences—and as yet we don't know just what all those differences are.

"Well, just take the obvious examples. How do we know what native foods we can eat and what is poisonous to us? We just have to try everything out first, by chemical analysis or by using Terrestrial animals. Then there are the native animals—which of them can we tame and use, and which are hopeless? The natives could tell us a lot of things we need to know.

"And eventually we have to understand the way the whole planet works, and fit ourselves into it. Little things like the exact composition of the soil, the bacteria in it, the insects that fertilize some plants, the spectral distribution of sunlight—all that will make a big difference in the success of agriculture. We haven't had too much success so far in growing Terrestrial plants on Nerthus, for precisely that reason. They're working in the labs at Stellamont, developing new varieties of staple plants like corn and potatoes—Nerthusian varieties, that will fit in here. It'll be done, too, but it's a big job and it'll take time. Meanwhile, we colonists have to make out the best we can."

Pete nodded. Uncle Gunnar was fun to talk to, though it was hard to follow him sometimes.

Anyway, the trip from Stellamont had been so interesting that Pete wasn't tired any more. He was all on fire to see the place.

"Well, it isn't long till supper," said Aunt Edith. "I suppose you menfolk might as well loaf around for a while."

"Come on, then," said Uncle Gunnar, and he and Pete went outside.

The house was low and white, with a high, peaked roof—on Earth it would have been funny, it looked so ancient, but here it blended with the trees and the sky and the big open fields. As you came out on the front porch, you saw a broad space of turf and wooded clumps, flowers nodding in the breeze, the tall forest beyond. On one side, the fields began, rolling away toward far blue hills, on the other side and toward the rear the lawn sloped off to the farm buildings.

As they walked toward the barn, someone stepped out of it and approached them. Someone—no, something. Pete caught his breath as he saw that it was an alien.

He looked like a short, squat man with very wide shoulders and long arms, but he was completely hairless and his skin was blue. A round, flat-nosed, earless, wide-mouthed head sat on a short thick neck. He wore the usual pouched belt, as well as baggy pants around his bowed legs, and nothing else. Huge eyes that were pools of blackness gleamed at them as he came up and smiled.

"Hello," he said. His voice was deep and heavy, with a funny sort of accent that no human throat could have had.

"Hello, Tobur," said Uncle Gunnar. "This is my nephew, Wilson Pete, who's going to stay with us awhile. You remember I told you about him. His father is an engineer on Earth who's been assigned to a project on Sol VIII. The planet not being fit to live on, Pete's folks have sent him here for the time being. Pete, this is Tobur of Javartenan, my old batman and now the hired man."

"P-pleased to meet you," said Pete uncertainly.

"Likewise, I say," grinned Tobur with an alarming flash of teeth. "How you like here, huh?"

"I—all right, I guess," answered Pete.

"Can you do this?" asked Tobur. He jumped up into the air—*way* into the air—clicked his heels and turned a somersault on the way down, and landed on his hands.

"N-no. Goshell, no."

"Then I winner," said Tobur. "Is custom on Javartenan for winner give prize to loser. Winner pay for glory, you see. So I give you prize. Here, take." He pulled a small knife out of one pouch. "Knife belong Queen of Astafogartistan once, I take after hard battle. Brings luck. Worshiped by natives as god. Keep for souvenir, Pete."

"Thanks! Thanks a googol!" Pete held the knife close. "Thanks, Tobur!"

The alien clapped him on the back. "Is nothing. Friends give presents, no? I have many other souvenirs of battles, sure."

Presently, the three of them went on toward the barn. Uncle Gunnar explained to Pete: "Tobur and I were together for many years. When I finally decided to settle down, he still followed me. We can at least gas over old times."

"But Cosmos, Uncle Gunnar, why did you stop exploring?"

"Oh—a man gets older, Pete. He's not quite up to it any more. And then I met your aunt and decided it was time I got a home of my own. Nerthus was wide open, it offered enough of a challenge for anyone. So we came here, and I've never regretted it."

They came into the cool dusk of the barn, where cows from Earth stood beside native bufoids. Going out the other door they emerged into a big corral where some of the six-legged, greenish-furred native "ponies" were kept.

"We've had pretty good luck taming those," said Uncle Gunnar. "It's handy. There isn't as much machinery available yet as we need, and they can substitute. Also, they can go places and do things that a car or tractor can't—into the woods, for instance."

He reached out and snagged the halter of one. "Here, Pete. I've been saving this one for you. He's yours."

A six-legged pony on an alien planet, an alien ex-spaceman and adventurer for a friend, a whole new world—Cosmos googolplex!

Pete rode around for a while, getting the feel of the animal. The middle pair of legs gave it a funny humping motion that was a little hard to get used to. They went down to look at the orchard and some of the pens, and glanced across the fence at the waving fields of avertigonite. From that plant came avertigon, the anti-space sickness drug, and it was Uncle Gunnar's chief money crop.

"But I'll be pretty busy when the harvest comes in," he said. "The neighbors—" he meant everyone within several hundred kilometers— "pool what machinery and labor they have to reap and thresh it, so I'll have to be away quite a bit. You and Tobur will have to look after Aunt Edith and the farm, Pete."

"We'll do that," promised Pete, swapping a glance with Tobur. The Javartenanian grinned back at him.

The sun was low in the west, filling the air with shining gold and slipping long blue shadows over the ground, when they heard Aunt Edith calling them to supper. "Let's go," said Tobur, smacking his lips, and waddling quickly ahead.

Something tinkled in the high grass, a ripple of little glass bells, sweet and laughing in the gentle sunset air. Pete had a glimpse of a green-furred small thing that skittered away from them, chiming and singing as it danced.

"What's *that?*" he asked, very softly.

Uncle Gunnar shrugged. "We call 'em tinklers," he said. "They're found everywhere hereabouts, making that noise. Don't ask me what they do for a living. Damn nuisance, I think."

Pete stared after the retreating tinkler. It gamboled off, stopping now and then to look after them, and the laughter of bells filled the quiet evening.

They had given him a room to himself, a big cool chamber at the rear of the house, and sent him to bed there not long after supper. He lay for a while thinking of all that there would be to do, thinking about his luck in having Thorleifsson Gunnar for an uncle, thinking about the way he would tell of all this when he got back to Earth. Pretty soon he dropped into a light doze, but it wasn't long before he woke up again and was thirsty.

For a little while, he just lay there, feeling too lazy to get up for a drink. But that only made him more wide awake than before. He looked around the room; it was all black and white with moonglow, the ghostly curtains fluttered in the breeze, and he could hear the faint noises of the night murmuring out there.

Well, sunspots! He wanted some water bad. So he got up and walked across to the door. The floor was cool and hard under his bare feet, and shadows slid around behind and in front of him, and the wind blew in a faint tingle of unearthly smells. Another world! You couldn't even see the sun of Nerthus from Sol's planets—and here he was!

He went quietly down the corridor toward the bathroom and got his drink. As he came out again, he noticed light coming from around the bend in the hall, from the living room, and he heard a low mutter of voices. His aunt and uncle must still be sitting up, talking.

It would be fun to sneak up and listen in, the way the Patrolman had listened in on the Scordians in that stereo. It'd be good practice for the time when he would be having adventures, and shoot, it wouldn't do any harm—He went very softly down the hall and stood just beyond the open living-room door.

"—I still don't think they should have done it," said Aunt Edith.

"Why not?" rumbled Uncle Gunnar's deep voice. "Cathy would naturally want to be with her husband, and you can't have kids along on that devil's planet. They had to send him somewhere, and this is a healthy sort of place for a youngster."

"Oh, Peter is a sweet boy—" Pete's ears burned—"and I'm glad to see him. But this planet healthy? I wonder!"

"What in the Galaxy could be dangerous here?"

"I don't know. That's just the trouble, I don't know. If we did, we could guard against it. But Nerthus is still too much a mystery, Gunnar. Diseases, maybe—"

"Edith, I've told you a million times that the probability of any local germ finding a congenial host in man is vanishingly small. Sure, they did have one epidemic here, of native origin, but that particular thing was soon licked. The chance that another organism can survive a metabolism as alien as ours is so slight that we've got a considerably better prospect of being hit by a meteorite."

"Well—wild animals—"

"Come now, sweetheart, you also know that potentially dangerous life-forms have been eliminated around all our settlements. I haven't seen a large carnivore in the woods here for at least two years now." Uncle Gunnar got up and came across to where she sat; Pete could hear his slow heavy footsteps and feel the floor quivering ever so faintly under them. "Besides, Pete's under orders to stay on the farm grounds, where even you will agree there's no danger. And Tobur will keep an eye on him too."

"Oh, I know it, Gunnar, I know it all. But why have all those other children vanished off farms? What became of them?"

"I don't know. I wish I did. Perhaps there are dangers in the woods that we don't know about. My guess is their parents got careless and let them go off alone. That's not going to happen with Pete. Now for Cosmos' sake, honey, stop worrying—"

Pete stole back toward his room, not caring to listen any more. He felt a little mad about it—as if he couldn't take care of himself! But he'd obey orders like a good spaceman, if only to save the folks from worry and himself from a licking.

As he got back into the room, he heard a noise from outside. He went to the window and leaned out.

It was a strange, magic scene, a fairyland of streaming moonlight and whispering trees and unknown constellations. There were two moons in the sky, pouring their cold silver light down over the grass to glitter in the dew, throwing weird double shadows of trees. One moon was so close you could almost see it move, could almost see its shadows crawling like live things, as if the world stirred restlessly in its sleep. The stars flashed and gleamed high overhead, sprawling in new figures. Only the pale flood of the Milky Way looked the same.

The night murmured. Pete knew the nights of Earth and their noises, out in the silence far from man—buzz of insects, chirp of crickets, hoarse croaking of frogs, a million little sounds all blending into one great quiet voice. Nerthus had its language too, but it wasn't Earth's; all the tiny parts of it were different and they added up to a strange whisper, the voice of an alien world.

Insects were there, thrumming and humming. Something was singing, a sweet liquid trill running up and down the scale, and something else screamed harshly, far away in the woods and swamps. There was a far-off pattering like the rapid thunder of a small drum, there was a shrill scrape as of metal, there was brief maniac laughter, there was hooting and hissing and chuckling and bubbling, all at the very edge of hearing. And—something else—

Yes, there it came again. Pete remembered now, harked back to the thing which had chimed and laughed at him in the sunset.

It came bobbing and dancing out of the shadows and the forest, jumping, bouncing, swatting after the elfin lamps of night-glowing insects, and a million little bells came with it. Pete listened, straining out the window, enchanted by the night and the music.

He couldn't see the tinkler very well. It was a dim whiteness in the shifting, tricky moonlight, a small thing that danced under his window and called to him to come out and play. But he could hear it, the bells came high and sweet now.

They were like silver sleigh-bells on a frosty night, like a sunlit rain-shower, like the laughter of young girls. It was a rush of chiming, a pizzicato on a string of glass, gay and joyous and drunken with life. *Come out, come out, come out*—come out and run in the moonlight with me!

"No," said Pete all at once, and yawned. He was sleepy. Some other time, maybe. Perhaps Tobur would come along—somehow, he didn't think the bells of Faerie would chime for Uncle Gunnar, but Tobur might understand.

After all, grownups thought the tinklers were just a nuisance. They came dancing around the house of nights and spoiled your sleep with their wistful laughter. You had to listen to them—

Tobur leaned back more comfortably against the wall of the shed. "—and there was I," he went on. "Spacesuit leaking, poison air and minus two hundred degrees all around, natives after me—"

"Gollikers!" whispered Pete.

They sat in the shade, letting dinner settle inside them while a hot early-afternoon sun danced and glimmered beyond and the air was drowsy with humming bugs. Tobur had another story to tell.

The being from Javartenan was always ready to drop what he was doing and talk to a fellow, always glad to make some little thing for you or show you how to do a job in the best and easiest way, letting you help him so you could learn. And he was even more fun to listen to than Uncle Gunnar, with his odd accent and his exciting stories. He'd told Pete a lot in the last few days.

Of course, when you considered how Uncle Gunnar had taken him from Javartenan as a servant to begin with, and how they'd been together ever since, it was funny how many adventures he'd had all by himself, how many planets he'd been on that Uncle Gunnar never mentioned—but Cosmos, he was sure a fine storyteller and he wouldn't lie to a fellow.

"Well, what I do?" said Tobur now. "There I was, trapped 'gainst cliff of frozen nitrogen, spacesuit leaking, powerpack near gone, blaster 'most empty, and all those hundreds of natives coming up at me. What I do? I give up Sacred Jewel of Pashtu? Save my life that way?" He looked hard at Pete.

"Cosmos, what else could you do but surrender?" asked Pete, since that was the answer Tobur seemed to expect.

"And betray trust in me? Go back on oath? Not Tobur! Die is little thing, small Pete, but honor much. Also, I began to have idea. I began thinking mighty hard there, you bet. I had Jewel to defend, near out of blaster charges, but still plenty brains, yes. I—"

"Tobur!"

The Javartenanian started guiltily as Uncle Gunnar's voice bellowed through the still air.

"Tobur! Where in the name of Valdaoth are you—Oh, there!" Uncle Gunnar came around the corner of the shed and saw them. His cold blue eyes flashed under his bristling red eyebrows.

"Loafing again, huh? I told you we had to get that bottom land fenced in before the harvest starts. Which means today. Where's the truck? What've you been doing besides sitting on your fat tail?"

"Been watching small Pete like you told me," said Tobur sulkily.

"Nothing to stop you working while you did, was there? Now get up and help me, or before Cosmos I'll bounce you out of here. Up!"

Tobur rose, scowling, and slouched into the shed. Uncle Gunnar lingered behind with Pete to whisper with a twinkle: "He's a good old cuss, but if I didn't blow my top once in a while and yell at him, he'd never get anything done." He added, "You might as well come with us and watch."

"All right," said Pete, though he was a little mad himself at being pulled out of the shade and having the story broken off that way. Now Tobur would be too grouchy to finish it for the rest of the day.

They went into the shadowy cavern of the shed after the truck. Machinery filled it, the semirobot machinery that made it possible for three beings to run this enormous place alone. But most of the things still needed intelligent beings at the controls; Uncle Gunnar couldn't afford too many automatics yet.

The truck had a small plastic cab and a long flat back. Tobur had the sides off by now, and he and Uncle Gunnar grunted as they lifted the fencing machine up and bolted it in place. They racked as many of the metal posts as they thought they'd need on it, added three big rolls of wire, and got into the cab. Pete said he'd rather ride in back.

So they bounced off over the fields, around trees and low hillocks, till the house was out of sight and they reached the bottom land. This was a forty-hectare patch of low-lying meadow on the edge of the great forest, covered with high lush grass that rippled in a faint wind. Uncle Gunnar wanted to make a pasture of it.

"I'll drive for a while and you guide the machine, Tobur," he said. "Pete, keep in sight of us."

It was fun to watch at first. The truck went slowly along the boundary, while the machine rammed down a long spike to make a hole, drove in the post, tamped down the earth around it, and strung three taut lines of wire, all in one dazzle of metal arms. Tobur had to walk alongside the truck, guiding the rammer and the post-setter. Pete brought up the rear.

But it got tiresome after a while, the same thing over and over again, and the day was warm and quiet, not meant for working. Pete yawned and lagged.

"I'll spell you there," said Uncle Gunnar presently.

"No need. Not tired," said Tobur, still sulky. Uncle Gunnar shrugged and drove on.

Pete sat down on a hummock and looked around him. From here

you couldn't see the house. There was just the meadowland, sloping upward toward the cultivated fields on one side. On the other side was the forest. It was very still and lonely.

He lay down, feeling the soft turf give under his weight like a mattress. He crossed his hands under his head and looked upward. Tall white clouds walked through a sky of far clear blue, the sun wheeled on its slow horizonward way, the grass whispered and rustled around him, there was a drowsy murmur and buzz in the air. For a while, he picked shapes out of the clouds, a spaceship, a horse, a robot, Uncle Gunnar with his nose getting longer—He giggled and looked around him.

Only, the grass waving above his head, its smell rich and green and not quite like the smell of grass on Earth. There was a little patch of wild flowers too, blue as if they were fallen pieces of sky, sweet and nose-tickling in their scent. An insect flew past his face with its wings a million colored shards of broken sunlight. Somewhere a bird was singing.

Pete wriggled deeper down into the grass and the earth and the summer warmth.

All of a sudden, he heard the bells again, very near, high and thin and sweet. He sat up and looked wildly around.

The truck was far down the line, almost out of sight behind a jutting neck of trees. Otherwise he couldn't see anything—no, wait—

Pete sat very still, hardly breathing, and in a moment the tinkler came into view. It was no bigger than a rabbit, fat and pale-green and fuzzy, with little black eyes that twinkled merrily. It skipped around him, twitching its nose and going *ding-ding-ding* and then breaking into a rain of crystal chiming.

Pete thought back to what he'd asked Uncle Gunnar about the tinklers the first morning after he'd seen one. What were they, where did they come from, why did they make that noise and how?

"Nobody knows, or cares very much either, Pete," Uncle Gunnar had said. "There are a lot of them, running around all over this part of the continent. I shot and dissected one once to find how its vocal organs work—a matter of tympani and vibrating strings—but it wasn't very good eating and its hide was too thin to be useful either. So now I just let them alone."

"You shouldn't 'a killed it, Uncle Gunnar," said Pete, shocked. "That's like shooting a—an elf."

"Sure, an elf," put in Tobur. "And there a big old troll in the woods too, and fairy castles. I know."

"You know too damn many things, Tobur," said Uncle Gunnar. "No, this is just another little animal."

"But what do the tinklers do?" Pete asked.

"I don't know," said Uncle Gunnar. "They have the teeth and digestive system of meat-eaters, but they're too small and weak to kill anything for themselves, and in fact I should think a fat juicy tinkler would be in some danger from carnivores itself. Especially with that silly music it makes—you can hear it half a kilometer away. Offhand, I should think they eat carrion, and reproduce like fury to keep up their numbers and keep their natural enemies fed."

That was all, except that Pete had seen them often, and heard them still more often, and never had a close look at one—till now.

He sat still, not daring to move, and pretty soon the tinkler quieted down and crouched less than a meter from him, wiggled its impudent nose and twinkled with its eyes.

"Hello," whispered Pete. "Hello, there."

The tinkler skipped to its feet and let go a happy carillon.

"Come here," said Pete. "Come here, fella. I won't hurt you."

The tinkler danced closer. Almost, Pete's outstretched hand touched it, the whiskers brushed his fingers, and then it was away and laughing at him.

Pete had to laugh too. He got up, very softly and slowly so as not to scare it. The tinkler waited for him and then skipped another meter away.

He walked slowly toward it. The tinkler wriggled with delight and jumped over the wild hedge at the boundary of the woods.

Without thinking, Pete followed it in under the trees. It danced close to him, brushed its soft nose against his leg, and then before he could grab it was off again, deeper into the forest.

Pete hesitated, looking around him. He wasn't supposed to go in here—

The trees stood tall around him, their trunks reaching up and up to a whispering vaulted roof of green and gold. It was cool and shadowy under them, speckled with sunlight and small bright flowers.

A bird was trilling its gladness, and only the faint rustle of leaves answered it through the quiet—that, and the happy peal of elfin bells as the tinkler came back to Pete.

It circled around him, chiming and dancing, a little figure of laughter. It wanted him to follow it—yes, there it went, off again, stopping to look back over its shoulder at him.

Well, gollikers, it wouldn't hurt to go just a ways onward. Maybe it wanted to show him something. And it was nice here in the woods.

The bells chimed eagerly as Pete started off. The tinkler came back, nudged him, bounded in a gleeful circle around his feet, and shot away into the farther shadows.

He trudged on for a while under the trees. It was like an enchanted forest, cool and dim and green, little spots and shafts of sunlight streaming down to pick out mossy rocks and colored fungi, and flowers hiding under fallen logs. Once in a while, a strange thing would streak off from his path, and there was a sudden rush of birdsong as he approached a gnarled old tree. Cosmos, what could go wrong in here, what were the grownups afraid of?

The tinkler bounded eagerly ahead, shaking sound out of its throat like a snowstorm turned to music, stopping now and then to look after him and wait for him with a shivering impatience. *Come on, Pete, come on, come on!*

But where was it going, anyway, what was it leading him to?

The notion came suddenly to Pete, so suddenly that he stopped in his tracks with the awe and amazement of it. Why, sure—sure—that could be it—what else could it be?

Nerthus *wasn't* uninhabited, and man wasn't alone on it. There was a native race, a race of little furry elves who spoke in silver chimes, only the humans who roared out of the sky in their great steel ships frightened them. They hid away, deep in the shadowy quiet of their forests, they waited and watched—

Intelligent life!

And *he* had discovered it!

He hurried after his guide now, running, scrambling over logs and dodging past thickets. The tinkler darted ahead, a white streak in the shades; you'd never have thought the fat little fellow could move that quick. But when it saw he couldn't keep up, it stopped and waited.

Pete had to slow down after a while. He was panting and his

heartbeat was loud in his ears. But he still shivered with the excitement of his tremendous discovery.

Sure, the tinklers were intelligent. Why else would this one be so plainly guiding him on? Intelligent, with a dancing, joyous, fairy mind that sang like its voice, a mind of moonlight and magic remote from the slow ponderous brain of man. They had been frightened, they had hidden away, but had spied out the newcomers simply by pretending to be animals. And now they had decided the time was ripe to reveal themselves.

Only they wouldn't approach just anybody. It had to be someone they could trust, someone who would understand. A human who could tell them about his race with an insider's viewpoint, and who could still feel the way they did, keep their secrets, act as a go-between—a kid. Sure!

Wilson Pete, first ambassador of man to the tinklers of Nerthus!

He went on, deeper and deeper into the woods, and the tinkler rang and pealed and leaped before him. And what was it saying in its own strange language?

Welcome, Pete, welcome to Nerthus and the Old Dwellers, welcome to the realms of Faerie.

Another tinkler popped out of the dripping underbrush. The two of them gamboled together, darted back toward Pete, and ran on, tinkling furiously. Two of them—! Why, that must mean he was approaching their village.

It couldn't be far now. They'd lead him into the ring of little thatch houses; the whole population would swarm out in joy, torches and fireflies would bob and flare in the dark. They'd dance around him, singing their songs of welcome to the stranger from the stars, they'd bring him food in a golden dish and put him to bed on sweet-smelling moss. And when he came back next day with his tremendous news, the folks would forget they were mad at him.

The ground squished under his feet. Shadows were rising out of the earth, shadows and a thin steaming mist. He stumbled over logs and splashed into pools. Two more tinklers came out of the deeper darkness and frolicked around him.

They sure picked a nasty swamp to live in. Only maybe they had to do that, for protection from their enemies. Pete groped his way on, too weary to think straight any more. He only wanted sleep,

The sun was down now, darkness was whelming the world, but a last sullen ember glowed red between the trees. As he came out on the bank of the lake, it gleamed like a pool of blood.

He couldn't see far over it. The water was thick and scummy, and trees and hummocks grew out of it. He plodded squashily along the muck of the bank, feeling a little ill from the dank smell of swamp and rot. The fog was thickening, swirling its tendrils around him. Here and there, phosphorescent fungi glowed blue in the murky twilight. The tinklers led the way, dancing and skipping over the dreary mudbanks—there was a whole crowd of them, pushing and jostling, swarming about him. Their belling filled the heavy air with a harsher note than he had heard before.

Something stirred, out there in the crimson water. Pete couldn't see very well what it was. But after a moment, he made out a vague bulk by the shore, something looming and dark and misshapen. A dead stump? A small hummock? A—

The tinklers darted all around, shoving, crowding, pushing him now, and their eager noise drowned his thoughts. Only—they were urging him toward that thing—

Suddenly, Pete didn't want to go any farther. He stopped, and his heart was like a lump in him. "No," he gulped. "No."

The tinklers swarmed around, thrusting him on by their weight, and the last red light glistened on their eyes and their little sharp fangs.

Something closed around Pete's ankle, cold and hard and rubbery. He screamed. The tinklers danced with glee, *ting-ting-ting-a-ting-ting!*

The monster's tentacle dragged Pete through the mud, up toward the beak that snapped and grinned in its black lump of a body. He screamed and screamed. Help, help, help, Uncle Gunnar, Mother, help, help, *wake me up*—

It slid from the bank and pulled him under water. He drew a breath to howl and the rotten water rushed in, filled his lungs, his head roared and swam and whirled down into darkness, down and down and down.

Something else, a hand closing around his arm, a wild moment of struggle—Pete kicked out, lashing in a crazy howling darkness of thunder and horror, and then he was gulping air into his lungs, coughing and choking with fire in his chest.

* * *

He came to himself on the bank, and Uncle Gunnar's shape, huge and dark in the gloom, was holding him. He screamed and shuddered himself against the man's breast.

"There, Pete." The deep voice sobbed, vibrating through his shivering body. "All right, fella, it's all right now—"

Something of his training in self-integration came back, psycho-physiological habits, a shaking sort of calm. He huddled in his uncle's arms and watched where the lake roiled and bubbled.

"Why did you do it?" groaned the man. "Why did you do it? We trailed you as soon as we saw you were gone, Tobur and I, we followed you and guessed our way and came here in time to see that thing dragging you under water—but *why?*"

"The—t-t-t-tinkler—"

"What?"

"The-the t-t-t-tinkler—it led me—I th-thought it w-w-was intel—" Pete began crying.

"So—" Uncle Gunnar's voice was soft and cold and terrible. "So that's it. That's how they live. When we arrived, a whole pack of the little fiends was crouched on the bank, watching—

"They lure animals out here, carnivores, curious ones, and then that thing in the water kills the prey and shares with them—Maybe that's where some of those other kids went, to that devil's symbiosis—Tobur!" The last word was wrenched out of him.

"T-tobur?" whispered Pete.

The lake seethed and churned with struggle. "He's down there, fighting it," said Uncle Gunnar. "He leaped after you, got you free—passed you over to me, and then the monster dragged him under—He's fighting for his life down there, and I can't go help him. If the thing got both of us, there'd be no one to take you home. I can't help him, oh Cosmos, I can't help him!"

They sat waiting for a long time as night closed in on the swamp. Once a little bell tinkled in the dark. Pete screamed and huddled against Uncle Gunnar.

The man swore softly, brokenly.

The lake quieted. In the last gleam of light, Pete thought he could see blood on its surface.

Nothing came out of it.

Uncle Gunnar stood up. "I'm going down," he said in a harsh, strange voice. "Wait here. I'll be right back."

He stepped into the lake and his head went under. Pete shivered on the bank and tried not to scream. Another little chime pealed, he clutched the muddy ground with his hands and held his jaws shut with all the strength that was in him.

Uncle Gunnar came up again and waded back to shore. He moved slowly and wearily, like an old man, and flopped down as if all the strength had gone from him.

"They're both dead," he whispered. "I felt them down there. Tobur knifed it to death, but it broke his neck in the last struggle. They're both dead." Suddenly he rolled over and buried his face in his hands.

"Oh, Tobur, Tobur, you old windbag, it's going to be an empty world without you!"

Pete sat very quiet, for he had never seen a man cry before.

If fair is sometimes foul, is the reverse also true? How can humans distinguish friend from foe on such a beguilingly beautiful world as Nerthus?

The Green Thumb

PETE FELT SO BAD about Tobur getting killed on his account that Uncle Gunnar and Aunt Edith were afraid at first they'd have take him to a psychiatrist in Stellamont. But they finally talked him around.

"It wasn't your fault, Pete," Uncle Gunnar said again and again. "It was just one of those things. How could you know—or anyone know—that the harmless little tinklers were bait leading to that thing in the swamp? Maybe you shouldn't have gone off by yourself, but we should have kept an eye on you too—" And so on for days, meanwhile always behaving so Pete could be sure he meant what he said. Uncle Gunnar was really swell.

"We just don't know enough about this planet," he kept saying. "People—" he meant nonhumans like Tobur, too— "are going to die because of storms and earthquakes and wild beasts; disease and poison; and every other way they can die, here on Nerthus and on a thousand other worlds, till we get to know them. Till we understand the whole of a geology, and an ecology different from Earth's, in the million big and little ways that some two billion years of separate evolution can create. It's the price we pay. Because Tobur died, we now know what a menace the tinklers represent—we can save some of those children who kept disappearing as you did, Pete—we're just a little more secure on this planet. Sure, I'll miss him; all my life I'm going to miss his ugly old face—but he didn't die for nothing."

So Pete's visit stretched on some more.

It was hard to think that so beautiful a planet as Nerthus could kill people. Nerthus was almost another Earth. Sunlight spilled out of a high blue sky over plains and hills and shining rivers; woods rustled and whispered; the long, sad winds blew over more kilometers of loneliness and peace than a man could imagine. There weren't many colonists here yet—Stellamont was the only town—not a very big one either—and the farms were sprinkled thinly. When you had an aircar and a televisor, you weren't far from anyone in time, but your neighbor was still far off in space and the nights were big and lonely.

So Pete was surprised when Joe came walking in.

It happened one afternoon when he was alone in that fifty-hectare stretch of forest and lawn which they called the front yard. Aunt Edith was in the house, which Pete could glimpse through the trees; and Uncle Gunnar was working in back somewhere repairing one of the semirobot machines. Pete had grown tired of watching him and had wandered off to where he was now—flat on his stomach watching a colony of formicoids making one of their big nests.

Joe came very quietly. Suddenly he just was there, a shadow falling athwart the streaming sunlight, tall and thin and not moving. Pete looked up and gulped a little and felt his heart speed up. This was an alien.

"H-hello," he said, getting to his feet.

"How do you do," said the stranger. He spoke Terran with the flat perfection that showed he had learned it by psychophonic means; his only accent was what the shape of his vocal apparatus forced on him, a hissing lisp you could barely hear.

Pete looked him up and down. He wasn't human, nor did he belong to any other race Pete had ever heard of. But there are so many races knocking around the Galaxy these days—with more being discovered all the time—that nobody pretends to know them all.

He was very tall, about two-point-three meters, with long legs and a skinny frame—classifiable as "humanoid" except that he had four arms, one pair smaller than, and below, the other. His head was big and round, with long pointed ears and large, yellow eyes—between which were the noseless nostrils, and above which waved two feathery antennae. Except for a pouched belt, he was naked, but sleek greenish fur covered his whole body. He looked sort of like a Vashtrian or maybe a Kennacor, but he wasn't.

"Who are you?" asked Pete. Then he remembered his manners—after all, he was going on eleven—and said: "Pardon. I am Wilson Pete of Sol, and this place belongs to my uncle Thorleifsson Gunnar. Can I help you?"

"Perhaps so," said the stranger. "I understand your uncle is looking for an assistant."

Now Uncle Gunnar *did* need somebody pretty badly. Even with all the automatics and semirobots he had, one man just couldn't run a place this size alone. After Tobur's death, he had put an ad on the telecast for a hired hand, but he hadn't expected much result. Labor was still scarce on Nerthus, and what new men did arrive generally went to work in Stellamont at fancy wages. So—Cosmos rocketblast, this was luck!

"You bet he does," said Pete. "Come on!" And he ran on ahead, the stranger's long legs keeping up without hurrying.

They found Uncle Gunnar perspiring and oily in the machine-shed. He looked up, wiped the sweat off his red-bearded face, and said a polite hello. When he heard that the newcomer wanted to work for him, his eyes lit up; but he only nodded. "Come on in and talk about it," he suggested.

So they went into the house, and Uncle Gunnar peeled off his greasy clothes—as any sensible person did on warm day like this. Aunt Edith was surprised to see the alien; she wasn't used to nonhumans the way an old space-explorer like Uncle Gunnar would be, and she didn't quite know how to behave. But the stranger didn't seem to mind.

Uncle Gunnar hesitated when it came to introductions. "I am from Astan IV," said the newcomer. "My designation—well, call me Joe."

"Astan IV—can't say I've ever of it," said Uncle Gunnar. "Newly discovered?"

"Not quite. Galactic explorers landed several years ago. But being, on the whole, a race without much interest in technology or foreign adventure, we have remained obscure. I am one of the few of us who really cares to see what the Galaxy and its civilization are like. So I am working my—it is the best way to learn." Joe's voice was very gentle and quiet, and there was something in his luminous eyes which Pete liked.

"Why didn't you stay at Stellamont to work? You could earn more money there than I can pay you," said Uncle Gunnar.

"I have seen other colony-towns; they are very much alike. This time I wanted an insight into colonial life itself—also, a chance to rest from confining mechanical environments. I heard your advertisement and walked over here."

"From Stellamont? Through unexplored forest? That's a several weeks' walk; I haven't had the ad that long."

"Oh, a colonist gave me a ride part of the way. The forest does not frighten me; it is friendly. My home world is forested."

"Well—" Uncle Gunnar scratched his head. You could see he was wondering whether to take a chance on an alien who might not be any use at all—who might even be a fugitive from the law. But he did need help a lot, and Joe was so nice and soft-spoken.

"Well—blazes, why not?" Uncle Gunnar smiled. "We'll see how it works, Joe. Sit down and rest a while. Edith, where in space is that whisky?"

The hired man didn't really go to work till the next morning, but Uncle Gunnar spent a while the evening before showing him around. Pete tagged along with his eyes popping. This would be something else to tell the kids about when he got back to Earth. "There was a real alien working for us. He came from so far away that even my uncle had never heard of his planet, and he had four arms and no nose and we called him Joe."

They went down to the animals. Uncle Gunnar had only a few from Earth—a couple of cows, some pigs and chickens. He was more interested in taming the native life, and had had pretty good luck with a couple of the six-legged mammalian species. There were some "steers" that were good for meat and leather; some "ponies" that could be ridden through the woods where a car or tractor wouldn't go, and he was working with the winged, four-legged fowl, too.

"A lot of the colonists here are importing all their stuff—animals and plants alike—and trying to raise them as if Nerthus were Earth," he explained. "It won't work. We can't put them into a wholly different ecology without a long period of careful breeding. Little things will affect them: certain insect bites poison them; the grass and soil don't have quite the right composition; trace elements are missing—the result is poor stock. Look at those cows of mine, for instance. Runty, and that in spite of my buying feed from Earth to supplement their diet. But the native critters are all fat and sassy.

"We have to use cut and try, figuring out what species it will be practical to domesticate. It took man on Earth a long time to find out that the horse and the wild cow could be tamed, while the bison and the zebra could not—but the result was worth waiting for. Man won't ever be really at home on Nerthus till he's become part of it himself,"

The cows stamped and rolled their eyes in the gloom of the stable; Joe made them a little nervous. But the native animals stood quietly. Some tiny difference in smell, no doubt.

"But can man. your race, eat native foods without suffering from the same deficiencies?" asked Joe.

"That's a good question," said Uncle Gunnar. "It's one of our major problems. First, of course, we have to find out what plants and flesh are actually poisonous to us—that's a matter for chemical analysis, or for experiment with animals from Earth. Then we have to learn what vitamins, minerals, and trace-elements we need are lacking in the food we can eat. At present, we supplement our diets with tablets containing the missing factors, and that works well enough. But ultimately we have to change some of the native stock—by mutation and selective breeding—and we ourselves will have to change to a certain degree, too. The latter will accomplish itself in a few generations.

"We're an adaptable breed, and everyone born here will change just a little bit because of the differences acting on him from conception onward. Natural selection will change the heredity—say in the course of a thousand years or so. Nobody will die, but those people whose heredity is a little better adapted to Nerthus will have more children."

"So that ultimately you will become—Nerthusians," said Joe.

"That's right. Just as man colonizing other worlds will adapt to them. Just as man, back on Earth, adapted racially to different environments. The old Eskimos, for instance, got so they could be perfectly healthy on a straight meat diet. The Kalahari Bushmen became able to drink brackish water, and little enough of that, and developed a water-storing steatopygia." Uncle Gunnar had quite a library on the subject of adaptation.

"And there is no native race here?" asked Joe.

"Intelligent life? No. This planet was checked pretty thoroughly for such beings before it was opened to colonization, and no sign was found. No villages; no artifacts; not even stone tools. It'd have been nice if there had been natives; they could have told us a lot of things we've had to find out for ourselves. But then, if there had been aborigines the law would have forbidden colonization."

"That is a—humane attitude."

"Also a sensible one. In the early days, men did settle on planets with primitive native races. It only led to conflict in which man, though always the victor, often paid a heavy price. And the worst of it was, that once colonization was begun it couldn't be stopped; you can't evacuate people who've built their lives in a certain place. The struggle just had to continue until some compromise—not very satisfactory to either side—could be worked out."

Joe nodded, slowly, his eyes shining in the half-darkness with strange yellow lights.

In the next few days, it became pretty plain that Joe just wasn't any good with machinery. He tried, but he only made a mess of things; he never could learn the simplest principles of repair and maintenance. He was all thumbs and muttering awkwardness. When he drove a truck or tractor, he got tensed up till you'd think he would explode, and the machine veered off to one side and snarled at his handling.

But it was another story with the animals and the plants. He could make the ponies—still half-wild—do things no one else had dreamed of. He had them hauling carts without a driver, coming when he whistled, and standing quiet while he curried their gleaming greenish-gray hides. He went into the woods and came back with a basketful of grasses which the fowl gobbled up: they began to get fat so quick you could almost see the flesh building. When Uncle Gunnar asked Joe how he knew about that, he shrugged.

"We of Astan IV live closer to wild nature than your people," he said. "Now I knew your fowl ordinarily live in certain meadow areas; I noticed that on my way here. It occurred to me that their natural food would be some plant common in such regions, so I looked for types which would probably be nutritious."

He studied the garden, and the orchard and the fields, too, and came up with some funny ideas. "Plant some of this," he said, holding up a small blue flower, "with your native grain; you will have a better yield."

"Why so?" asked Uncle Gunnar. "It's just a weed."

"Yes, but it is always found growing side-by-side with the wild prototypes of the grain. I suspect there is a symbiosis of some kind; try it, anyway."

Uncle Gunnar shrugged, but let Joe sow some of the flowers in a field. It wasn't long before you could see that the grain there was healthier than anywhere else.

"Joe must belong to an odd race," said Uncle Gunnar. "They're morons where it comes to mechanical things, but they have a feel for living systems which we humans will never match."

"Maybe our race could use some of it," said Aunt Edith. She had grown quite fond of Joe—especially when he found a mixture of grass and clay which could be worked into baskets and pottery. She didn't like the plastic stuff they made at Stellamont, and imports from Earth cost too much.

"Every species to its own strength," answered Uncle Gunnar. "I've seen races like his—here and there in the Galaxy—living in so close a symbiosis with nature that they never had to develop any mechanical technology. But they weren't the less intelligent for that. Still—the machine-minded races, like ours, have their part to play, too."

Pete wandered out, looking for the hired hand. He found him setting out native lycopersiconoid plants in the garden. They had good berries, but humans had never been able to grow them. Joe had brought some back from the Woods and they grew all right for him.

"He just has a green thumb," Aunt Edith said, smiling.

"Or else," suggested Uncle Gunnar, "one of our hormones, excreted in very small quantities through the skin, kills the seeds—and Joe's metabolism doesn't include that hormone."

The alien looked up and his mouth twisted in the wry way that was his smile, "Hello, Pete," he said.

"Hello," said Pete, hunkering down beside him. "Aren't you tired?"

"No," said Joe, going on with his work; his hands were swift and gentle among the frail stems. "No, this I like. Sunshine and open air and the sweet smell of life—how can one grow weary?" He shook his big round head. "How can you shut yourselves away from life, you humans?"

Joe didn't come into the house much, except for meals. He slept outside, under a tree—even when it rained.

"Oh, a spaceship is all right," said Pete.

Joe shuddered a little. He raised his eyes again, sweeping the broad horizon and the whispering, sun-dappled forest. "And would you really make this world over?" he asked. "Would you really cut down the trees and wound the earth with mines and shut away the sky with cities?"

"Well, not too much, I guess," said Pete. "Earth is pretty woodsy these days too. But o' course, there'll be a lot more people here, and they'll have to build and plant."

"I know a little of your god," said Joe. "Your all-pervading primordial Cosmos, whom you do not even pretend to understand. That is a machine god, Pete—a mathematician's god. Have you ever wondered if there might not be other gods, if the old spirits of a land might not have something to say?"

"I don't know," mumbled Pete. Sometimes Joe talked oddly.

"Out in the cold great dark of space, between the flaming suns, one might know Cosmos," said Joe. "Awe and wonder and impersonal magnificence—yes. But it is in the forests and the rivers and the small winds that my gods live—gods of life, Pete, not of flame and vacuum. Little gods, maybe, concerned with a tree or a flower or a dreaming brain—not with meaningless hugeness; not with a universe which is mostly incandescent gas. But I still think that on the last day my gods will speak louder."

Pete didn't know what to answer. He thought maybe Joe was afraid men would settle on Astan IV, so he said quickly, "You got your own planet; nobody's ever going to take it away from you. Man won't, and he won't let anyone else do it either."

"Perhaps not," agreed Joe. "But I wonder. Even with the best intentions in the universe, you could conquer other races—not physically, but by sheer dominance, forcing them to imitate your ways or become insignificant. If we started having mines and factories on our own world—even if the mines were our own—it would never be the same planet again, and we would not be the same race. We would have chosen an alien destiny."

"What's Astan IV like?" asked Pete.

"Oh—like Nerthus. Wild and open and almost empty. There aren't many of us, but we like room. I can't explain very well."

"Were you ever on Earth?"

"No, nor on any of the great worlds of the Galaxy. I simply worked my way along the odd trade-lanes, seeing obscure and backward planets. I fear I would have little of interest to tell you."

"Oh." Pete was disappointed. Uncle Gunnar was full of stories about his travels, and so had Tobur been. Joe was nice, but he wasn't as much fun as Tobur.

"In fact," said Joe, "I will be the one to ask questions. I came to learn, since I have all too little to teach—or, rather, men would never listen to anything I tried to teach. How many humans are there, all in all?"

"Gosh, I dunno. I don't think anybody does; they're spread over so many worlds. But lemme see—" Pete thought back to what he had learned in astrography or from books and films or from listening to grownups talk. Before long, he was telling Joe all he knew, while the alien nodded and asked questions. It was the first time Pete had ever explained things to anyone except a littler kid, and he nearly burst with the importance of it.

"I see," said Joe. "It is a very loose arrangement, and Nerthus has little direct contact with Earth. But tell me, Pete; if Earth's civilization is as satisfactory as you say, why do men come here at all? What can they gain by it?"

"Oh—different things, I guess. A lot of settlers never were on Earth; they were born on other planets, and haven't ever been conditioned to the setup at home. They wouldn't be very happy living there, you got to grow up in an integrate civilization to like it."

"Those are big words for a boy of your age," smiled Joe.

"I don't understand it all," admitted Pete. "But they say I will someday. Well, anyway, there are people who like lots of room, and people who want to be doing something different all the time, and—oh, all sorts of people."

"But what economic motive is there? There is little outside trade, you told me—the avertigonite harvests barely pay for the imports you must have. What economic value to your civilization is a colony like this?"

"Mostly it gives living room for people. They got to go somewhere, you know. And they want a home, land of their own, a place to belong. They say—uh—the social value of an enterprise takes pre—*precedence* over the economic value. That means if people are happy it doesn't matter if they aren't making much credit."

"I see. A commendable attitude, I suppose—though it seems to have taken your race a fantastically long time to discover a self-evident fact. But you mean that the colonists—here on Nerthus, for instance—are determined to stay at all costs?"

"Why, sure. What sort of pioneers would it be who couldn't take a little trouble without quitting?"

Joe shook his head. "You humans will go far," he murmured. "You are still fighting animals. You will even fight for your happiness." He straightened. "Well, that takes care of the plants. Let's go round up the 'steers', shall we?"

Sometimes when the moons were full, Pete couldn't sleep.

He woke up now and lay for a while in the shadows of his room. The cold, strange light slanted through the windows and streamed along the floor, casting double shadows that were as sharp and black as if someone had cut them out with a knife. There was a breeze blowing in the open windows, billowing the curtains like pale ghosts; he could hear its low mournful voice in the trees outside. And there were things talking and singing in the night—birds and insects unknown to Earth, a high sweet trill and a soft liquid laughter and the chiming of little glass bells. Pete lay quiet and listened to the night.

Then he thought he'd get up and look out, as long as he was awake. He leaned on the windowsill and the moonlight was like cold colorless day; he could see just as clear to the edge of the woods.

All at once he stiffened. There was a tall, thin shape walking over the lawn, black against the moonglow. Why, that was Joe . . . only what was he doing?

The alien stopped at the boundary of the forest and whistled, a funny soft trill sliding up and down the scale and along Pete's backbone. Maybe he was singing to himself, thought Pete; maybe he liked to walk alone under the moons and talk to the night.

All of a sudden, Pete thought it would be fun to sneak up on Joe and watch him and maybe jump out and say "Boo!" Maybe afterward they'd sit under Joe's tree, with moonlight speckling the shadows around them, and talk about the planets in outer space. Joe was nice to talk to.

So Pete turned and went down the hall to the front door and slipped quietly out and around the house. He felt wide awake now, but in a funny way as if the moonbeams shone inside his head. He laughed to himself at the way Joe would jump when he hollered.

Trees and bushes on the lawn gave plenty of cover. Pete slipped softly across the cool wet grass, half blinded by the flooding moonlight, until he was crouched in the shadow of a great bole only some three meters from where Joe was standing.

The alien was still a high, gaunt outline with too many arms, and for a minute Pete was just a little bit afraid. The night was so full of voices and eyes and sliding darknesses, and the house was only a vague blur between the trees.

Now Joe whistled again, and no human could have whistled just the way he did. And wings came down out of the sky.

It was a great night-flying strigiformoid, Pete knew—he'd heard their weird hooting in the woods, caught glimpses of huge yellow eyes out of shadow. This one whispered down to close one pair of great talons on one of Joe's wrists. There it sat while he stroked it with another hand and murmured to it in a soft, throaty tongue. Pete watched, without daring to move. He hardly dared to breathe, or those terrible eyes might turn around and look at him.

Joe fished in a pouch with his other two hands, brought out a narrow roll of paperite, and tied it around one of the bird's legs. Then he laughed, softly and not very humanly, and tossed his burden into the air.

Black wings against the stars, then silence.

Pete moved, without meaning to. And Joe was on him in one long jump.

He loomed over the boy with his head seeming to scrape the moons, and his own eyes burned with yellow fire. Pete shrank away.

"Why—why, Pete!" Suddenly Joe stepped back, so that the moonlight fell on his face. He smiled, a little shakily. "Pete, you startled me. What are you doing here?"

"I—I came out—for a walk—" mumbled Pete, not looking up.

"When you should have been in bed? Tchk, tchk." Joe shook his head. "Your aunt and uncle would not like that, Pete."

"I saw you were walking around, and came out to talk with you—"

"Any time, Pete. Except your bedtime. Now get up to the house, and I won't tell anybody."

"But what were you doing with that bird?"

"That? Oh, he's a pet of mine. He comes when I call."

"I didn't think they could be tamed. Uncle Gunnar knows a man who tried to tame one, for hunting—and it wouldn't."

"I just had better luck, Pete. Now, come along." Joe laid a hand on his shoulder and steered him toward the house.

Pete wasn't afraid right now, so he piped up again: "What were you tying that message on it for?"

"That wasn't a message. It was just a roll of paperite. I was experimenting to see whether the *orvish*—the strigiformoid can be trained to carry letters. They are very intelligent birds, I think they can be taught to go from place to place."

"But who needs that? Everybody's got a 'visor."

"The 'visors might break down, you know."

"No, they wouldn't; if they did, somebody would soon come to see why we weren't heard from."

"Well, that shows how little I know about it," laughed Joe. "But I may want to take some strigiformoids back to Astan IV with me to use that way. I told you we don't want machines there."

They were quite near the house now, so Joe stopped. "Run on in, Pete. Dry your feet; they are soaking with dew. And if you won't tell anyone about your coming out at night—you know you are not supposed to—then I won't." He turned away. "Goodnight, Pete."

When Pete woke up next day, he thought that perhaps it had been a dream. But then he decided it wasn't; there were still grass-stains on his feet.

Joe was nice and quiet as ever, at breakfast. After chores he didn't have anything to do right away, so he went back to his books. He'd borrowed a lot of texts from Uncle Gunnar—books on biological subjects, all of them—and studied them every chance he got. He was especially interested in biochemistry and biophysics, which told him things he'd never known before, in spite of his people being so good at the life sciences.

"What's the matter, Peter?" asked Aunt Edith. She always did call him by that sissy name. "You look a little sad today."

"Just thinking," he said.

He had a lot to think about. He hadn't got very far in psychology yet

in school, but he had learned the basics of multiordinal evaluation—
which meant you had to look at everything twice and think it through
for yourself, instead of just taking somebody else's word. So he was still
wondering about Joe.

He found his favorite place—a big, mossy rock warmed by the
sun—and sat down with his back against it, letting his mind wander
for a while. Pretty soon, it went of its own accord to what Joe had done
and said.

Sure, Joe was nice, but there were a lot of things about him which
didn't fit. Little things. Like the way he always dodged talking about
planets he'd been to, even his home world. Like what he'd been doing
last night—and his explanation had been pretty silly, when you looked
at it again, as if he'd made it up just then. If he meant to wander on
from there, he couldn't go lugging a cageful of strigiformoids with
him—anyway, the people of Astan IV must have some better ways for
communicating than messenger birds.

Well, alien psychologies weren't human, and you could get habits
and customs and training which made them odder yet. But even so—

Come to think of it, Joe claimed his home world was very like Earth
or Nerthus. But they were both the third planets of GO dwarfs;
wouldn't the fourth planet be pretty cold? The systems of similar stars
were usually very much alike—especially where it came to the spacing
of planets. Astan *could* be an exception, sure—but—

Suppose, now, just suppose Joe was lying. Suppose he—well,
shucks, suppose he belonged to a civilization outside our own. Man,
and the races allied with man, didn't really know much about the
Galaxy; it was too big. Man had found several other species which had
developed interstellar travel on their own, and there was no reason to
suppose he'd found them all.

If such an outlying culture wanted to spy out our own without
revealing itself—either because it had hostile ideas, or because it was
just cautious—what would it do? The answer was ready-made: Pete
had seen a dozen stereofilms with that motif. They'd send their agents
into our territory to pose as harmless tourists, students, workers from
some or other of the thousand backwoods planets nobody had ever
heard about, but which do belong with us.

Joe could have been landed from a spaceship which was now
somewhere out in the unvisited forest. He could be transmitting

information by bird, for fear of a radio set being overheard—or simply because a plain wanderer such as he claimed to be wouldn't be carrying around a radio. And when he had all the information he wanted—

Would Nerthus make a good base for the aliens? It had no defenses; one warship could take it over.

Maybe he was making too much out of a little thing. Uncle Gunnar would laugh and advise him to stay away from thrillers for a while. But Cosmos' whiskers, a guy couldn't just sit and do nothing even if he wasn't sure!

After a while, Pete figured out what a good detective would do, and sat for a while shivering with excitement. It would be easy enough, too, and it would settle the question and warn the other people—It was just plain swickerjack, that idea!

Only—wait. He had to do it secretly, because he knew how little grownups would believe him. Or if they did believe, and let him make that call, Joe might be somewhere around and might use his nameless powers to stop them.

Or suppose that didn't happen either; suppose they let him go through with it, and then Joe turned out to be just what he said he was— that would make a fellow look awfully silly. So Pete had to wait till night.

That day dragged on forever; it seemed as if the sun were stuck up in the sky and would never sink. And Joe was around the house, working, saying no word but always having his big eyes open.

"What's the matter, Peter?" asked Aunt Edith at lunch. "You don't look well at all."

"Oh, I'm all right," he muttered. "Honest I am."

"Strain," said Joe, who sat right next to him. "What are you worrying about, Pete?"

"Nothing. Nothing at all," said Pete.

Joe buttered a piece of bread—funny he should be doing that, every day, while the remembrance of alien suns burned in his skull. "You ought to be doing something to clear your mind," he said. "Why don't you come with me this afternoon? I am going into the forest for some humus. Your aunt's wagtail flowers are not doing at all well, and I suspect their soil is deficient."

"Oh, no—I can't," gasped Pete, and his heart seemed about to burst through his ribs.

"'Certainly you can," said Uncle Gunnar. "Do you good."

Pete fought not to stand up and scream that he couldn't; that he didn't dare; that Joe knew he knew, and would murder him out in the green silence. Because maybe Joe wouldn't.

"All right," he said. "But excuse me a minute first."

He went to his room and scrawled a note which he left in his drawer where it could be found. *Joe is an alien agent. If I don't come back, it's because he don't want me to talk. Love, Pete.*

He thought how his uncle and aunt would feel when they saw that brave little message, and tears filled his own eyes. Then he remembered that, in psych training, you were warned against such thoughts; he went slowly back to meet Joe.

So they took a pony and a wagon, and went into the forest; nothing happened all afternoon. Joe talked on as he always did, mostly about how it was a shame for people to come and disturb the quiet woods, and cut down the windy trees on high hills. And once he looked at Pete in a strange sorrowful way and shook his head, very slowly. But that was all, and they were back in time for supper.

Pete fumed and fidgeted away the endless hours; now the worst of it was that he was no longer sure. Joe just didn't act the way you'd expect a nonhuman spy to act. Come to think of it, what in all space was there to spy on out here?

Only—Joe still didn't ring true.

The sun went down in a mist of fire and shortly afterward Pete was sent to bed. He lay for another century or two while the grownups sat in the living room. And, even after the lights were out, he waited until he couldn't stand it any longer and slipped out of the covers.

He risked a glance at the moonlit lawn. It was all white and gray and sliding black shadow, the singing of the night, and the far glitter of the stars. No sign of Joe; maybe he was asleep under his tree. Please let him be asleep!

Down the hall went Pete, and into the living room. The moonlight didn't come in much on this side of the house; the room was a pit of darkness through which he felt his way to the televisor in the corner. Once something creaked, as if under a footstep, and he stood shaking; but the place stayed silent.

He worked the luminous dial as quietly as he could. The screen flickered to life, its glow picking out the furniture which had loomed like so many crouching beasts. He wanted to call the central office of the spaceport at Stellamont. He didn't know just what time of day or night it would be there, but being the only spaceport on the planet it ran on a continuous schedule, anyway.

After a while he got a young woman, "Please," he whispered, "I'm calling for my uncle, Thorleifsson Gunnar."

"Pardon me?" she asked in a voice that seemed to shake the walls. "I can't hear what you're saying."

Pete shook as he turned down the volume. But he still had to raise his own voice and repeat himself. Cosmos, this was making noise enough to rouse the planet.

"My uncle would like some information," he went on. He was getting less nervous now; his trained cortex was taking over in his psychosomatic system. "Only he's busy and asked me to get it instead."

"Certainly." All the world, it seemed, knew Uncle Gunnar.

"You got a Galactic Catalogue, haven't you? A cross-indexed list of all known planets, with descriptions?"

"Naturally. All ports have them."

"Is yours up to date?"

"Well, it can't be much more than a year behind the official reports. What would you like to know?"

"Look—is there a planet called Astan IV? That's prob'ly the native name, though I'm not sure."

"That doesn't matter; the Catalogue gives names in all languages. But can you tell me more about it?"

"Well, it's Earth-type and was supposed to have been discovered several years ago. The natives—" He described Joe as well as he could, ending with the remark that their culture was nonmechanical. "Uncle would also like to know if any native of that planet, or any being answering that description—" he stumbled a little over the big words in his hurry— "has come into Stellamont lately."

"I can check passenger-registers for that. But may I ask why your uncle wanted to know all this?"

"He—oh, he's writing a book, and he's not sure about that planet—"

"I see. Well, just wait a few minutes, please, while I consult the robofiles."

"Sure. An' thanks!"

The girl's head slipped out of the screen. Pete looked around, trembling a little with relief.

"Do you not trust me, Pete?" asked Joe.

Pete shuddered back, stumbling toward the corner.

Joe's tall gaunt form leaned against the doorway, all four arms folded, a smile on his face that wasn't a human smile. In the dim half-light of the glowing screen his eyes were like amber moons.

He spoke very softly, so that the alien lisp stood out clear in the humming stillness. "What do you think I am, Pete?"

"I—I—" Pete opened his mouth to scream.

"Don't," said Joe. Suddenly there was a weapon in one hand.

Pete caught himself and tried to stop the feverish shaking of his body. "What do you want?" he gasped. "What're you here for?"

"I noticed light in the living room, and thought I had better have a look," said Joe. He padded across the room, toward the bookshelves. "But why are you asking those questions of the female?"

"You're an alien," said Pete through clapping teeth. "You're an enemy spy—"

"From where?" Joe's voice was as soft and easy as ever. Over in the shadowy corner, where he now was, you could hardly see him.

"I don't know. But now I can prove it—"

"Of course. The records will show that no such planet as Astan IV has ever been described, and no being of my description has landed at Stellamont; therefore I am proved a liar. But does it follow that I am your enemy?"

Pete didn't answer. Presently Joe sighed. "Turn off the 'visor, Pete," he said. "The female may suspect something is wrong, but I will be gone before any action could be taken."

He began taking books off the shelves with two free hands. "I fear I am also turning out to be a thief," he said. "But it cannot be helped; I need those texts."

"'What're you gonna do?" whispered Pete. "What're you gonna do?"

"Why, I don't know." Joe smiled, a brief flash of white teeth in the gloom. His eyes were golden lanterns out of that dimness. "It depends on my nature, doesn't it? If I am the monstrous invader as in your cheap entertainments, then I should kill everyone in the house now, should I not? But that may not be my nature. What do you think I am, Pete? Where did I come from?"

"I don't know, how could I know—please, Joe—"

"Tell me what you think. Quickly, now!"

So Pete blurted it out fast, the words tumbling over each other to escape. And Joe nodded.

"You are shrewd, Pete," he said. "Yes, you have guessed it. Only we are from further away than you thought, and our intentions are not evil. We are simply studying your culture from the inside before making open contact.

"I have to go now; my spaceship is waiting, out in the forest. My report will be one of many, on the basis of which our leaders will decide whether to reveal ourselves to you or not. I would suggest that you keep this a secret. The more chance we get to study you without fear of detection, the more likely we are to find out your good points. I have found many in my stay here, which is one reason why I am not going to kill you. Now goodbye. Pete."

"*No.*"

Joe stood very still and his eyes glowed across the room. Uncle Gunnar's huge shadowy form stood in the doorway and the vague light gleamed off the gun in his hand.

"I've been listening for a while," said Uncle Gunnar, heavily. "You'll stay right there, Joe."

"I will do nothing of the sort," replied Joe evenly. "Before you could kill me, my weapon could be fired; it would get both you and the boy. Let me out."

"Nothing doing. I've got the drop on you. This magnum slug'll get you by hydrostatic shock before you can squeeze that trigger. And I can't let a potential menace go free."

"You forget that there is an armed spaceship waiting for my return," said Joe, just as calmly as before. "My comrades won't like it if I am slain; they will take revenge. Now—let me out."

He started walking across the room, not raising the weapon in his hand but still having his finger curled on its trigger. "Perhaps you can get me first," he said; "but will you risk the boy's life in the attempt?"

"Let's be reasonable," said Uncle Gunnar. "I'll go out to that ship with you and talk to your friends."

"No." said Joe. "We are departing tonight."

He was almost up to Uncle Gunnar. And suddenly he sprang, a great dark blur of motion. There, was a moment of wild tangle, then Uncle Gunnar went spinning halfway across the room and Joe was out through the door.

Uncle Gunnar plunged after him. Joe fired his weapon—a great glare of light and thunder of noise—but it was at the closed front door. He blew it off its hinges and leaped out.

Uncle Gunnar's gun snarled, but Joe was already another shadow on the moonlit lawn. And then he was into the woods and away.

The next thing Pete remembered, he was crying on Aunt Edith's breast while Uncle Gunnar patted him clumsily and mumbled something about his being a brave kid. "But you should've told me," he said. "You should've told me. I heard noises in here and came and listened—but if you'd told me beforehand—"

So Pete gulped out the whole story of how he'd come to suspect Joe, and in the end Uncle Gunnar nodded his red head with a grim look in his eyes.

Aunt Edith was white, "So he's going back to his warship," she whispered. "Back to his planet—"

"Maybe." Uncle Gunnar walked around the room. It was still hazed with smoke from the charred door. "Maybe so. But why did he take my books?" He looked at the empty places on the shelves. "Biological texts—the application of physical science to biology—but Joe already knew more about living things than any man ever did."

He scratched his head. "I can't figure it out, Edith. He wanted to fill the gaps in his knowledge, I suppose. The physical-science angle of biology. That proves his race is backward in physics and chemistry— which I knew already from his awkwardness with an ignorance of machinery—

"*But how could a race without such knowledge build spaceships?*"

"Maybe some other race is involved," suggested Aunt Edith. "Maybe they build and run ships of that particular culture."

"Maybe." Uncle Gunnar sounded doubtful. "But it still doesn't ring true, somehow—"

He stopped, and stood for a long, long minute where he was, and his face went white. "Oh, almighty Cosmos," he whispered at last. "*That's* the answer!"

"What is?" Aunt Edith's voice was near breaking with strain.

"Joe—Joe—he lied. *How* he lied! And when his first lie broke down, he used another—Sunblaze, the being's a genius!"

"What do you mean? Who is he? *What* is he?"

Uncle Gunnar fought for control. Then his tones came out, unnaturally steady. "It all fits in. Most of the vertebrate life on this planet has six limbs. The mammals have greenish fur. So does Joe."

"You mean—oh, no!"

"Yes, dear. That's also why our native animals weren't alarmed by his smell—why he knew so much about botany, Nerthusian botany— the green thumb—sure!"

"Joe is a native of this planet." There was a very long silence. Then Uncle Gunnar laughed harshly and went on: "They must be a non-mechanical culture, beings living in the woods—but not savages. This whole business was too sophisticated for a savage. I think they must have evolved tools, may live in the boles of trees—anyway, they didn't have anything which our first explorers would recognize as belonging to intelligent life. Especially since they were suspicious of us. They hid from us. All this time, when we thought, we were alone, they've been watching us—

"They could easily have stolen things. 'Visors, psychophone equipment, books—enough to get an idea of our culture, to learn our language—and then they finally sent an agent to live with us and really get to know us. . . . Joe."

He laughed again. "Oh, it was brilliant. Joe knew we probably wouldn't get around to checking up on him—and we wouldn't have if it hadn't been for Pete here. Even when we did, he almost had us believing he came from outer space. He'd have had mankind scouring the Galaxy for his mythical home planet—turning the universe inside out, looking everywhere but right here under our own noses!

"And he's still won. He's escaped with as much information as he could use. He's taken my books, which will teach his people enough additional biology to put them centuries ahead of us. If they get to thinking about biological warfare—And we still don't know a thing about them! Not their numbers, or where they live, or how they think, or what they want—not a thing!"

Aunt Edith held Pete close to her. She replied in a dry whisper: "But Joe was so—nice—"

"Oh, sure." Uncle Gunnar looked moodily out at the eerie white night. "Oh, sure. A pleasant fellow, who may or may not be typical of his kind. Who may or may not have been posing. He's gotten away, though.

"His race is in one hell of a good bargaining position. We'll hunt for them—of course we will—but they'll have plenty of time to prepare themselves."

"They won't choose war?" asked Aunt Edith. "They know they can't win against the whole Galaxy."

"No. But they can blackmail all kinds of concessions out of the Galaxy by threatening war against its colonists here. If they want to."

He shrugged wearily. "Maybe they won't want to; maybe they'll decide to cooperate with us. Between man and Nerthusian, this planet could be made a paradise for all races. But we don't know what they're like, Edith, Pete—we just don't know—"

The settlers on Nerthus—and elsewhere—did learn to join the web of native life on their planet and make themselves fully at home. Nerthus grew into a prosperous hub of its galactic sector, attracting visitors from other worlds and cultures. It even hosted a regional base of the Stellar Union's peace-keeping Coordination Service.

Meanwhile, 200 light-years away on the other side of a deadly trepidation vortex that warped space unpredictably, lay another human settlement utterly isolated and untouched.

Virgin Planet

CORPORAL Maiden Barbara Whitley of Freetoon, hereditary huntress, wing leader of the crossbow cavalry, and novice in the Mysteries, halted her orsper and peered through a screen of brush. Breath sucked sharply between her teeth.

From this edge of the forest, the Ridge mountains rolled away in a green blaze of grass to the wide floor of the Holy River valley. Tall white clouds walked in a windy sky. With midsummer approaching, both suns were visible. Ay was a spark so bright it hurt the eyes, following the great golden fireball of Bee down toward the western horizon. Minos was waxing, huge and banded, in its eternal station a little south of the zenith. The moon Ariadne was a pale half-disc. The other moons had not yet risen, or were drowned by daylight, but the six hours of night to come would be bright.

It was on the thing in the valley, five kilometers away, that Barbara focused her eyes.

It stood upright, like a lean finless war-dart, and she estimated its height as 40 meters. That was much smaller than the Ship of Father. But it was nearly the same shape, if the hints dropped by initiates were truthful . . . and it had been *seen* this morning, descending from the sky.

A chill went along her nerves. She was not especially pious; none of the Whitleys were. But this was Mystery. They had always said it, they sang it in the rituals and they told it to children on rainy nights when the fires leaped high on the barracks hearths—

Some day the Men will come to claim us.

If this was the Men.

Barbara's hand strayed to the horn slung at her waist. She could call the others. Claudia, the Old Udall, had sent out the whole army to look for the shining thing, and there must be others within earshot.

The stillness of that big metal beast was unnerving. It could well be a vessel of the Monsters. The Monsters were half folk-tale, it was said they lived on the stars like the Men and had dealings with the Men, sometimes friendly and sometimes otherwise.

A stray lock of rusty-red hair blew from under Barbara's morion and tickled her nose. She sneezed. It seemed to crystallize decision.

Surely there were Monsters in that thing! The Men would arrive much more portentously, landing first at the Ship of Father and then at the various towns. And there would be haloes and other prodigies about them, and creatures of shining steel in attendance.

Barbara was rather frightened at the idea of Monsters—she felt her heart thump beneath the iron breastshields—but they were less awesome than Men. If she merely went back to town and reported, she knew exactly how Claudia Udall would take charge—the army would move according to tactics which were, well, simply *rotten*, like the time when it had been led directly into a Greendale ambush. And a mere corporal would be just nobody.

She checked her equipment with rapid, professional care: iron helmet, reinforced leather cuirass and kilt, boots, ax, knife, lasso. She cocked her spring-wound repeating crossbow and tucked it in the crook of her left arm. Her right hand picked up the reins, and she clucked to the orsper.

It trotted downhill at the swift rocking pace of its breed, the feathered head, beaked and crested, erect. The wind blew in her face, murmuring of the sea and the Ship whence it came. The object grew nearer—still not a sound from it, not a stirring. Barbara grew quite convinced that there were Monsters aboard. Men would have been out long ago. It was a less terrifying prospect. Monsters had unknown powers, but they were still mortal, limited creatures, but Men . . .

Barbara had never thought a great deal about the Men. Now the songs and rituals came back to her. "The Men are the males of the human race. We were coming to join them, but the Ship went astray because of our sins. The Men are taller and stronger than we, infinitely wiser and more virtuous, and they have hair on their chins and no breasts . . ."

She came up into the long shadow of the—boat? "Hoy, there!" she cried. No answer. A flock of gray rangers went overhead, calling to each other, incredibly unconcerned.

Barbara rode several times around the thing. There was a circular door in the hull, out of her reach and smoothly closed, and there were blank ports. Not a face in any of them. Really, it was getting ridiculous! Fear vanished in a gust of temper.

The startled screech of the orsper jerked her back to reality. There was someone running from the west.

She spurred her mount forward. The person was approaching the boat . . . must have been looking around when she arrived. . . . Person? No!

It was strangely dressed in some kind of tunic, the legs sheathed in cloth, a small packsack on the shoulders. But the form of it was grotesque, inhuman. Broad shoulders—not unpleasing, that, but the hips were of an ugly narrowness. There was yellow hair cropped short, and a lean face with too much nose and chin, altogether too much bone and too little flesh.

Barbara knew what all the 500 families looked like, and this wasn't any of them. She remembered from the old stories that Monsters had many shapes, but some of them looked like deformed humans.

"Hoy-aaa!" she yelled. "What are you doing here?"

The Monster drew a small tube from a holster and pointed it at her. Dashing close, Barbara saw that its crimson tunic was open at the neck, the chest was flat and hairy and there was thick hair on the arms—

Then she hardly had time to think. The Monster might or might not be peaceful, and she couldn't just shoot it down. But she knew better than to take unnecessary risks.

Her knees guided the leaping bird and her hands whirled up the lariat.

The Monster stood there gaping.

She heard words in a distorted, alien accent: "Holy Cosmos, what's going on here?" No human had so deep a voice!

Then the lasso snaked out, fell, and drew taut.

Corporal Maiden Barbara Whitley galloped in triumph toward Freetoon, dragging the Monster behind her.

DEFINITIONS AND REFERENCES

"Delta Capitis Lupi: Double. (Coordinates given, indicating its distance from Nerthus as about 200 light-years; Nerthus is a Service base planet, ca. 300 parsecs from Sol.) Primary of type AO, mass 4 Sol, luminosity 81 Sol. Companion Sol-type, average distance from primary 98 Astronomical Units. Unexplored due to trepidation vortex in neighborhood . . ."
    —*Pilot's Manual, Argus*
    293 Region (with much expansion of abbreviations)

"Trepidation Vortex: Traveling region of warped space, primary effect being that of violently shifting gravitational fields. Responsible for some planetary perturbations. Spaceships on hyperdrive encountering a vortex are thrown far off course and usually destroyed . . ."
    —*General Encyclopedic Dictionary*

". . . Davis Bertram. Born in Sigma Hominis Volantis system, where father had grown wealthy. (Odd how anachronisms like private ostentation redevelop on the frontier, isn't it?) Basic schooling on Earth; astronautical training on Thunderhouse (the most notoriously slack academy in the known Galaxy—must assemble data and file a complaint when I get the time). Having bought his own robotic cruiser, he came to Nerthus to start a career in stellagraphic survey by going to Delta Wolf's Head—alone! As far as I could gather, his preparations here consisted mostly of bottle hoisting, skirt chasing, and a little amateur landscape painting.

"I could not legally refuse him clearance, since he had the training and a sufficient goodwill quotient to protect any natives he might encounter. I checked the physiological data, hoping for an excuse, but somatically he is first-rate; I presume he makes himself exercise regularly to attract women, but the law does not make this any of my business. He is, in fact (or was), quite a large, good-looking young man of the vanishing Nordic type; his brain is excellent, if he only cared to use it; how can I extrapolate disaster on the basis of mere cocksureness and flippancy?

"I warned him of the vortex, and that the Service did not plan to visit Delta until it was safely gone from the region, in about 30 years. He replied that it was probably safe as of now. I told him that if he did not come back, we could not hazard lives in a rescue party. He could not conceive that he might not return. What he wanted, of course, was the glory. If Delta turns out to have intelligent autochthones or be an uninhabited, colonizable planet, he will go down in history with Carsten.

"In the end, then, he left, and his *At Venture* is now somewhere near the vortex. If he avoids that, and avoids hostile natives, wild beasts, poison, disease—the million traps a new planet lays for us—he will come back and have all the adoring females he can use. So much for Man's Starward Yearning, or am I merely envious in this winter of my own lifetime?"

—*Diary of Yamagata Tetsuo,*
   Chief of Coordination Service,
   Argus 293 Region, Stellamont, Nerthus

Minos was full, drenching Freetoon with cold amber light, and the air had grown chilly. Barbara Whitley walked through silent streets, between darkened buildings, to the cavalry barracks. It formed one side of a square around a courtyard, the stables and arsenal completing the ring. Her boots thudded on the cobbles as she led her orsper to its stall.

A stone lamp on a shelf showed the snoring grooms—all Nicholsons, a stupid family used only for menial work—stirring uneasily on the straw as she tramped in. She nudged one of the stocky, tangle-haired women awake with her toe. "Food," she demanded. "And beer. And take care of the bird."

Afterward, she undressed and washed herself in the courtyard trough. She regarded her face complacently in the water. The Minoslight distorted colors, ruddy hair and long green eyes became something else, but the freckled snub nose and the wide mouth and the small square chin were more pleasing than . . . oh, than that Dyckman build. Dyckmans were just *sloppy.*

The dying hearthfire within the barrack showed long-limbed forms sprawled on straw ticks. She stowed her weapons and armor, trying to be quiet. But Whitleys were light sleepers, and her cousin Valeria woke up.

"Oh, it's you. Two left feet as always," snarled Valeria, "and each one bigger than the other. Where did you park your fat rump all day?"

Barbara looked at the face which mirrored her own. They were the only Whitleys in Freetoon, their mothers and four aunts having perished in the Greendale ambush 15 years ago, and they should have been as close as relatives normally were. But it was a trigger-tempered breed, and when a new wing leader corporal was required, the sacred dice had chosen Barbara. Valeria could not forgive that.

"I took my two left feet and my fat rump—if you must describe yourself that way—into the valley and captured a Monster in a star ship," said Barbara sweetly. "Goodnight." She lay down on her pallet and closed her eyes, leaving her twin to speculate . . .

Bee had not even risen when there was a clank of metal in the doorway and Ginny Latvala shouted: "Up, Corporal Maiden Barbara Whitley! You're wanted at the Big House."

"Do you have to wake everyone else on that account?" snapped Valeria, but not very loud. The entire company had been roused, and Captain Kim was a martinet, like all Trevors.

Barbara got to her feet, feeling her heart knock. Yesterday seemed unreal, like a wild dream. Ginny leaned on her spear, waiting. "The Old Udall is pretty mad at you, dear," she confided. "We may have all sorts of trouble coming because you roped that Monster." The Latvalas were slim blonde girls, handy with a javelin and so made hereditary bodyguards in most towns.

"I was never ordered not to lasso a Monster," said Barbara huffily.

She let the barracks buzz around her while she dressed for the occasion: a short white skirt, an embroidered green cloak, sandals, and dagger. The air was still cold and the fields below the town white with mist when she came out. A pale rosy light lifted above the eastern Ridge, and Minos was waning. The moon Theseus was red sickle caught in the sunrise.

There were not many people up. A patrol tramped past, all of them husky Macklins, and the farmhands yawned out of their barracks on the way to a day's hoeing. The street climbed steeply upward from the cavalry house, and Barbara took it with a mountaineer's long slow stride. They went by the weavery, she glimpsed looms and spinning wheels within the door, but it didn't register on her mind—low-caste work. The smithy, a most respected shop, lay beyond, also empty; the Holloways still slept in their adjoining home.

Passing a window of the maternity hospital, Barbara heard a small wail. Must be Sarah Cohen's kid, born a few days ago. The sound broke through her worry with an odd little tug at her soul. In another year or so, she would be an initiate, and make the journey to the Ship. And when she came back, no longer called Maiden, there would be another redhaired Whitley beneath her heart. Babies were a nuisance, she'd have to stay within the town till hers was weaned and—and—it was hard to wait.

The stockade bulked above her, great sharp stakes lashed together and six Latvalas on guard at the gate. Inside, there was a broad cobbled yard with several buildings: barracks, stables, sheds, the Father chapel. All were in the normal Freetoon style, long log houses with peaked sod roofs. The hall, in the middle, was much the same, but immensely bigger, its beam-ends carved into birds of prey.

Henrietta Udall stood at its door. She was the oldest of Claudia's three daughters: big and blocky, with sagging breasts and harsh black hair, small pale eyes under tufted brows, a lump for a nose and a gash for a mouth. The finery of embroidered skirt and feather cloak was wasted on her, Barbara thought. None of the Udalls could ever be handsome. But they could lead!

"Halt! Your hair is a mess," said Henrietta. "Do those braids over."

Barbara bit her lip and began uncoiling the bronze mane. It was hacked off just below her shoulders. *Spiteful blowhard,* she thought. *I'm barren if I do and barren if I don't. Come the day, dear Henrietta, you won't find me on your side.*

The death of an Udall was always the signal for turmoil. Theoretically, the power went to her oldest daughter. In practice, the sisters were likely to fight it out between themselves; a defeated survivor fled into the wilderness with her followers and tried to start a new settlement. Daydreams of heading into unknown country for a fresh start drove the sulkiness from Barbara. If, say, she rose high in the favor of Gertrude or Anne . . .

"All right," said Henrietta as Bee rose. She led the way inside.

The main room of the Big House was long and gloomy. Sconced torches guttered above the Old Udall's seat. Servants scurried around, serving breakfast to her and to the middle-aged high-caste women on the bench below the throne.

"Well!" said Claudia. "It took you long enough."

Barbara had learned the hard way never to blame an Udall for anything. "I'm sorry, ma'm," she muttered, saluting.

The Old Udall leaned back and let her chambermaid comb the stiff gray hair. Elinor Dyckman had gotten that job; an Udall usually took a Dyckman for a lover.

Elinor was in her middle twenties; her baby was dead and she hadn't asked for another. Dyckmans had scant mother instinct. She was medium tall, with a soft curving body and soft bluish-black hair. Her small heart-shaped face smiled sweetly on the chief, and she combed with long slow strokes.

"You'll have to be punished for that," said Claudia. "Suggestions, Elinor, dear?" She laughed.

Elinor blinked incredible lashes over melting dark eyes and said: "Not too severe, ma'm. I'm sure Babs means well. A little KP—"

Barbara's hand fell to her dagger. "I'm in the army, you milk-livered trull!" she exploded. "*Dishwashing*, by Father—!"

"Watch your language," said counsellor Marian Burke.

Elinor smiled and went on combing. "It was only a joke, ma'm," she murmured. "Hadn't we better get down to business?"

The Old Udall gazed at Barbara. *Trying to stare me down, are you?* thought the girl savagely. She would not look away.

"Enough," said Claudia at length. "Yes, Elinor, you're right as usual, we can't stop to quarrel now."

She leaned ponderously forward. "I've heard reports from the scouts who met you," she went on.

Barbara remained silent, not trusting her tongue. Captain Janet Lundgard had emerged from the woods with some troopers and taken charge: set a guard on the ship, slung the unconscious Monster on a spare orsper, and ridden to town with the rest of them for escort. She had reported directly to the Big House—but what had she told? The Lundgards were not as predictable as most families; that was one reason they were hereditary army officers.

"Apparently you attacked the Monster unprovoked," said Claudia coldly. "Father knows what revenge it may take."

"It had drawn a weapon on me, ma'm," answered Barbara. "If I hadn't lassoed it, maybe it would have destroyed all Freetoon. As it is, we have the thing a prisoner now, don't we?"

"It may have friends," whispered Elinor, her eyes very large. A shiver went through the hall.

"Then we have a hostage," snapped Barbara.

The Old Udall nodded. "Yes . . . there is that. I've had relays of guards sent to its ship. None of them report any sign of life. It, the Monster, must have been alone."

"How many other ships have landed, all over Atlantis?" wondered Henrietta.

"That's what we have to find out," said Claudia. "I'm sending a party to the Ship of Father to ask the Doctors about this. We'll also have to send scouts to the nearest other towns, find out if they've been visited too."

Both missions would be dangerous enough. Barbara thought with a tingling what her punishment would be. As a non-initiate, she couldn't go to the Ship, but she would be sent toward Greendale, Highbridge, or Blockhouse, to spy. *But that's terrific! When do we start?*

The Udall smiled grimly. "And meanwhile, for weeks perhaps, we'll have the Monster to deal with . . . and our own people. The whole town must already be getting into a panic.

"We have to learn the truth about the Monster—yes, and all the people had better know the facts. We'll do it this way. The carpenters will set up a cage for the Monster, right in the plaza, and while everybody not on duty watches, someone will go into that cage and we'll see what happens."

"Who's going to volunteer for *that* job?" grumbled Marian Burke.

Elinor smiled gently. "Why, who but our brave Corporal Whitley?" she answered.

Davis Bertram woke when the door was opened and lay there for a minute, trying to remember why his flesh ached in a hundred places. Then he got his eyes unglued.

There was a boot in front of his nose. He rolled over, cautiously, and sent a bleared gaze upward. Above the boot was a shapely knee, and above that a leather-strip kilt reinforced with iron bands; then a belt supporting a knife and pouch, a cuirass of laminated leather with

Poul Anderson

an iron bust bucket, a slim neck, a lot of yellow hair braided under a
helmet, and a rather attractive suntanned face.

Cosmos! That girl on the nightmare bird, the lariat and—

"What's going on?" croaked Davis. "Who are you?"

"Father!" stammered one of the girls. "It talks!"

She spoke Basic—a slurred archaic form, but it was the Basic of all
human-settled planets. She must be human, thought Davis groggily;
no alien was that anthropoid.

A handsome wench, too, though a bit muscular for his taste. He
began to smile through bruised lips at all ten of them.

"Gak!" he said.

The ten were identical.

Well, not quite . . . some leaned on spears and some bore light,
wicked-looking axes, and some had a beltful of needle-nosed darts.

He shuddered and grew aware that he had been stripped mother
naked. Between the cuts and abrasions, he started to blush, more or
less all over. He scrambled to his feet. A jerk at the wrists told him his
hands were tied behind his back. He sat down again, lifting his knees
and glaring across them.

"I imagine Monsters would have learned the Men language, Ginny,"
said one of his visitors. On closer observation, Davis saw that she was
older and had a scar on one cheek. Some kind of insigne was painted
on her breastplate . . . sunblaze, it was the six-pointed star of an
astrogator's mate!

"It *looks* fairly harmless," said one of the others doubtfully.

"You, Monster!" The officer raised her battle ax. "Up!" She was
tense as a drawn wire. Davis rose.

They marched him out of the shed. He saw a courtyard, rudely
paved with stones, a number of primitive wooden buildings, and a
high palisade around all. There was a catwalk beneath the stakes, and
warriors posted on it with some kind of crossbow.

Beyond the gate, Davis saw quite a small army, alert for whatever
he might try to pull. Some were on foot, some mounted on birds like
the one he'd seen before: larger and stouter than ostriches, with feathers
of blue-tipped white and cruel hawk heads. He decided not to pull
anything.

A rutted unpaved street snaked downhill between big, clumsy
houses. Outside town it became a road of sorts, wandering through

cultivated grainfields. They covered a sloping plateau, which dipped off into forest toward the river valley. Behind the castle, the mountains rose steep and wooded.

Ignoring botanical details, this might almost have been Earth of some elder age. But not when you looked at the sky. It was blue and clear, yes, with towering white clouds in the west; overhead, though, were two crescents, dim by daylight: one almost twice the apparent size of Luna seen from Earth, the other half again as big. And there was the emperor planet, the world of which *this* was only another satellite. When full, it would sprawl across 14 times as much sky as Luna. Now it was a narrow sickle, pale amber. The morning sun was approaching it. That is, the smaller, Sol-type sun, Delta Capitis Lupi B, about which the giant planet moved. The primary sun, bluish-white A, had not yet risen; it would never seem more than the brightest of the stars.

Davis shook an aching head and wrenched his attention back to the ground. Be sundered if this was like Earth, after all, even with the women and children clustered around. Not just their dress—the civilians wore a short skirt, the kids nothing. Their *likeness*. Women and children—all female, the children—seemed to be cast from a few hundred molds. Take two from the same mold, like those gawping dairy-maid types over there, and the only difference was age and scars.

Cosmos, but he was thirsty!

At the farther end of a broad open space were some thousands of civilians, jammed together, craning their necks, held back by a line of guards. Their high-pitched, excited voices sawed on his nerves. In the middle of the square was a large wooden cage.

"In there," said the blonde captain. She drew her knife and cut his bonds.

Davis shuffled through the cage door. "Is this a zoo?" he asked. "Where are all the men, anyway?"

"Don't *you* know?" the captain asked acidly.

"Very well, Babs, let's see how you get out of this one!"

It was a new voice, pleasantly husky in spite of its jeering note. Davis looked through the bars and saw a redhaired girl among the cavalry. Holy Valdaoth, the same one who'd roped him yesterday!

Or was she? Her twin, also in armor, came walking slowly forth across the square. Davis stepped warily back as the newcomer entered. The blonde officer latched the door behind them.

The girl touched her dagger. He could have gone for her in better circumstances. Her greenish eyes widened, and she breathed hard. It would have been an interesting sight if it hadn't been for that iron bra.

"I'll fight if I must," she whispered.

Four women approached the cage, all of the same unprepossessing genotype. The oldest wore a headdress of plumes. "Well, Corporal," she snapped, "question it."

"Y-yes, ma'm," said the girl in a small voice. "I . . . I am Corporal Maiden Barbara Whitley, Monster."

"The same who captured you," said one of the hags.

"Be quiet, Henrietta," said the oldest witch. With a certain fearless pride: "I am Claudia, the Udall of Freetoon."

"Honored, Citizen," said the man. "My name is Davis Bertram."

"Why . . . that could almost be a human name," said Barbara shyly.

"What else should it be?" asked Davis.

"Oh . . . oh, yes, the stories do say you Monsters learned the arts from the Men." She smiled, the least little bit.

"But I—Who said I was a monster?" He was not, Davis told himself, vain; but more than one woman had informed him she liked his face.

"You are! *Look* at you!"

"Blast it, I'm as human as you are!"

"With all that hair?" rapped Henrietta Udall.

Davis gave her an unfriendly glance.

"Look here," said Barbara reasonably, "we're not blind. I admit you have two legs and five fingers and no feathers. But you're bigger than any of us, and haven't got any more breasts than a ten-year-old."

"I should hope not!" said Davis.

"In fact—" Barbara scratched her neck, puzzledly, and pointed. "Just what *is* that? Do you fight with it?"

"It doesn't look prehensile," said the blonde captain.

Davis told himself wildly that he had not gone insane, that he really was here on the Earth-sized third satellite of Delta Capitis Lupi B I. But somehow it seemed to slip through his fingers.

He put his face in his palms and shuddered.

"Poor Monster." Barbara trod impulsively forward.

He looked up. She paled a little with fright, under the smooth brown skin, and made half a step back. Then her lips—unfairly attractive lips—stiffened, and she stayed where she was.

"We had no way of knowing," she said. "Some Monsters are friendly with the Men and some aren't. We couldn't take chances."

"But I am a man!" shouted Davis.

A groan went through the crowd. Somebody screamed.

Barbara clenched her fists. "Why did you say that?" she asked in a wobbly voice.

"Can't you *see*, girl?"

"But the Men . . . the Men are powerful, and beautiful, and—"

"Oh, Evil!" Davis took her fingers and laid them against his cheek. "Feel that? I haven't got much yet in the way of whiskers, but—"

Barbara turned faintly toward the Udall. "It's true, ma'm," she whispered. "There's hair starting to grow out of his face."

"But you *captured* him!" protested the blonde captain.

Davis took hold of his sanity with both hands. "Look, kenno," he began between clenched teeth. "Let's be reasonable about this. Just what the jumping blue blazes do you think a man is?"

"A Man is . . . is . . . a human male." He could barely hear the Barbara girl's reply.

"All right. Now, have you ever seen a human male before?"

"Certainly not." Her courage was returning. "You must indeed be from far away, Monster, There are no Men on all Atlantis."

"Oh . . . is that what you've called this world? But how do you manage—how long since—"

"Humans came here some 300 years ago. That is, by a year I mean the time Minos needs to go once around the sun Bee."

Minos . . . the big planet, of course. Davis had measured from space that it was about one Astronomical Unit from B, which had nearly the same mass as Sol. So one Minos year was approximately one Earth year. Three centuries—why, they were barely starting to colonize then! The hyperdrive was newly invented and—

"But you have children," he said feebly.

"Oh, yes. By the grace of Father, the Doctors at His Ship can—I don't know any more. I've never been there."

Davis took a while to swallow that one.

Something came back to him. In the few hours he'd been on Atlantis, before this Barbara wench caught him, he had seen plenty of animal life: reptiles, fish, insects, flying and flightless birds. Some of the earthbound avians had been the size of buffalo.

But no mammals. In all those flocks and herds, not a mammal.

Excitement gripped him. "Wait a minute!" he cried. "Are there any . . . I mean, well, does Atlantis harbor any warm-blooded animals with hair that give live birth and suckle their young?"

"Why, no," said Barbara. "Except us humans, of course."

"Ahhh-*ha*. Mammals never evolved here, then. And they're the only terrestroid form where the males are . . . hm—" Davis blushed. "Obviously male. No wonder you didn't recognize—I mean, uh—"

"What do you mean?" asked Barbara innocently.

"This is ridiculous," barked the Old Udall. "It's well understood that the Men will come in all their power and glory. This wretch is a Monster, and the only question is what to do about it."

Another girl trod forth. Even now, Davis felt his eyes bug out. She was dark, throaty-voiced, with gold bangles on slender arms and red flowers in her long hair, high in the prow and walking like a sine wave. "Please ma'm," she said. "I have an idea."

Claudia smiled at her. "Yes, Elinor?"

"It says it is a Man." Elinor waggled her eyelashes at Davis. "Let it prove it."

"How?" demanded Davis.

"By fertilizing the corporal," said Elinor with scientific detachment.

"*What?*"

Barbara stepped back, white-faced. "No!" she gasped.

"Corporal Whitley," said Claudia earnestly, "we've had our little differences, but now the future of Freetoon may depend on you. You won't fail your duty."

"Unless you're afraid, darling," murmured Elinor.

Davis saw Barbara flush red. She knotted her fists. After a very long minute, she looked squarely at him with an air of having but one life to give for her country.

"Yes," she said defiantly. "You may fertilize me, Davis—if you can!"

He looked at several thousand interested faces.

How did you explain the effect of social conditioning to a tribe which had never heard of such matters?

"Not now," he begged hoarsely. "Give me time . . . privacy, for Cosmos' sake . . . can't do anything *here*—"

The Old Udall lifted a skeptical brow.

"Oh, never mind," said Davis. "Have it your way. I'm a monster."

Barbara was not happy.

That sorry business in the plaza had won her a good deal of respect, but she didn't enjoy baiting captives, even Monsters. In the four days since, a growing moodiness had driven her to get permission to go out alone after game. It was not quite safe, but she felt somehow that a companion would be more of a hazard.

We Whitleys are a crotchety lot, she admitted. For once the reflection was less arrogant than gloomy. She had not, before, felt it a loss to have no sweetheart, not even a close friend, and to be forever at odds with her only kinswoman in Freetoon. But suddenly she wanted her mother back . . . Or someone. She couldn't understand the pull she felt, as if her thirteen-year-old self were reaching across seven years of time to invade a body gone all soft and unsure. Ever since those moments in the Monster's cage . . . *Damn* the Monster! Had the thing psyched her?

She headed northward into the woods and steeps of the Ridge, spoored a stamper herd on the second day and caught up to it on the third and shot one of the great grazing birds. She didn't have it cut up before dark, and wasn't sleepy even then.

And she saw that the night was cool, a bright mystery where dewed leaves sparkled gold beneath Minos, a scent of young blossoms, the High Gaunt rearing its stern stone peak among the stars. An irrational happiness lifted in her, she gathered armfuls of sweetbird and fernish, crooned, threw her arms about a slim white tree and rubbed a hot cheek against it and was near crying when a night-triller began to sing. There was a tingle all through her.

And this was not to be understood either. All at once she wanted very much the harsh sweaty comfort of the barracks. The trail had arced, she could be in Freetoon tonight if she rode hard.

Sleep was no problem. Normally you slept about four hours out of the twelve between a sunset and a sunset, but huntresses could go for days on birdnaps. Barbara loaded her pack orsper, mounted the other, and started at Bee-rise. She ate in the saddle, not stopping even for the holy time of eclipse, when Bee went behind Minos and the stars came out. Ay and Ariadne gave light enough for those ten-plus minutes, and a muttered prayer to Father met minimum requirements.

Shortly afterward she struck the Ironhill road. It was wider than most—all towns, however hostile, met at the mining settlement to trade. Jogging along in her own apprehension, she forgot all care. She rounded a bend and could have been shot by the Greendalers before realizing they were there.

A dozen of them, in full armor, riding toward Freetoon . . . Barbara reined in, gasping, and stared at the crossbows as they swiveled around.

The Greendale leader, a middle-aged Macklin with a broken nose, laughed. "We won't harm you today, darling, if you behave yourself," she said. "Freetooner, aren't you? We're on embassy."

Barbara nodded distantly and joined them. She felt no hatred, but war was as normal a part of life as the harvest festival. She had been in several raids and skirmishes since gaining her growth, and her kin were dead at Greendale hands.

There was a Whitley sergeant among them, about fifty years old. "I'm Gail," she introduced herself.

"What's your mission?" asked Barbara, rather snappishly.

"What do you think?" answered Gail. "You people ought to know better than to send spies our way when I'm on patrol duty."

"Oh . . . you bushwhacked them, then." Barbara felt a chill.

"Every one. Caught three of them alive. One, Avis Damon, got pretty much cut up in the fracas, and rather than bleed to death she told us what she knew."

It was bad news, very bad, but Barbara's first reaction was scorn. "I always claimed those Damons aren't fit for combat." Then, slowly: "So what do you think you learned?"

"A star ship landed in your country." Gail said it with care. "There was a Man aboard."

"A Monster," corrected Barbara. "We made it admit that."

"Mmm . . . yes . . . I thought so myself. You couldn't have captured a Man against his will."

A thin, dark-haired Burke interrupted softly: "Are you sure it was against his will? Maybe as a test of faith, he—"

That was trouble with the Burkes. They thought too much. Barbara's hands felt clammy. "We've sent to the Doctors, of course, to ask what we ought to do," she said defensively.

"And meanwhile you have the Monster and its ship." Anger writhed across the Macklin's leathery face. "Do you think we're going to stand by and let you make an ally of the Monster?"

"What do you want?" replied Barbara.

"We're bringing an ultimatum," said Gail Whitley. "Your Udall has damned well got to turn the Monster over to a joint guard till we get word from the Doctors. If you don't—war."

Barbara thought about if for a while. She ought to make a break for it, try to reach Freetoon ahead of this gang . . . no, that would earn her nothing more than a bolt in the back. There was plaguey well going to be a war, no Udall would cough up a prize like the Monster. *Well, who says we can't defend our own fields? Hell and thunder, we'll toss them out on their fat cans and chase them all the way home.*

The battle would probably start tomorrow. It was about thirty hours' ride to Greendale, but the enemy soldiers must already have left and be bivouacked somewhere in the Ridge.

So be it! Barbara felt a welcome tension, almost an eagerness. It was a pleasant change from her eldritch moods of the past days. She chatted amiably with the others for the rest of the trip.

Bee and Ay were under the horizon when they clattered by the patrols up to Freetoon, but Minos, Ariadne, Theseus, and tiny Aegeus gave plenty of light. The embassy had dismounted in the courtyard and stamped into the Big House when Barbara realized her usefulness was over. She turned her kill over to the servants and put the two orspers in the castle barn. Poor birds, they were so tired. Then she ought to go tell her barracks mates, but—

"Where's the Monster being kept?" she asked, before thinking.

"In the shed under the north wall, ma'm," said the Nicholson groom. "Didn't dare have him anywhere else, they didn't, though he ain't done no harm yet but you can't never tell."

"*He!*" said Barbara with a flash of anger. "Why call it 'he?'"

"Well, he says he's a male, ma'm, and, uh, well, he says—"

Barbara walked off. No reason why the Monster shouldn't be male. They were Man and woman, the wise happy people of the stars, and doubtless Monsters too—But why should the thought of this Davis creature's maleness be so odd, half frightening and therefore resented?

She grew suddenly aware that she had rounded the Big House and was in its multiple shadow looking toward the Monster's prison.

A door of wooden bars had been erected for the shed. It . . . he . . . Davis stood against the bars, flooded with cool Minoslight and moonlight. He showed sharp and clear in the radiance, and somehow the hollow cheeks and flat hairy breast and bulging muscles were no longer ugly. They had given him clothes, kilt, cloak, and sandals, his hair was combed and a yellow beard was growing out on his face.

He was holding hands between the bars with a girl in a long feather cloak. Their faces drifted to Barbara—Elinor Dyckman, of all foul pests!

"Oh, I really must be going, Bertie. Those awful Greendalers . . . didn't you see them come in? Claudia will be just *furious*."

"Stick around, beautiful." The Monster's low chuckle was paralyzing, Barbara could not have moved after hearing it. "It's worth all my woes, just to get you here alone at last."

"Really . . . Bertie, let go, you scare me." Elinor tittered.

"Aw, now, macushla. I'm not going to eat you. Let me only feast on your silken hair, your starry eyes, your—" Etc., etc.

"You say *such* things." Elinor leaned closer against the bars. "Nobody says such things here."

"Ah, nobody is able to appreciate you, my little one. To think I crossed the stars and found you. Come here . . . lend me that adorable mouth—"

"Bert! I . . . I . . . mmmmm—"

The night blurred before Barbara. She wondered why, gulped, realized it was tears, and cursed herself.

"I *mustn't*, Bertie, dear! Why you're a—"

"A man. And you're a woman."

"But you said—"

"I had no choice then." Davis leered. "But come in here and I'll prove it to you this time."

"Oh, I can't, Bertie, I just can't! You're locked in and—"

"You can swipe the key, can't you? Here, give me another kiss."

It was too much. And a Whitley was no sneaking spy like a, a, a Dyckman. Barbara strode across the yard, jingling her spurs as noisily as possible. "What's going on here?" she yelled.

"Oh!" Elinor squealed. "Oh . . . Babs, is it? Babs, dear, I was only—"

"I know what you were only. Get out before I knock your teeth down your throat!"

Elinor wailed and fled.

Barbara turned furiously on Davis. "What were you plotting?" she snarled.

The Monster sighed, shrugged, and gave her a rueful grin. "Nothing very evil," he said. "You again, eh?"

Heat and cold chased each other across Barbara's face.

"You know," went on Davis, "this is the kind of thing I used to daydream about in my teens. A brand new world, like Earth but more beautiful, and I the only man among a million women. And holy Cosmos, I've found it, and I want out!"

Barbara raised a fist. "Yes, so you can go home and call your friends to come raiding."

"Look," said Davis earnestly, "we want to help you—blast it all, we're not your kind of bloodthirsty pirate. And I *am* a man, as human as you. If you'd not come along, Elinor Dyckman would have found that out . . . nine months afterward, at most!" His smile grew altogether insolent. "Maybe you'd like to give me another chance? Honestly, you're one of the best-looking girls I've seen anywhere."

"Hell spit me out if I do!" Barbara turned her back.

"Don't go away," begged Davis. "It's lonesome as space here. All I've done is argue with that barrel-shaped queen of yours."

Barbara couldn't help laughing. The epithet was too good.

"That's better," said Davis. "Shall we be friends?"

"Why do you claim to be a Man?" she countered hastily. "You've already admitted you aren't."

"I had no choice then, blast it! You and . . . the other girl . . . only ones who might give me a chance to convince them. I tell Siz Claudia that I'm a benevolent Monster and if they'll let me at my boat—under guard, if they want—I'll go home and bring the Men. I mean it, too."

"But she doesn't dare," said Barbara slowly.

"Well, not so far. Can't really say I blame her. Say, have you found my blaster?"

"Your what?"

"My weapon. I had it in a hip holster, dropped it when you—No? I suppose it must be lying out in the grass somewhere. You won't find much in my pack. Medical kit, lighter, camera, a few such gadgets. I've offered to demonstrate them, but the old sow won't let me."

"What were you doing when I . . . found you?" asked Barbara. Really, she thought, he wasn't a bad Monster at heart.

"Just looking around. I analyzed basic surface conditions from space, then came down to let my robots check on the biochemistry, bacteriology, and ecology. That looked safe too, so I violated all doctrine and went for a stroll. I was just coming back to the boat when—Oh, Evil, I don't imagine you understand a word." Davis smiled gently. "Poor kid. Poor little Amazon."

"I can take care of myself!" she flared.

"No doubt. But come over here. I won't hurt you."

Barbara went to the door. He held her hands and pressed his face against the bars. What right had that hairy, jut-nosed, thin-lipped face to look beautiful? Her temples hammered.

"I want to show you something," he said in a grave tone. "Maybe that way . . . one kiss, Barbara."

She couldn't help it, she felt bonelessly weak and leaned toward him.

The main door of the Big House crashed open. Torchlight spilled on the cobbles, Minos became suddenly wan. The Greendale Macklin strode angrily forth, her women bristling about her.

The voice jerked Barbara to awareness, she sprang from the Monster and grabbed for the crossbow slung at her shoulder.

"This means war!"

Civilians and movable property were brought inside the stockade that night, and armed females streamed forth. But the fighting didn't start till well after sunrise.

Davis could just hear the horns and shouts and clash of metal. There was a good-sized battle on the edge of the forest, he guessed. He looked across a courtyard littered with women, children, and assorted dry goods and wondered what the desolation to do.

Claudia Udall tramped over to his jail, in full armor and toting a battle ax. Elinor Dyckman undulated in her wake, thinly clad and scared. Davis would rather have looked at her but thought it more tactful to meet the queen's eyes.

"Well, Monster, now a war has started on your account," said Claudia grimly.

Davis gave her a weak smile. "It wasn't my idea . . . uh, ma'm. What do they want me for, anyway?"

"The power, of course! Any town which had you and your ship could conquer the rest in days. Now we'll have those Greendale pests chased away by eclipse. Then will you help us?"

Davis hesitated. Union law was unreasonably strict about one's relationship with primitives. You could fight in self-defense, but using atomic guns to help a local aggression meant a stiff sentence.

"Let me aboard my boat—" he began.

"Of course," beamed Claudia. "Under guard."

"Hm, yeh, that's what I was afraid of." Davis had intended only to light out for Nerthus and never come back. Let the Service disentangle this Atlantean mess. He gulped and shook his head. "Sorry, I can't use the boat to fight with. You see, uh, well—"

"Bertie!" Elinor wobbled toward him. Her white indoor face was beaded with sweat. "Bertie, darling, you've got to help us. It's death for me if the Greendalers take this place."

"Hm?"

"Don't you understand? The Greendale Udall already has two Dyckman lovers. They won't want a third . . . they'll see to it . . . *Ber-r-rtie!*"

Davis got the idea. A queen's favorite dropped the word to some unsentimental captain—

"Nonsense, child." Claudia glared jealously. "Monster, right now the Greendalers do hold the area where your ship is. Can they get in?"

Davis laughed nervously. "Axes and crowbars against inert steel? I'd like to see them try!"

Short of atomic tools, there was only one way to open that airlock. He had set it to respond to himself whistling a few bars of a certain ballad. And *The Jolly Tinker* was not a song which any lady ought to know.

"You won't help us?" Claudia narrowed her eyes.

Davis began a long, thoroughly mendacious speech about friends who would avenge any harm done to him. He was just getting to the section on gunboats when Claudia snorted.

"If *we* can't have you, Monster, I might decide not to let anybody have you." She swung on her heel and walked off. Elinor followed, throwing imploring looks across her shoulder.

Davis sat down on the straw and groaned. As if he didn't have troubles enough, that sex machine had to slither around in a thin skirt and few beads . . . just out of reach.

Then he found himself wondering about Barbara Whitley. He hoped very much she wouldn't be hurt.

Eclipse came. It happened daily, at high noon in this longitude, when Atlantis, eternally facing her primary, got Minos between B and herself. An impressive sight: the planet, dimly lit by the remote companion sun, fourteen times as wide as Earth's moon, brimmed with fiery light refracted through the dense atmosphere . . . dusk on the ground and night in the sky. Davis looked hungrily at the stars. Civilized, urbane, *pleasant* stars! . . .

An hour later, the battle had ended and the Freetoon girls came back to the castle. Davis noticed that the warriors were divided into about thirty genotypes. When everyone in a single line of descent was genetically identical, a caste system was a natural development. And, yes, he could see why the Atlanteans had reverted to the old custom of putting surnames last. Family in the normal sense couldn't be very important here. For a moment the image of his father drifted across Davis' memory. He'd been rather a disappointment to the old man; it occurred to him that he had spent most of his life trying to justify himself in his father's eyes. But his chromosomes had never intended him for a solid citizen.

The armored lasses, foot and orsper (horse bird?) troops, clamored for lunch and beer. They had casualties and prisoners with them. There weren't many dead or seriously wounded—couldn't be, with these clumsy weapons powered by female muscles—but some had been killed, by ax, knife, dart, bolt—

"Barbara!" Davis whooped it forth.

The tall redhead looked his way and strolled over through the crowd. Her left hand was wrapped in a wet crimson bandage. "Barbara! Cosmos, I'm glad to see you're all right!"

She gave him an unfriendly grin. "Mistake, Monster. I'm her cousin Valeria."

"Oh. Well, how is she?"

"No damage. She's helping mount guard on your ship."

"Then you did win."

"For now. We beat them back into the woods, but they haven't quit." Valeria gave him a hard green stare. "Now I know you're a Monster. The Men would fight."

"Why can't you tribes compromise?"

"Who ever heard of an Udall compromising?" laughed Valeria.

"Then why do you obey them?"

"Why? Why, they're the . . . the *Udalls!*" Valeria was shocked. "When I took arms, I swore—"

"Why did you swear? My people have learned better than to allow absolute rulers. You've got a whole world here. What is there to fight about?"

"A gutless Monster would say that." Valeria spat and left.

The day dragged. Davis was fed, otherwise ignored. Night came, and he tried to sleep, but the refugees made too much noise.

Toward morning he fell into a doze, huddled under his feather quilts against the upland chill. A racket of trumpets and hurrying feet woke him.

Another battle! He strained against the bars, into darkness. And wasn't it getting closer? The sentries were shooting and—

Elinor screamed her way across the courtyard.

The multiple shadows thrown by Minos and the other moons rippled weirdly before her. "Bertie, you've got to help! They're driving us back!"

He reached out and patted her in a not very brotherly fashion. "There, there." When it made her hysterics worse, he shouted. After a struggle, he got some facts.

The Greendalers had returned with allies. Outnumbered three to one, the Freetooners were being hammered back through their own streets.

Newburgh, Blockhouse, and Highbridge banners flew beyond the walls. It was clear enough to Davis. Having learned about the spaceship, and well aware she couldn't take it alone, the Greendale Udall had sent for help, days ago, probably. And the prize looked great enough to unite even these factions for a while.

"But now Claudia will have to make terms," he blurted.

"It's too late!" sobbed Elinor. She moaned and ran toward the Big House. Only warriors were to be seen, the artisans and helots had retreated into their sheds. Davis told himself to stop shaking.

The fighting didn't halt even for eclipse. At mid-afternoon the gates opened and Freetoon's army poured into the court.

Step by step, their rearguard followed. Davis saw Barbara at the end of the line. She had a round wooden shield on one arm and swung a

light long-shafted ax. A red lock fell from under the battered morion
and plastered itself to a small, drawn face.

A burly warrior pushed against her. Barbara caught the
descending ax-blow on her shield. Her own weapon chopped for the
neck, missed, and bit at the leather cuirass. It didn't go through; low-
carbon steel got blunted almighty fast. The other woman grinned
and began hailing blows. Barbara sprang back and threw her ax
between the enemy's legs. Down went the woman. Barbara's dagger
jumped into her hand, she fell on top of the other and made a deft
slicing motion.

Davis got to his pot barely in time.

When he came back to the door, there was a lull in the battle. The
Freetooners had been pumping bolts and javelins from the catwalk,
discouraging the allies long enough for the gates to be closed.

Presently Barbara herself came to him. She was a-shiver with
weariness, and the eyes regarding him had dark rims beneath. There
was blood splashed on her breastplate and arms.

"How is it for you?" she asked hoarsely.

"I'm all right," said Davis. With more anxiety than a neutral party
ought to feel: "Are you hurt?"

"No. But I'm afraid this is the end."

"What . . . what do you think will happen? To you, I mean?"

"I'll get away at the last if I can." Her voice was numb.

Davis told himself sternly that this mess wasn't his fault. He had
seen from space that there were small towns and agriculture on this
continent, and had landed to bring the gift of Union civilization to all
its natives. The last thing he wanted was—

The *first* thing he wanted, he thought in self-abasement, had been
the glory of finding a new inhabited planet. And the money prizes,
and the lucrative survey commissions, and the adoring women.

"Cosmos curse it," he shouted, "I can't help your stupidity!"

Barbara gave him a blind, dazed look and wandered off.

At B-set the battle resumed. Trumpets howled, and by Minoslight
he saw Claudia hurry toward the gate.

Its wood groaned. The ladies from Greendale must be using a
battering ram. Fire kindled outside, flame ran up and splashed the sky.
Somehow a house had been touched off. The top of the stockade
loomed black across the blaze, like a row of teeth, the warriors on the

catwalk were silhouetted devils. Davis wondered crazily which of them was Barbara, if Barbara was still alive.

The main gate shuddered and a hinge pulled loose.

Someone galloped toward him on a frantic orsper, leading two others. She jumped from the saddle. "Barbara!" he whispered.

"Valeria again." The girl laughed with scant humor. "Stand aside, I'm going to get you out."

Her ax thudded against the bolt.

"But what—why—"

"We're finished," snapped Valeria. "For now, anyway. For always, unless you can help us. I'm going to get you out, Monster. We'll escape if we can, and see if you can remedy matters."

"But I'm neutral!" gibbered Davis.

Valeria grinned unpleasantly. "I have an ax and a knife, my dear, and nothing to lose. Are you still neutral?"

"No," gulped Davis. "Not if you feel that way about it."

Another orsper ran from the stables, with a rider who led a spare mount. Valeria turned, lifted her ax. "Oh, you."

"Same idea, I see," answered Barbara. *Of course,* thought Davis, *genetic twins normally think alike.* He saw that Barbara strove not to weep. It could be no fun to watch your country conquered.

"Put on your cloak, Monster," ordered Valeria between blows. "Pull the hood up. They won't bother with three people trying to get away . . . unless they know what you are!"

The bolt gave way. Valeria threw the door open. Davis stumbled out, got a foot in a stirrup and swung himself aboard. Valeria mounted another bird at his side. Barbara took the lead. They jogged toward the broken gate where Claudia and a few guards still smote forlornly at a ring of enemies. The orsper's pace was not so smooth as a horse's, and Davis was painfully reminded that a mounted man does well to wear tight pants. This silly kilt was no help. He stood up in the stirrups, swearing.

Someone ran from the Big House. "Help! Ohhh—" Davis glimpsed Elinor's face, blind with terror. He leaned over, caught her wrist, and whirled her toward a spare orsper.

"Get that pantywaist out of here!" yelled Valeria.

Elinor scrambled up. Barbara freed her ax and broke into a gallop. Willy-nilly, Davis followed.

A band of women stood before them. A bolt hummed maliciously past his ear. Barbara's orsper kicked with a gruesomely clawed foot. Davis' mount stumbled on something. Valeria leaned over and swung at a shadowy form, sparks showered.

Then they were out of the melee, on the street, into the fields and the forest beyond.

Davis woke up after eclipse. For a moment he knew only one pulsing ache, then memory of his all-night ride came back and he gasped.

Barbara, crouched over a little smokeless fire, preparing a meal from what supplies and equipment had been in the saddlebags, smiled at him. "How are you?" she asked.

"I'm not sure. Oof!" Davis crawled from his bedroll. His legs were so sore from standing as he rode that he didn't think he would ever walk again.

Dousing his head in a nearby spring helped, and he looked around. They had come a goodly ways from Freetoon, into a tall country of ancient woods and steep hillsides. Northward the land climbed higher still, with snow on the peaks. The day was clear and windy, sunlight spilled across green slopes and Minos brooded remotely overhead. Ay was a searing spark to the east, daily overtaking the closer sun.

"Bertie!"

Davis lurched to his feet as Elinor came from the forest, sleeking back her long hair. She fell into his arms and kissed him.

"Bertie, you saved my life, oh, I'm *so* grateful . . . do you know, Bertie, *I* believe you're a Man!"

"You might come slice your Man some bread," said Barbara acidly. "Why did you bring her, Davis? Of all the useless— And good women are dead back in Freetoon!"

Valeria strolled into sight, crossbow on her shoulder and a plump bird in one hand. "Hell," she drawled, "all we need to do is leave the Dyckman beast here. Let her make her own way back."

"I'll die!" screamed Elinor. "There are jacklins in these woods! I'll be killed! You can't—*Bertie!*"

"Keep out of this, Davis," snapped Valeria.

He blew up. "I'll be damned to Evil if I will!" he roared. "I've been pushed around long enough!"

In his present mood, he would have welcomed an excuse to clip that coppertopped hellion on the jaw, but Barbara intervened just as Valeria pulled a knife. "Enough out of all of you," she said. "We have to stick together. Davis, if you insist, we'll let this ... Elinor come along till we reach some town. Now sit down and eat!"

"Yes, ma'm," said Davis meekly.

The food was strengthening, it seemed to give him back his manhood. Now that he was out of that filthy jail, he ought to start exercising some choice. He would have given much for a cup of coffee and a cigarette, but neither being available, he opened the council. "What are your plans?" he asked.

"I don't know," said Valeria. Both Whitleys had calmed down as fast as they'd flared up, though Elinor remained tactfully inconspicuous. "Last night I only thought about getting away."

Davis tugged his beard. It itched. "Just what will happen at Freetoon?" he asked. "No massacres, I hope."

"Oh, no," said Barbara. "There've been conquests before. As far as the lower castes are concerned, it's only a change of bosses. And some of the soldiers will take a fresh oath to the new Udall—Damons, Burkes, Hausers—" She snorted the names. "But families like us, who don't switch loyalties so easily, have to be killed. Though I imagine a lot of our sort got away into the woods. Outlaw life—" She shrugged, woefully.

"All right," said Davis. "But what do you want to *do*? Claudia and her daughters are most likely dead now. You haven't got any chief to be loyal to."

The cousins stared at him and each other, as if suddenly bewildered. It was a moment before Valeria said savagely:

"Well, the powers of your ship aren't going to be used for Bess Udall of Greendale! Not after she killed barracks mates of mine."

Davis nodded, thinking his own thoughts. If Bess got her hooks on him, the situation would return to what it had been. He wouldn't lift gravs for her without a spear at his back and strict orders to destroy some town which Union law said he must die rather than bombard. He might well be tortured by way of inducement.

Therefore he must recapture his boat, somehow, despite all the guards the victorious allies would mount over it ... big joke!

Barbara looked at the northern ranges. "We've scant hope of

finding help this side of Smoky Pass," she said. "But nobody's crossed the mountains for, oh, generations. They say there are some strange folk living over there. If they'd help . . . we could promise them the loot from the enemy—"

"Wait a minute!" Davis' brain whirred. He was not forbidden by law to use violence against primitives, if it would save himself or rectify an obviously bad turn of affairs. But he doubted that a Coordinator board would see eye to eye with Barbara on what constituted rectification. "Look, look here," he stammered. "Wasn't there a message already sent to this, uh, holy Ship of yours?"

"To the Doctors? Yes," said Valeria. "They would decide—"

"Ah, ha!" Whoever these mysterious Doctors were, they knew enough science to operate a parthenogenesis machine. He'd have a better chance of convincing them of the truth than anyone else. And they could order his boat returned to him!

"Let's go to the Doctors," he said quickly. "They have the final disposition of the case anyway, and we'd be safe there."

"We can't!" said Valeria, quite aghast. "Barbara and I are only Maidens. And *you*—the Ship is sacred to Father!"

"But I'm a man," argued Davis. "Or a monster, if you insist. The rules don't apply to me." He glanced at Elinor. "You're an initiate, aren't you?" She nodded eagerly. "All right. You can escort me through the taboo area."

It took a good deal of wrangling. Being roared down out of bigger lungs was a salutary new experience for the Whitleys. Eventually they agreed, reserving the right to find allies if the Doctors, who seldom mixed in politics, would not order Freetoon liberated. The meaning of "liberation" in such a context was vague to Davis, but the poor lost kids needed something to hope for.

"We'll have to continue north," said Valeria. "Over Smokey Pass and down through the valleys on the other side to the coast . . . because the Holy River route, all this region, will be full of people hunting you, Davis. Once we reach the coast, we can maybe get passage with the sea-dwellers, back to the Ship at Holy River mouth."

The prospect looked strenuous, thought the man dismally.

At least it was summer. The Atlantean seasons were due only to the eccentricity of Minos' orbit, but he had gathered that hereabouts the variation of weather was considerable. A satellite always facing its primary: permanent tidal bulge, terrific mountains on the inner hemisphere and mostly ocean on the outer . . . oh, well.

He remembered an item. "Do you have a sewing kit?" he asked. "I'll need a, uh—" he blushed— "special garment."

"I'll make it for you," said Barbara helpfully. "Just let me get the measurements."

Davis' ears glowed cadmium red. "No, thanks! You wouldn't understand."

Elinor, who had picked up a little self-confidence, piped: "This trip will take just weeks, won't it? But the Freetoon couriers will have reached the Ship pretty soon. The Doctors will send word back. Why, we may meet one of their legates!"

"That's all right," said Valeria. "Just so we don't fall into Greendale hands." She drew a finger across her throat.

"Must you?" said Elinor faintly.

Davis glanced up at Minos. The big planet, 5000 Earth masses, was almost half full, its amber face blurred by a crushingly thick hydrogen atmosphere, cloudy bands of dull green and blue and brown, dark blots which were storms large enough to swallow Terra whole. He shivered. It was a long, lonesome way home; the Service wouldn't visit Delta of its own accord for decades, and he didn't think he could survive that long. Why, missing his antigeriatric treatments would alone cut his life down to a lousy century! *In short, me boy, you've got no choice. You're jolly well on the Whitley team.*

He looked at the cousins and then at Elinor; she smiled back at him. It could be a lot worse, he reflected. One man alone with three beautiful girls—if he couldn't make a good thing out of that, he didn't deserve to . . .

Some days later, Davis Bertram shivered on the heights of the Ridge with Elinor.

It had been a cruel trek, through the forests and then up over the glaciers to this pass. Davis wanted to help with the twins' pot-hunting, at least—he soon mastered the spring-powered repeating crossbow— but Valeria told him coldly that he walked too loud. Maybe that had been the worst of the situation, the feeling of uselessness. He had always before taken the lead while women watched and made admiring noises.

However, as they rested atop Smoky Pass, in a mordant wind and whirl of dry snow, Elinor shared his ragged cloak.

The range dropped even more steeply on its north side than the southern approach. Davis looked across a downward-rolling immensity of green, veined by rivers, here and there the flash of a lake, and wished for his paints.

"I don't see any signs of man . . . uh, woman . . . down there," he said, "but there must be some. Haven't you any idea what the people are like? Seems you'd all meet at the Ship."

"Oh, no," replied Elinor. "You see, Bertie, each town sends its own parties to be fertilized. It's seldom that two groups are at the Ship at the same time, and even if they are, they don't talk to—Oh, I mustn't say more. But it's *thrilling!*" She clasped her hands. "And safe. Nobody would dare attack a party going to or from the Ship. If anyone did, why, the Doctors would refuse to fertilize that whole town forever after."

Which would be one form of excommunication that really worked, though Davis. He gave Elinor a sidelong glance. Her nose was frostbitten and peeling, she had lost weight, but she was still an interesting lesson in solid geometry. And he wanted a lot more information from her, whether it was taboo to non-initiates or not. He was going to enjoy persuading her.

Meanwhile, though, they had to get down where it was warm.

Later he remembered the next two days only as a nightmare of struggle. He could hardly believe it when they reached timberline and the nearly vertical descent began to flatten.

This was a conifer forest, trees not unlike jack pines though the smell was different, sweeter and headier. The ground was thick with brown needles, the orsper footfalls a muted *pad-pad*. They saw only small birds, darting red and gold between bluish-green branches, but there was spoor of big game.

At the end of the day, they reached a king-sized lake. It blinked amiably in the low sunshine, reeds rustled on the banks and fish leaped in the water. "We couldn't find a better campsite," said Barbara.

"Skeeterbugs," said Valeria.

"Not this early in the year."

"Yeh? See here, rockhead, I've seen them when—"

There were no skeeterbugs that night. This did not improve Valeria's temper.

In the morning, both Whitleys went out afoot after game. Davis and Elinor were to watch the camp and try for fish: there were hooks and lines in the saddlebags. It was a cool, sun-drenched day and a flock of birds with particularly good voices were tuning up nearby. Davis' grin spread.

"What are you so happy about?" Elinor looked grumpily up from scouring the utensils.

"At having you all to myself," admitted Davis candidly. He knew her type. "Let's take a stroll."

"Bertie! No!" Elinor pouted. "I'm so tired."

"As you wish." He sauntered off. In a moment she pattered after him. He took her hand, squeezing it rather more than necessary.

"Bertie! Bertie, be careful, you're so *strong*—"

Davis wandered along the lakeshore, eyes alert for a secluded spot. He was in no hurry: all day before him, and he was going to enjoy the fishing too.

"You're a brave little girl, Elinor," he said. "Coming all this way and—" he paused, took a deep breath, and prepared the Big Lie—"never a complaint from you."

"I could complain," she said bitterly. "Those awful Whitleys. Skin and bones and nasty red hair and tongues like files. They're just jealous."

It might have been profitable to agree, but for some reason Davis couldn't backbite Barbara. "I hope the worst is over," he said. "You ought to tell me what to expect when we reach the Ship."

"I can't, Bertie. I mustn't. Nobody who's been there is allowed to talk about it to anyone who hasn't."

"But I'm a Man," he argued. "You do believe that, don't you?"

"Yes . . . you must be . . . even if your whiskers *tickle*."

Davis stroked his short yellow beard patriarchally. "Well, then," he said, "since the Doctors are only filling in for men . . . I mean . . . Sunblaze!" He backed up and started over. "What are they like, the Doctors?"

"I can't—" Davis stopped for some agreeable physical persuasion. "I mustn't—Mmmmm! Bertie!" After a while: "I really *can't* say. They have this big beautiful town, with the Ship in the very middle. But I never saw a Doctor's face. They're always veiled. Bertie, please! I *mustn't* tell you anything!"

"I can guess. The, uh, fertilizing rite—it involves a machine, doesn't it? A lot of tubes and wires and things?"

"If you know that much," said Elinor, "yes."

Davis nodded absently. The picture was taking shape.

Three hundred years ago, the hyperdrive was new and colonization more art than science. You couldn't trust an apparently Earthlike planet; chances were its biochemistry would be lethal to man. It was rare good luck to find a world like Atlantis. Therefore doctrine enjoined caution. First the planet was thoroughly surveyed. Then an all-male party landed, spent two or three years building, analyzing, testing in detail. Finally the women came.

Somewhere in the Service archives of three centuries back lay a record of a female transport with a female crew; you didn't mix the sexes on such a journey unless you wanted trouble. Judging from names, its complement had been purely North American. The ship was bound for a new colony, but vanished. A trepidation vortex, of course, perhaps the same one he had managed to avoid. That was back before anybody knew of such a thing.

The Ship had not been destroyed. It had been tossed at an unthinkable pseudovelocity across hundreds of light-years. The hyperdrive must have been ruined, since it didn't return home. It must have emerged quite near Delta Capitis Lupi, or it would have drifted endlessly at sublight speed till the women died.

Pure good fortune that Atlantis was habitable. But probably the ship had been wrecked in landing, because it seemed never to have lifted gravs again. And there they were, cut off, no way to call for help and no way to get back.

They had little machinery, no weapons, scant technical knowledge. They did their best—discovered what the edible grains and domesticable fowl were, located mines and established crude smelters, named the planets and moons in classical tradition—but that was all, and their knowledge slipped from them in a few illiterate lifetimes.

But in the first generation there must have been a biochemist. The thought of aging and dying, one by one, with nobody to help the last feeble survivors, was unwelcome. Human parthenogenesis was an ancient technique, though little used. The biochemist had taken what equipment was in the ship to make such a machine.

The right chemicals under the right conditions would cause a single ovum to divide. Once that process was initiated, it followed the normal course, and in nine months a child was born, genetically identical with the mother.

"Three hundred years of virgin birth!" mumbled Davis. "An appalling situation. It will have to be remedied."

"What are you talking about?" asked Elinor.

"You'll find out," he grinned.

They had come to a little bay, with soft grass down to the water's edge, rustling shade trees, the mountains looming titanic above. Flowers blossomed fiery underfoot and small waves chuckled against the shore.

It was, in short, an ideal spot for a seduction.

Davis planted his fishing pole in a forked twig, laid aside his weapons, sat down, and extended an invitational arm. Elinor sighed and snuggled up to him.

"Just think," she whispered. "The first Man in three hundred years!"

"High time, isn't it?" said Davis thickly.

"Ah . . . your kilt. . . what's the matter?"

"Never mind." Davis gathered her in. Their necking became furious. He fumbled at her belt buckle. She closed her eyes, breathing hard. His other hand slid up her thigh.

Something roared behind him.

Davis leaped a meter in the air from a prone position. Elinor screamed.

The thing looked like a saw-beaked, penguin-feathered seal, but bigger. It had swallowed his hook and was quite indignant. The flippers shot it up on the shore and over the grass at express speed.

Elinor tried to get to her feet. The fluke-like legs batted out. She went rolling and lay still. Davis clawed for his ax. He chopped wildly, saw blood run, but the damned soft iron wouldn't bite on that thick skull.

The seal-bird knocked him down and snapped at his face. Jaws closed on the ax haft and crunched it across. Davis got a hand on the upper and lower mandibles, threw a leg over the long sleek back and heaved. The brute roared and writhed. He felt his strength pour out of him, the teeth were closing on his fingers.

A crossbow bolt hummed and buried itself in the wet flank. Another and another. Barbara ran over the grass, shooting as she went. The monster turned its head and Davis yanked his hands free.

"Get away!" yelled Barbara.

Her bow was empty now. She crouched, drawing her knife, and plunged toward the creature. It reared up. She jammed her left arm under its beak, forced the head back, and slashed.

The seal-bird fell on her. Davis glimpsed a slim leg beneath its belly. He picked up his own bow and fired pointblank, again and again, hardly aware of what he did. Blood gurgled in the monster's voice.

Then it slumped, and the arterial spurting was only a red flow across slippery grass.

"Barbara—" Davis tugged at the weight, feeble and futile. His own throat rattled.

The leg stirred. Barbara forced her way out from under.

She stood up, gasping, adrip with blood, and stared at him. His knees gave way.

"Are you all right?" she whispered. "Bert, darling, are you all right?"

"Yeh." His palms were lacerated, but it was nothing serious. "You?"

"Oh, th-th-this isn't my blood." She laughed shortly, sank to her knees before him, and burst into tears.

"There, there." He patted the bronze head, clumsy and unsure of himself. "It's all over, Barbara, it's finished now . . . Sunblaze, we've got meat for the pot—"

She shook herself, wiped her eyes, and gave him an angry stare. "You *fool!*" she snuffled. "If I hadn't h-h-happened to be near . . . heard the noise . . . oh, you blind gruntbrain!"

"Guess I've got that coming," said Davis.

Elinor stirred, looked around, and started to cry. Since she wasn't much hurt, she got no attention. "Well!" she muttered.

Barbara swallowed her rage. "I never saw a thing like this before," she admitted. "I suppose you couldn't have known, Bert. You were giving it a hell of a good fight. And it *is* meat."

"Thanks," he said weakly. . . .

When Valeria had blown off enough pressure by a magnificent description of Davis' altogether negligible intelligence, she finished: "We'll start out again tomorrow."

"Oh, yes!" babbled Elinor. "Those *things* in the lake—"

"What about the orspers?" demanded Barbara.

"Ride 'em till they drop, child, and continue on foot," said Valeria. "It'll be quicker."

"Don't call me child!" exploded Barbara. "I'm only three days younger than you, and my brain is twenty years older!"

"Girls, girls," began Davis. Valeria's scarred left hand dropped to her dagger, and he shut up and let the twins argue.

Barbara gave in at last, against her better judgment . . . after all, if they camped longer, Davis and Elinor were sure to— Only why should she care? What was a Monster to her?

She regarded him with concern. He had seemed such a big coward, she reflected; and yet he had fought the lake bird to save Elinor's life . . . Damn Elinor! If Davis had died on her account—Maybe, she thought, his unwillingness to fight was only a different way of thinking. A Man wouldn't think like a woman.

But it was heresy to admit this creature barely two meters tall, who could sweat and bleed and be afraid, was a Man!

And yet, when you got used to him, he was a beautiful creature, beard like spun gold and blue eyes that crinkled when he laughed . . . his hand brushed her knee, accidentally, and for a moment it seemed to burn and she got all weak and the world wobbled. What was wrong with her? She wanted to laugh and cry at the same time. Vague dreams chased through her head, she performed heroic deeds before his eyes, now they were together under a full Minos—

"Damn!" said Barbara.

"What's the matter?" asked Davis.

"Oh, nothing." His gaze made her want to squirm. "Leave me alone, will you?— No, I didn't mean that!"

All the next day, as they rode deeper into the valley, she churned over a new thought. Just suppose Davis *was* really a Man. What then? Yes . . . voice the thought, wait for Father's thunderbolt . . . when none came, Barbara's universe quivered and lost a few bricks.

He was at least a very dear Monster, with his songs and laughter, and he came from the stars. The stars! Man or no, he could bring the Men, and Atlantis would never be the same again.

Even if no Men ever came, she thought with sudden tears, her own Atlantis was dead. Let her return in triumph, driving out the enemy from Freetoon, return to the comradeship of the barracks and the unforgotten forest, Holy River below her like a dawn knife and the remote lance of the High Gaunt wreathed with cloud—for her, after knowing Davis, it would be too narrow and lonesome. She could never really go home.

She wanted to blurt her woe to him. It was not the Whitley way, but there would be a strange comfort, like having her mother back . . . only he would not hold her like her mother—

For lack of anyone else, she confided in Valeria. They were sitting up by the campfire while the others slept.

"It would be better if the Men came," agreed her cousin. "We've never lived as Father meant us to. We've just hung on, hoping, for three hundred years."

Barbara felt a smile tug her mouth. "It would be fun to have a Man-child," she murmured. "A kid like his father—like both of us mixed together—" Suddenly: "Val! I've been thinking . . . I almost believe Bert *is* a Man!"

"Rotten specimen of one, then," snapped Valeria.

Barbara felt puzzled. Her twin was an obstinate nuisance, yes, but so was she. They had never thought so unlike before now.

On the following day, the descent became so steep that they had to lead the orspers. Toward evening they found themselves on the stony floor of a large canyon. The river flowing through it was broad as a lake, brown and swift, toppling in a kilometer-high waterfall over a cliff behind them. The air was subtropically warm, this was a much lower country than Freetoon's.

"These birds are about finished if they don't get a long rest," ventured Elinor. She sighed. "So am I."

"Maybe we can find someone around here who'll trade us," suggested Davis. "Look, whether you believe I'm a Man or not, I can sure as Evil act the part, overawe them, demand their help."

"It's blasphemy!" said Valeria.

Barbara looked down at her own tanned form, saw no signs of shriveling, and grew skeptical of Father with a speed that astonished her. "Are you afraid to try, Val?" she purred.

"All right, then!" snarled the other Whitley. "If this oaf can act like a Man, all right."

They were up before Bee-rise the next day, trudging downstream along the barren riverbank. The first dawn-glow showed the end of their search.

An island, some ten kilometers across, lifted sheer cliffs from the water to a luxuriance of trees on its crown. There was no access but a suspension bridge from the shore to the heights. Barbara's crossbow clanked into position. "So we've found somebody," she murmured.

"The question," said Valeria, "is who, and what can we talk them out of? Go to it, Davis."

He advanced to the foot of the bridge, cupped hands around his mouth, and bawled: "Hello, up there! We come in peace!" Echoes clamored from the canyon wall. There was a waiting.

Then a slender girl clad in long brown hair and a few flowers stepped from beneath the trees to the bridgehead. She carried an arbalest, but didn't aim it. "Who are you?" she called timidly.

"She's a Craig," muttered Barbara to Davis. "At home they're all poets and weavers. Now why would a Craig be on sentry-go?"

Davis drew himself up. "Know that I am a Man, come from Earth to redeem the old promise," he intoned. Barbara smothered a giggle.

"Oh!" The Craig dropped her bow and broke into a tremble. "A Man—*Ohhhh!*"

"I come as the vanguard of all the Men, that they may return to their loyal women and drive evil from Atlantis," boomed Davis. "Let me cross your bridge that I may, uh, claim your help in my, er, crusade. Yes, that's it, crusade."

The Craig squeaked and fell on her face. Davis led his tatterdemalion party over the bridge. The timing was perfect: Bee just rising in a golden blaze over the great waterfall above them. On the other side of the bridge, there was a downward path. The island was cup-shaped, holding trees in orderly groves, clipped grass, brilliant flowerbeds.

A few more women emerged from the foliage. They were as sleek, sun-tanned, and informally clad as the first one. And their reactions were just as satisfactory, a spectrum from abasement to awed gaping.

"More Craigs, couple of Salmons, a Holloway, an O'Brien," murmured Valeria. "Artist, artisan, entertainer classes at home—where are the warriors?"

A Holloway cleared her throat shyly and blushed. "We never thought there would be such an honor for us," she said. "We thought when the Men came, they'd—I mean—"

Davis puffed himself up. "Do you doubt I am a Man?" he roared.

"Oh, no, ma'm!" The Holloway cringed back from possible thunderbolts. Her voice, like that of all the islanders, had a melodiousness which betokened long training.

"Where's your Udall?" asked Valeria impatiently.

"Udall, ma'm?" The Craig they had first seen looked confused. "No Udalls here. Just us, ma'm."

No Udall! Barbara's mind staggered. But, but it wasn't possible!

"We'll take you to Prezden Yvonne Craig, ma'm," offered the Holloway.

"Do so." Davis beamed. "Incidentally, 'sir' would be more suitable than 'ma'm'. And don't . . . I mean, be not afraid. Rejoice!"

Another puzzling alienness—the islanders needed no more than the Man's consent to start rejoicing! Like children! When they had walked through two kilometers of parkscape, the whole population swarmed out to meet them, laughing, singing, dancing, striking up music for them. Altogether they numbered about a thousand, including children, and all bore plain signs of good, easy living.

Their village was surprisingly large. Barbara decided dazedly that they didn't have barracks at all. Each of these simple grass huts was for no more than one woman and her children. The concept of privacy was so new it felt like a hammerblow.

She was led to a hut, and goggle-eyed girls brought her eggs, fruits, small sweet cakes, and sang to her while she ate. Only slowly did her mind stumble from the wreckage of its own axioms and wonder what Davis was up to. . . .

As a matter of fact, Davis, the past weeks catching up with him, had gone to sleep. He woke near sunset, donned the embroidered kilt, plumed headdress, and gold ornaments laid out for him, and strolled from the shack to find a banquet in preparation.

Valeria stood waiting for him in the long mellow B-light. She had loosened her red hair and discarded armor for a kilt and lei, but the scarred left hand rested on her dagger. They started together across the green toward a dais draped with feather cloaks, where Barbara stood talking to a Craig who held a carved staff.

"We seem to have found the kind of place we deserve," he said.

Valeria snorted. "Oh, yes, they're friendly enough—but gutless.

This island is *too* easy to defend. They fish, raise fowl, have fruits the year round, all the metal they need . . . spend their time on arts, poetry, craft, music—" She ended her list with a vulgarity.

Glancing at delicately sculptured wood, subtly designed decoration, intricate figure dancing, listening to choral music which was genuinely excellent, Davis got fed up with Valeria. Narrow-minded witch! Her own rather repulsive virtues, hardihood and fearlessness, would be as redundant here as fangs on a turtle.

"What's the place called?" he asked coldly.

"Lysum. There was a conquered town about a hundred years ago that a lot of its people ran away from. Up the river there's a settlement of nothing but Burkes. These people are all from the same class . . . Oh, here we are. Prezden Yvonne Craig, Davis Bert."

The woman stood up for him. She was in her middle thirties, and given a stronger chin would have been quite pretty—though Barbara, in kilt and lei, was unfair competition. "Be welcome among us, Man." Now that the first shock had worn off, she spoke with confidence. "Atlantis has never known a happier day. Oh, we're so thrilled!"

Davis looked around. "Where's Elinor?"

"Still pounding her ear," clipped Barbara. "Want to wait?"

"Cosmos, no! When do we—I mean, let the banquet begin."

Rank, as the women of Lysum settled themselves on the grass, seemed strictly according to age. It was pleasant to be in a casteless society again. The food was delicious, and there was course after course of it, and the wooden winebowls were kept filled.

Suppressing a burp, Davis leaned toward Yvonne. "I am pleased with what I have seen here," he told her.

"You are *so* sweet . . . er, gracious," she trilled happily.

"But elsewhere there is devilment on the loose. I am only the vanguard of the Men. Before all of them can come, the wrongdoers of Atlantis must be punished."

Yvonne looked alarmed. Valeria, flanking Davis on the seat with Barbara, leaned over and hissed: "No help here. I told this featherbelly we'd want some spears to follow us, and she damn near fainted."

"Mmmm . . . yes." Davis felt a moment's grimness. He couldn't stay holed up here forever. No wonder Val was so down on the islanders. Not a bad girl, Val, in her waspish way. Davis tilted his winebowl. His free arm stole around Barbara's waist. She regarded him mistily.

"Strong, this drink," she said. "Not beer. Wha's it called?"

"A jug of wine, and thou," smiled Davis.

"Bubbles in my head . . ." Barbara leaned against him.

The Prezden gave him a large-eyed look. Minoslight streamed over sprawling feminine shapes. "Will you take your pleasure of us all tonight, sir?" she inquired.

"Yipe!" said Davis.

"Like hell you will!" Barbara sat straight up and glared at him.

Yvonne looked bewildered. Barbara was quite tight enough to start an argument, which would never do. Davis gritted his teeth and said: "No, thanks. Tonight I must, urp, think on weighty problems. I would be alone."

Yvonne bent her long-tressed head. "As the Man wishes. My house is his." Her dignity collapsed in a titter. "I am his, too, if he changes his mind. Any of us would be so *thrilled*—" She rose and clapped her hands. "The Man wishes to be alone tonight," she called. "All you girls scat!"

Davis gaped. It was not what he had meant. Too late now, of course. A god couldn't say, "Hoy, wait!"

Valeria stood up, put an arm under Barbara's shoulders, and raised her tottery cousin. "I'll see her to bed," she said frostily.

Davis watched them disappear into one of the huts. "Death and destruction!" he said, and poured himself another drink.

He was tipsy, but there was no sleep in him. Presently he wandered off across a dewed sward, under the light-spattered shade of high trees, and stood on the island rim looking across a broken wilderness of stone and water and moonlight.

The fact is, me boy, and we might as well face it with our usual modesty, Barbara is in love with me. Maybe she doesn't quite realize it yet, but I know the symptoms. Well?

Well, so if they could only shake that Valeria hornet and that rather cloying Elinor, they could have a lot of fun. Only somehow Barbara Whitley wasn't a person you could simply have fun with. Davis grew a little scared. Cosmos sunder it, he didn't want to be tied down yet!

So, since he couldn't get away from her, he'd have to remove temptation by curing her of her feelings. In the absence of electronic psychadjusters, he thought woozily, he could do that by making her mad at him—say, by exercising his Man's prerogatives with, yes, with

Yvonne . . . who must be very disappointed in him . . . he grinned and started down toward the village.

As he emerged from a grove into the unreal light, he stopped short. A tall form approached him. "Barbara," he stammered.

She came to him, smiling and shaking the loose red hair down over her back, but her eyes were big, solemn, a little afraid. "Bert," she said. "I have to talk to you." She halted and stood with hands clasped behind her, like a child. Davis swallowed, because she was not at all like a child in other respects.

"Uh . . . sure . . . you got rid of that spitcat cousin of yours, I see," he began feebly.

"She's asleep. I wanted this to be between us two."

"Uh, yes, of course. Can't settle anything with Valeria around. Ask her a civil question and you get a civil war."

"Val . . . oh." Light and shadow flowed across the girl. Suddenly: "What do you have against Valeria?"

"She's just a natural-born shrew, I suppose," he shrugged.

"She means well. It's only that she—never quite knows what to say . . . we are of the same blood, I know her and—"

"Scuttle Valeria!" said Davis impulsively. "Come here, you!"

She crept into his arms, her hands stole around his neck and he kissed her. She responded with an endearing clumsiness.

"I couldn't stand it, Bertie," she gulped. "You and all those other women—what's happened to me?"

"Poor little Babs." He stroked her hair. "Sit down."

They spent a while without words. He was delighted to see how fast she learned. Here in the shadow of the frondtrees, she was only a warm breathing shape close to him.

After a time, she blurted: "Do whatever you want, Bertie."

Davis reached for her—and pulled up cold.

It was one thing to seduce an Elinor or an Yvonne. Barbara was a different case entirely: too whole-hearted, it would hurt her too much when he finally left. And . . . and . . . oh, there were all the practical objections, a long dangerous road ahead and so on. At the same time— no he *could* not rebuff her or humiliate her into storming off.

"Well?" she asked with a hint of testiness.

"Well, this is a serious matter," said Davis frantically. "You should think it over . . . look here . . . but—"

"But nothing!" Small calloused hands closed on his wrists.

Davis talked. And talked. And talked. He wasn't sure what he said, but it included words like sanctity. At the end, sweating, he asked her if she understood at all.

"No," she sighed. "But I imagine you know best."

"I wonder—never mind! Of course I do."

"There'll be other times, darling. Whenever you want to fer—"

"Cut that out!" groaned Davis. "Give me a kiss and go to bed."

She gave him a lengthy one. Then, rising: "There's one thing, dearest. The others in our party—you know it could make trouble—don't let's let on to *anyone*. Don't even talk to me about it unless I say the coast is clear."

"All right. That does make sense. Run along, sweetheart."

"Goodnight, Bertie. I care for you."

"The word," he said, "is 'love.'"

"I love you, then." She laughed, with a little sob, and sped off.

She ran like a deer, Davis thought. Evil, why couldn't she be trained for spatial survey? Married teams were common enough.

The girl stumbled. She spread her hands, regained balance, and continued.

Davis felt the wind go out of him. There had been a scar on her left hand. . . .

Barbara woke up and wished she hadn't. What had she been *drinking?*

She rolled over on her stomach and buried her face in her hands. Foggy recollections came back, yes, Val had helped her to bed and then she passed out . . . Davis making eyes at that Yvonne trollop—Father!

A young O'Brien entered with breakfast, which helped. Barbara tottered out into the open. It was a little past eclipse, and the islanders were going leisurely about their business. Prezden Yvonne ran warbling to greet her, received a bloodshot glare, and backed off. Barbara smoldered her way toward a fruit grove.

Valeria came into sight, wringing out her hair. "O, hello, little one," she grinned. "I recommend a swim. The water's fine."

"What have you got to be so Father-damned happy about?" grouched Barbara.

Valeria did a few steps of the soldier's ax dance. "Beautiful, beautiful day," she caroled. "I love this place!"

"Then it's too bad we're getting the hell out of here."

"Whatever for?"

"What reason is there to stay?" Barbara kicked miserably at the turf. "So Davis can make up to all the women in Lysum? I suppose he's still sleeping it off."

"Well, he did go to bed quite late, poor dear. But he just walked around, thinking." Valeria flushed at Barbara's look. "I couldn't sleep— sat up watching." Quickly, she jumped after a red fruit and crunched it between small white teeth. "Look, Babs, we do need a rest. So do our orspers; there aren't any here."

"Don't you know?" said Barbara. "One of those yuts told me yesterday. This river runs straight to the sea. They have boats here, we'll take one and make the trip twice as fast. The Lysumites get to the Ship that way—buy passage from—"

"Oh, hell, Babs. Life's too good to waste. I say let's stay here a few more days, at least." Valeria wandered off.

Barbara drifted glumly to the bridge. She didn't like the idea. That Yvonne—ugh!

A swim did help. Seated again on the rocky bank, she found her head clear enough to hold the problem. Which was that she wanted Davis for herself.

Just what that would mean, she wasn't sure, but the thought made her hot and cold by turns. She no longer doubted he was a Man, but it wasn't just any Man, it was *him*. Hell fry her if she let anyone else get him!

Then the thing to do was sneak out tonight, find him and— It took more courage than facing a wounded stamper. But to know where she stood and what she meant to do about it was like a fresh cup of that wine drink. She put her kilt back on and returned almost merrily.

Davis was just emerging from his hut. He looked wretched. Barbara's heart turned over with pity, she ran toward him calling his dear name and wondered why he jerked.

"Bert, what's the matter? Don't you feel well?"

"No," said Davis, hollowly.

Valeria joined them, walking in a new undulant fashion. Was everybody falling sick? "Lemme out of here," Davis muttered.

The musical winding of a horn interrupted them.

"Somebody's coming," said Barbara. "Over the bridge."

"It may not mean anything," said Valeria, "but let's get out of the way, just in case. Better collect the Dyckman."

Barbara nodded and ran off. Elinor, stretching herself langurously before a burly Holloway, found herself suddenly prodded up the slope at dagger point. Valeria and Davis joined them in a tanglewood stand on the rim. They stood peering through the leaves at a bustle down in the village, the Lysumites leaping to form ceremonial ranks.

"Father!" breathed Valeria. "It's a legate—messenger from the Doctors!"

The awe of a lifetime rose within Barbara. She had rarely seen a legate; now and then one had come to Freetoon to discuss such matters as the payment of annual tribute.

This was a tall woman. She wore a travel-stained uniform: hooded blue cloak, trousers and boots under a white gown, heavy veil. She was mounted on an orsper and led remounts and a packbird. As she stepped to earth, Yvonne prostrated herself.

Valeria snapped her fingers. "Of course!" she said excitedly. "Messengers from Freetoon to the Ship . . . remember? The Doctors must have sent to every town to inquire—"

"Well," said Davis. "Well, this is terrific! Our troubles are over, girls."

The veiled woman entered a hut. Her baggage was brought in after her, then she was alone. A party of women ran up the slope calling: "Man! Man, the legate wants to see you!"

Davis smiled importantly and led the way down. He seated himself on the dais, much to the shock of the crowded islanders—nobody sat in a Doctor's presence!—and waited. Stillness lay thick.

When the legate finally emerged, Barbara's knees bumped together.

The woman had changed into ceremonials: green robe, gloved hands holding a metal staff, a plumed mask in the shape of an orsper head covering her own and making it coldly unhuman.

Davis got up. "Hello, ma'm," he smiled. There was no answer. He faltered. "I am the Man," he stumbled. "You, uh, know about me?"

"Yes," said the legate. She had a low voice and a stiff accent. "The Ship and all Atlantis have awaited the Men for three hundred years. How many of you are there?"

"Just me," said Davis. "I need your help—the Doctors' help.

Otherwise," he finished dramatically, "there won't be any Men coming for a long time yet."

The legate neither moved nor spoke. Davis looked disconcerted, but launched into his story. He warmed up to it as he went along, and clenched his fists to emphasize the main point: the Doctors could order his boat returned to him, and he would fetch the Men. Barbara thought he looked much too smug, but lovable all the same.

At the end, the legate asked coolly: "Have you any weapons?"

"No, I told you. Just this dirk here. But—"

"I understand."

She strode from him, toward the bridge guards who stood holding their bows in what Barbara considered a miserable approximation of dress parade. Her voice rang out:

"This is no Man, it's a Monster. Kill it!"

For a moment nobody stirred.

The legate whirled on Yvonne. "I order you in the name of Father," she cried. "Kill the filthy thing!"

Barbara had no time to think. She jumped, snatched a bow from a half paralyzed guard, and lifted it to her shoulder. "The first one of you to move gets a bolt in the belly," she announced.

Valeria's dagger flared directly before the legate. "And this witch gets a slit throat," she added. Her voice cracked across. "Hold still, you!"

In Freetoon the arbalests would have been snapping already. But these were a timid folk who had not known battle for generations. "Drop your weapons," said Barbara. She swiveled her own from guard to guard. Armament clattered to the grass. A moan went through the densely packed crowd.

Davis shook a benumbed head. "What's the matter?" he croaked. "I am a Man. Give me a chance to prove it!"

"You've already proved yourself a Monster by assaulting the Ship's own envoy," shouted the legate. "Prezden, do your duty!"

Yvonne Craig shuddered her way backward, lifting helpless hands. "You mustn't," she whimpered. "You can't—"

Through a haze of terror, Barbara saw Davis shake himself. He spoke swiftly then: "Unless you want to die, lady, you'd better tell these people to obey us."

Valeria emphasized the request with a dagger flourish. Malevolence answered him: "So be it, then . . . for now! Don't think you'll escape Father."

Davis turned to the Whitleys. He was pale and breathed hard, but the words rattled from him: "We have to get out of here. Keep these people covered. I'll take charge. You, you, you, you—" his finger chose young, horror-smitten girls. "Fetch out all our stuff. And the legate's pack. And food, plenty of it. Elinor, pick up some bows."

"No—no, you Monster," she gasped.

"Suit yourself," he laughed harshly. "Stay here if you want to be torn to pieces as soon as we're gone."

Shaking, she collected an armful of weapons.

When the supplies were ready, Davis led his group up the path, a scared and sullen village trailing them several meters behind and staring into the Whitley bowsights. Once over the bridge, he cut the cable with a few hard ax strokes. The bridge collapsed into the water and broke up.

"How do we get back?" cried a young Holloway.

"You can swim out and let 'em lower ropes for you," said Davis. "Now, take us to those boats I heard somebody mention."

The burdened women trudged along the shaly bank while Yvonne stood on the cliffs and howled loyal curses. On the other side of a bluff, jutting into the river, a score of long slim bark canoes with carved stemposts were drawn up. Davis told his prisoners to load one. "And set the others afire," he added to Barbara.

She nodded mutely and took forth tinder and fire piston from her pouch. Flame licked across the hulls. Her mind felt gluey, she didn't know if she could have moved without him to think for her.

"All right," said Davis when the job was done. "Scram, you females. Boo!" He waved his arms and the youngsters fled screaming.

Barbara took a certain satisfaction in binding the legate's wrists and ankles and tossing her among the bundles. Elinor huddled near the captive, big help she'd be! They shoved the canoe into the river and climbed aboard. Davis demonstrated the use of paddles, set Valeria in the bow and Barbara in the stern, and said he and Elinor could spell them.

Ariadne rose above Ay-set, and Theseus was already up. It would be a bright night. Father! Barbara could have wished for clouds, she felt so exposed under the naked sky. There was a blotch on Minos like a great bloodshot eye glaring down at her.

No, she told herself, Father was a lie . . . at least, the stiff lightning-tossing Father of the Ship did not exist, or if he did then Bert with his long legs and blue eyes and tawny beard was a stronger god. Merely looking at him made her want to cry.

He grinned and wiped sweat off his face. "Holy Valdaoth, I don't want to go through that again!" he said.

Valeria looked over her shoulder. "But we got away," she whispered. "Thanks to you, we got away."

"To me? Thunderation! If you two hadn't— Well, let's take the cash and let the credit go." He regarded the legate thoughtfully. "I wonder what's beneath that helmet," he said.

He lifted the gilt orsper head. Barbara, who had half expected haloes or some such item, was almost disappointed when the ash-blonde hair and coldly regular features of a Trevor appeared.

Elinor covered her eyes and crouched shivering. "I d-d-didn't want to see, ma'm," she pleaded.

"You've fallen into bad company, child," said the Trevor. Then, to Davis: "Are you satisfied, Monster?"

"No." He ran a hand through unkempt yellow hair and asked plaintively: "What have you got against me? Don't you know I'm a Man? You must have *some* biological knowledge to operate that parthenogenetic wingding."

"You aren't a Man." The Trevor lay back, scowling in the light that spilled from the sky.

After a moment, Davis murmured: "I see. It's a common enough pattern in history. You Doctors have had it soft for a long time. You must always have dreaded the day when the Men would finally arrive and upset your little wagon. When I told you I'm alone and there won't be any others for a long time yet if I don't return—well, your bosses at the Ship must already have told you what to do if that was the case."

"You're a Monster!" said the Trevor. Dogmatic as ever.

"Even if you honestly thought I was, you wouldn't have ordered them to cut me down. Even a Monster could go home and call the true Men. No, no, my friend you're a pretty sophisticated lot at the Ship, and you've just decided to rub out the competition."

"Be still before Father strikes you dead!" she cried.

"Legates sent to every town," went on Davis. "Orders to learn what the facts are—dicker with the Men if there really are a number of them or if they can call for help; otherwise kill them and deny everything."

"I'd like to kill *her*," said Barbara between her teeth.

"Babs, have you any idea who the Doctors are . . . how many, what families?"

She frowned, trying to remember. A child always picked up scraps of information meant only for initiates . . . she overheard this, was blabbed that by a garrulous helot. "There are a few thousand of them, I believe. And they're said to be of the best families."

"Uh-huh. I thought so. Inferior types couldn't maintain this system. Even with that tremendous monopoly of theirs, there'd have been more conflict between Church and State unless— Yeh. Trevors, Whitleys, Burkes, that sort—the high castes of Freetoon, with the wits and courage and personality to override any local chief. Well."

Barbara shoved her paddle through murmurous moonlit waters. "But what are we going to do?" she asked in helplessness.

"I think—yes. I really think we can get away with it." Davis took a long breath. "The word from Lysum will be far behind us. Now, either of you two is about the size of this dame. You can pass for a legate yourself—"

Barbara choked. After a moment, Valeria shook her head. "No, Bert. It can't be done. Every child in the soldier families gets that idea as soon as it can talk: why not pass a Freetoon Whitley off as a Greendaler? There are countersigns to prevent just that."

"It isn't what I meant," said Davis. "Look here. How are the sea people to know you're not a genuine legate, bringing back a genuine Man? Only, on his behalf, you requisition an escort and a lot of fast orspers. We ride back to Freetoon, demand my own boat—oh, yes, our pseudo-legate can also order your town set free. Then we all hop into my spaceship and ride to Nerthus—and return with a thousand armed Men!"

Barbara thought dazedly that only he could have forged such a plan.

Eighteen Atlantean days later, the canoe nosed into Shield Skerry harbor.

The enormous, shifting tides raised by the other great moons turned the coasts into salt marshes at ebb, brackish lakes at flow. But the local life had adapted, there were even trees and grass, and a few of the low-caste families lived here, sunken to a naked neolithic stage but available as guides. Valeria, impressive in robe and veil, commandeered their help.

Davis had tried to quiz the legate. Beyond the information that her name was Joyce and he was a Monster destined for hell's hottest griddle, she would tell him nothing.

For Davis, lack of privacy and the weariness of incessant paddling had its good points. It staved off his own problem. The notion that someday he'd face it again—maybe alone in space with two jealous Whitleys, because he couldn't leave them defenseless against the Doctors' revenge—made his nerves curl up and quiver at the ends.

Unless he gave himself to a psychadjuster on Nerthus and had his own hankerings electronically exorcised—which he didn't want to do—he would have to pick one or the other. And now that he knew them both, he couldn't chose!

What have I done to deserve this?

Elinor had been very quiet on the trip. She made herself useful to Joyce, probably too scared of both sides to reach a decision. Davis felt sorry for her, in a patronizing fashion.

And then finally they were out of the marsh.

The chief Nicholson had told him in her barely intelligible argot that there were many many seafolk on many many islands, that Shield Skerry was only a port for the inland trade. Davis looked eagerly ahead. Behind him the swamps were a vaporous gray, low in the sea, a storm of shrieking birds made a white wing-cloud under Minos and the two suns—otherwise there were only the huge foam-flanked waves that marched out of the west. The water was a chill steely bluish-gray, the wind shrill in his ears.

The rock was nearly hidden by the stone walls erected on its back: massive blocks cut square, a primitive lighthouse where oil fires behind glass burned in front of polished copper reflectors, two long jetties enclosing a small harbor. As they entered this, Davis saw that a good-sized ship—by Atlantean standards—was in. A capstan-powered crane was unloading baled cargo. Strong suntanned women bustled about, barefoot, clad in wide trousers and halters, their hair cut off just below the ears. Beyond the dock were warehouses and dwelling units. They were of stone, with shingle roofs, in the same uncompromising angular style as the town wall and the pharos.

The ship was carvel-built, with a high poop and a corroded bronze winged-fish figurehead. Davis guessed it had a deep draught and a centerboard, to maintain freeway in these tricky waters. There was no mast, but a windmill arrangement turned idly amidships. What off Earth—? Otherwise the harbor held only a few boats, swift-looking, more or less yawl-rigged.

"Highest technology I've seen here," he remarked.

"What? Oh, you mean their skills," said Barbara. "Yes, they say the seafolk are the best smiths in the world. It's even said their captains can read writing, like Doctors."

Davis assumed that the pelagic colonies were old, founded perhaps before the final breakdown of castaway civilization. The sea held abundant food if you knew how to get it. "What kind of people are they?" he asked.

"We don't know much about them in the uplands," said Barbara.

"Well," said Davis, "we'll find out pretty quick." His stomach was a cold knot within him.

Work at the dock was grinding to a halt. Women swarmed from the buildings and hurried down tortuous cobbled streets. "*A legate, another legate, and who's that with her?*"

Valeria did not thank their guides, it wouldn't have been in character. She stepped haughtily onto the quay. Davis followed. Barbara nudged the wrist-bound Trevor with a knife and urged her after. Elinor slunk behind.

There was a crowd now, pushing and shoving. A few must be police or guards—they wore conical, visored helmets and scaly corselets above their pants. Davis noticed flamboyant tattoos, earrings, thick gold bracelets . . . and on all classes. A Nicholson stood arm in arm with a Latvala, a Craig pushed between a Whitley and a Burke, a Holloway carrying a blacksmith's hammer gave amiable backchat to a Trevor with spear and armor.

Valeria raised her staff. "Quiet!" she shouted.

The babble died away, bit by bit. A gray-haired woman, stocky and ugly, added a roar: "Shut up, you scupperheads!" She was an Udall, Davis recognized uneasily. She turned to Valeria and gave a crude salute.

"Are you in charge?" asked the girl.

"Reckon I am, ma'm, being the skipper of this tub . . . *Fishbird* out o' Farewell Island, she is. Nelly Udall, ma'm, at your service."

Joyce Trevor opened her mouth. She was white with anger. Barbara nudged her and she closed it again.

Valeria stood solemnly for a moment. It grew quiet enough to hear the waves bursting on the breakwater. Then she lifted her veiled face and cried: "Rejoice! I have brought a Man!"

It had the desired effect, though a somewhat explosive one. Davis was afraid his admirers would trample him to death. Nelly Udall cuffed back the most enthusiastic and bellowed at them. "Stand aside! Belay there! Show some respect, you—" What followed brought a maidenly blush to Barbara herself, and she was a cavalry girl.

When the racket had quieted somewhat, Davis decided to take charge. "I am a Man," he said in his deepest voice. "The legate found me in the hills and brought me here. She knows you are a pious people."

"Bless you, dearie," said the Udall through sudden tears. "Sure, we're pious as hell. Any Father-damned thing you want, ma'm, just say so."

"But there is evil afoot," boomed Davis. "Before all the Men can come, you must aid me to destroy the evil in Atlantis."

A certain awe began to penetrate those hard skulls. The show was rolling. Davis turned to Nelly Udall. "I would speak with you and your counselors in private," he said.

She looked confused. "Sure. . . sure, ma'm. Yes, your manship. You mean my first mate?"

"Oh . . . no authority here, is there? Well where does the Udall of the seas-dwellers live?"

"What Udall? I'm just me."

"Who is your queen, chief, president—who makes the decisions?"

"Why, why, Laura Macklin is the preemer, ma'm," stuttered Nelly. "She's at New Terra, that's the capital. Did you want everybody to come there and vote, ma'm?"

A republic was about the last thing Davis had expected to find. But it was plausible, now that he thought about it. Even under Atlantean conditions, it would be hard to establish despotism among a race of sailors. The cheapest catboat with a few disgruntled slaves aboard could sail as fast as the biggest warship.

"Never mind," he said majestically. "I'm afraid you misunderstood me, Captain Udall. Take us to a place where we can talk alone with you."

"Yes, *ma'm!*" Nelly's eyes came to light on Joyce Trevor's sullen face. She jerked a horny thumb toward the prisoner. "Enemy of yours, ma'm? I'll chop her up personally."

"That will not be required," said Davis. "Bring her along."

"Awright, awright, clear a way!" roared Nelly. "Stand aside there, you bilge drinkers!" Her fist emphasized the request, but nobody seemed to mind. Tough lot.

Davis led his party after her, through a narrow street to a smoky kennel with an anchor painted on the gable. "We'll use this tavern," said Nelly. "Break open a keg of— *No,* you fishbrains! This is private! Git!" She slammed the door in a hundred faces.

Davis coughed. When his eyes were through watering, he saw a room under sooty rafters, filled with benches and tables. A noble collection of casks lined one wall, otherwise the inn was hung with scrimshaw work and stuffed fish. A whole seal-bird roasted in the fireplace.

Nelly fetched heroic goblets and tapped a brandy cask. "Now then, your maledom, say away." She leaned back and sprawled columnar legs across the floor. "Death and corruption! A Man, after all these years."

Formality was wasted on her, Davis decided. He told her the same censored tale he had given Lysum.

"Heard of those wenches." Nelly snorted. "Well, ma'm . . . sorry, you said it was 'sir,' didn't you? What happened next?"

"This Trevor showed up," said Davis. "She was one of the agents of evil, the same who had whipped Greendale and the other towns into attacking Freetoon. She stirred up Lysum against me. I made her captive and we went down the river till we came here."

"Why didn't you see her gizzard, sir?"

"The Men are merciful," said Davis with a slight shudder. "Do you have a place where she can be held incommunicado?"

"A what? We've got a brig."

"That'll do." Davis continued with his demands: passage to the Holy River mouth and an escort to Freetoon, where the lady legate would give the orders of the Ship.

Nelly nodded. "Can do, sir. There are twenty good crewgirls on the *Fishbird*, and a causeway from the Ship over the swamps—"

"We needn't stop at the Ship," said Valeria quickly. "In fact, I'm commanded not to come near it till the rest of the Men arrive. And you understand, this has to be kept secret or we may have more trouble with the, uh, agents of hell."

"Awright, ma'm. We'll just leave the *Fishbird* at Bow Island and get orspers and ride straight to Freetoon. There's a ridge we can follow through the marshes."

Davis frowned. Whatever legate had gone to Freetoon might have planted a story that he really was a Monster, to be killed on sight. Or no, probably not . . . *that* legate had no way of knowing he was the only male human on Atlantis; she'd have to ride back for orders. . . .

"The faster the better," he said.

"We'll warp out at Bee-rise tomorrow, ma'm," said Nelly Udall. She shook her head and stared into her goblet. "A Man! A real live Man! Father damn it, I'm too old . . . but I've seen you, sir. That's enough for me, I reckon."

After Joyce Trevor had been safely locked in the town jail, with the guard ordered not to speak to her or let anyone else do so, Nelly led Davis' party down to the dock, where he made a short but telling speech to the assembled women. The inquiries of the preceding legate as to whether a Man had been seen had paved the way for his arrival; no one disbelieved him.

Cloud masses piled blackly out of the west, wind skirled, and scud stung his face. He felt the weariness of being hunted. "I would retire," he said.

"Yes, sir, this way, sir," said Nelly. She gave him a wistful look. "Sure you won't come down to the Anchor with us and fer—"

"Quite sure!" said Barbara and Valeria together.

The crowd trailed them to a long house reserved for ships' captains. Beyond a common room, there was a hall lined by small bedchambers. Elinor slipped into the first, then Valeria, then Davis, then Barbara . . . he closed the shutters against the gale, turned off the guttering oil lantern, and crept through a sudden heavy darkness into bed. Ahhh!

But it wasn't easy to sleep. Too much to think about . . . it would be good to be among men again . . . what to do about the Whitleys?—oh, blast, face that problem later . . . he'd be coming back to Atlantis, surely, to help these forlorn female devils through the difficult period of readjustment . . . *Hello, Dad! I seem to've been pounded into a sober well-integrated citizen after all* . . . But nobody mated to a Whitley would ever get *too* sober—

Drowsiness spilled from him when the door opened. He sat up. "Who's that?" Bare feet groped across the floor. His scalp prickled.

"Shhh!" The husky voice was almost in his ear. He reached and felt a warm roundedness. "Bertie, I just had to come to you—"

Davis made weak fending motions. The girl laughed shyly and slid under his blankets. Two strong arms closed about him.

His morality stood up in indignation, slipped, and tobogganed whooping down his spinal column. "C'mere!" he said hoarsely.

Her lips closed against his, still inexpert, her hands shuddered their way along his back. Well, he thought with an intoxicating sense of release, if Valeria chose to enter his bed, why, Val was a wonderful girl and he'd make a more or less honest woman of her when he got the chance.

"Bert . . . Bert, darling, I don't know what . . . what this is, to be with a Man . . . but I care for you so much—"

"I told you the word was 'love,'" he chuckled.

"Did you? When was that?"

"You remember, Val, sweetheart . . . you didn't fool me—"

"*Val!*" She sat bolt upright and screeched the name. "*Val?* What's been going on here?"

"Oh, no!" groaned Davis. "Barbara, listen, I can explain—"

"I'll explain you!" she yelled.

Davis scrambled to get free. The blankets trapped him. Barbara got her hands on his throat.

The door opened. The tall red-haired girl carried an ax in her right hand; the left, holding a lantern, was scarred.

"What's happening?" barked Valeria.

To the untrained eye, a wrestling match is superficially not unlike certain other sports. Valeria cursed, set down the lantern, and strode forward with lifted ax. Barbara sprang out of bed, snatched up Davis' knife, and confronted her twin.

"So you've been mucking around!" she shouted.

"I wouldn't talk," answered Valeria from clenched jaws. "The minute my back is turned, you come oozing in and—and—"

"Now, girls," stammered Davis. "Ladies, ladies, please!"

They whirled on him. Something intimated to him that this was not just the correct approach. He got out of bed one jump ahead of the ax and backed into a corner. "It's all a mistake!"

"The mistake was ever bringing you along," snarled Valeria.

The wind hooted and banged the shutters. Above it, suddenly, he heard a roar. It swept closer, boots racketing on cobblestones, clattering iron, a mob howl.

The Whitleys reacted fast. Valeria whirred her ax, Barbara darted back to her room for a bow. The vague light threw their shadows monstrous across the walls.

Feet pounded down the hall. Nelly Udall burst into the chamber. There were gashes on her squat body, and the ax in her hand dripped blood. "Hell and sulfur!" she bawled. "Grab your weapons! They're coming to kill you!"

A Macklin and a youthful Lundgard followed her. They were also wounded, hastily armed, and they were crying.

"What happened?" rattled Davis.

"I bolted the outer door," panted Nelly. "They'll break it down in a minute." A groan of abused wood came from behind her. "I believe you're a Man, dearie ... that's how I got these cuts ... but the Trevor— Why didn't you kill that snark when you had the chance?"

"*Trevor!*" Davis grabbed the Udall's shoulders. "Is she loose?"

"Yeh," said Nelly in a flat voice. "We was all down at the Anchor, drinking your health, and this Trevor walks in with that Dyckman of yours, says she's the legate and you're a Monster. Proves herself by running through the rites every mother knows are said at the Ship— challenges your Whitley to do the same—" Nelly shook her head. "It was quite a fight. We three here beat our way out o' the tavern and got here ahead of 'em."

"Elinor!" Barbara's voice seethed.

"She must have sneaked out," said Davis wanly. "Gone to the brig, told the guard she had new orders from me, set Joyce free. . . . Oh, almighty Cosmos, what're we going to do now?"

"Fight," answered Nelly. She planted herself in the doorway.

There was a final crash, and the mob came down the hall. A

Salmon leaped yelling, with drawn knife. Nelly's ax thundered down, the body rolled at her feet. A Hauser jabbed at her with a spear. Barbara shot the Hauser through the breast.

It dampened them. The women milled sullenly in the narrow corridor, the noise quieted to a tigerish grumble.

Davis stepped forward, trying not to shake. A scarred elderly Damon faced him boldly. "Will you call a truce?" she asked.

"Yes," said Davis. "Hold your fire, Barbara. Maybe we can—"

Joyce Trevor pushed her way through the crowd and regarded him over Nelly's shoulder. Ragged skirt and matted hair took away none of her frozen dignity. "I say you are a Monster," she declared.

"Elinor," said Davis, very quietly, still not believing it. "Elinor, why did you do this?"

He glimpsed her in the mob, thin, shaking, and enormous-eyed. Her lips were pale and stiff. "You are," she whispered. "You attacked a legate. The legate says you're a Monster."

Davis smiled wryly. "I was alone, and there were a lot of Doctors," he murmured. "That's why, isn't it?"

"Shut up, you Monster!" screamed Elinor. "You and those Whitleys kicked me around once too often!"

"This is a waste of time," snapped Joyce. "If that Whitley is a true legate, let her prove it by reciting the rites."

"Never mind," sighed Davis. "She isn't. But I am a Man. I can bring all the Men here. The legate lies about me because the Doctors don't want them. It would mean the end of Doctor power."

"I sort of thought that," muttered the Lundgard beside him.

"Let me go to my spaceship," said Davis. "That's all I ask."

Joyce whirled on the crowd. "Let him summon the other Monsters?" she yelled. "I lay eternal barrenness on anyone who helps this thing! I order you to kill it, now!"

Nelly hefted her ax, grinning. "Who's next?" she inquired.

Davis heard feet shuffle in the corridor, voices buzz and break, spears drag on the floor. And there was the sound of new arrivals, a few pro-Davis women stamping in and making their own threats. Women have slightly less tendency to act in mobs than men do; the crowd was wavering, uncertain, afraid.

He straightened, licked his lips, and walked forward. "I'm going out," he said. "Make way."

Barbara, Valeria, Nelly and her two companions, followed at his heels. A handful of determined roughnecks shoved through the pack, toward him, to join him. Otherwise no one stirred. Joyce boiled under the menace of Barbara's cocked bow, Elinor hid her eyes. If nothing broke this explosive quiet—

The wind raved in coalsack streets. A lonely score of women tramped in a circle about Davis, toward the dock. He heard the crowd follow, but it was too dark to see them.

Barbara—he felt the hard stock of her arbalest—whispered venomously: "Don't think I'm coming along for your sake, you slimy doubleface. I haven't any choice."

When they emerged from canyon-like walls, onto the wharf, enough light to see by trickled down from the pharos. Nelly led the way to her ship.

"I'm staking one hell of a lot on your really being a Man," she said desolately, into the wind. "I don't dare believe anything else."

The Shield Skerry folk swirled on the edge of darkness, still paralyzed. He had to get away before the shooting began. He crossed the gangplank to the deck. Valeria edged close to him and hissed: "Yes, I'll believe you're a Man too . . . and the hell with all Men! I'm only coming because I haven't any choice."

Nelly seemed to draw strength from the planks booming beneath her feet. "All aboard, you scuts! Man the capstan! Look lively now!"

She went aft, up on the poop to a nighted helm. The other women scurried about, doing incomprehensible things with ropes and pulleys. The great windmill jerked, gears whined as they engaged, there was a white threshing at the stern. The *Fishbird* moved slowly out of the harbor.

Morning was gray over an ice-gray sea, where waves snorted from horizon to horizon and the ship wallowed. Davis emerged from one of the little cabins under the poop to find the crew—mostly young women of the more war-like families—chattering happily. Barbara and Valeria sulked on opposite sides of the deck, elaborately ignoring him.

The windmill, facing into the stiff gusts, turned, driving a propeller through a set of gears and shafts. As he waited for breakfast, Davis tried to lose his gloom by admiring the arrangement—it made the ship independent of wind direction. Evil! Who cared?

Nelly Udall waddled into view. "Morning, dearie," she boomed. "Not seasick, I hope? No? Good—kind of hard to believe in a seasick Man, eh? Haw, haw, haw!" She slapped his back so he staggered. Then, seriously: "Come into my cabin. We got to talk."

They sat on her bunk. She took out a pipe and stuffed it with greenish flakes from a jar. "We can't go on to Holy River now, that's for sure, chick. That Father-damned legate's been preaching hellfire to 'em back at Shield. The boats must already be headed for the Ship to bring the glad tidings. With a wind like this, a yawl can sail rings around us. Time we get to Bow Island, even, all the country will be up in arms."

"Glutch!" strangled Davis.

Nelly kindled her pipe with a fire piston and blew nauseous clouds. "Sure you aren't seasick, duck? All of a sudden you don't look so good."

"We've got to raise help," mumbled Davis. "Somewhere, somehow."

Nelly nodded. "Figgered as much. I'm bound for Farewell, my home port. Got plenty of friends there, and nobody to conterdick whatever you say."

"But when they hear the Ship's against us—"

"I know a lot who'll still stick by us, dearie. Girls like our present crew. We've gotten almighty sick of the Doctors. We see more of 'em than the uplanders do, the—" Nelly went into a rich catalogue of the greed, arrogance, and general snottiness of the Doctors. Davis guessed that a mercantile culture like this would naturally resent paying tribute . . . and then, generations of sexual frustration had to be vented somehow.

The Doctors could not all be villains. Doubtless many were quite sincere. But Davis knew enough Union law to be sure that anything he did to them would be all right with the Coordination Service. It was they who stood between Atlantis and civilization—more important, a normal family life.

The idea grew slowly within him as the Udall rumbled on:

"I reckon we can raise quite a few shiploads, then go far up the coast and strike inland toward your boat."

"No!" said Davis. Words poured from him. "Too risky. It'll be guarded too heavily; and they may have tools enough left in the Ship to demolish it. We've got to act fast. If you think your friends are willing to hazard their lives to be free—"

Nelly smiled. "Chick, with that beard and that voice you can talk 'em into storming hell gate."

"It won't be quite that bad," said Davis. "I hope. What we're going to do is storm the Ship."

The rebel fleet lay to at Ship city at high tide, just after B-rise.

Davis stood on the *Fishbird's* deck and watched his forces move in. There were about forty vessels, their windmills and sails like gull wings across waters muddy-blue, rippled and streaked by an early breeze. At their sterns flew the new flag he had designed. His girls were quite taken with the Jolly Roger.

The rebels numbered some 2,000 women from the Farewell archipelago. There were more than that to guard the Ship, but less tough, less experienced in fighting—the seafolk were not above occasional piracy. The odds didn't look too bad.

Valeria stamped her feet so the deck thudded. "I'm going ashore," she said mutinously.

"No, you don't, chicakabiddy." Nelly Udall twirled a belaying pin. "Got to keep some guard over the Man. What's the bloody-be-damned use of it all if he gets himself skewered?"

Barbara nodded coldly. "She's right, as anyone but you could see," she added. "Not that I wouldn't rather guard a muck-bird!"

Davis sighed. In the three Atlantean weeks since they left Shield Skerry, neither of the cousins had spoken to him, or to each other without a curse. After the hundredth rebuff, he had given up. Evil take all women anyway! He just wanted to go home, go back and get roaring drunk and have the psych machine numb the pain which went with red hair and green eyes.

He twisted his mind elsewhere. The Ship must have been badly crippled, to land here; probably it had come down where it could, on the last gasp of broken engines. The walls which now enclosed it had been built on a hill that just barely stuck out over high tide. Eastward lay the marches, a dreary gray land where a stone causeway slashed through to the distance-blued peaks of the Ridge.

There must have been heavy construction equipment in the Ship's cargo. A few thousand women could not have raised this place by hand. The machines were long ago worn out, but their work remained.

The city was ringed by white concrete walls five meters high, with a square watchtower at each corner. The walls fell to the water of high tide or the mud of ebb: inaccessible save by the causeway entering the eastern gate or the wide quay built out from the west side. Against this dock the rebel boats were lying to. Gangplanks shot forth and armored women stormed onto the wharf.

Davis let his eyes wander back to the city, he could see the tops of buildings above the walls, the dome-roofed architecture of three centuries ago. And he could see the great whaleback of the Ship itself, 300 meters long from north wall to south wall, metal still bright but a buckled spot at the waist to show how hard it had landed.

Barbara looked wistfully at the yelling seafolk. She was clad like them: visored helmet on her ruddy hair, tunic of steely-scaled orcfish hide, trousers, spike-toed boots. The accessories included lasso, knife, ax, crossbow and quiver, she had become a walking meat grinder.

Davis, likewise armored, felt the same sense of uselessness. Not that he wanted to face edged metal, the thought dried out his mouth. But when women were ready to die for *his* sake—

Bee struck long rays into his eyes. Ay was so close as to be hidden by the glare of the nearer sun. Minos brooded overhead in the gigantic last quarter. There was a storm on the king planet—he could see how the bands and blotches writhed.

Horns blew on the walls, under the Red Cross flag. Women, lithe tough legates and acolytes, were appearing in cuirass, greaves, and masking helmet, all of burnished metal. Crossbows began to shoot.

There was no attempt to batter down the iron door at the end of the quay. A howling mass of sailors raised ladders and swarmed skyward.

"Cosmos!" choked Davis.

A Doctor shoved at one of the ladders, but there was a grapnel on its end. Davis saw her unlimber a long rapier. The first rebel up got it through the throat and tumbled, knocking off the woman below her, they fell hideously to the ground.

"Let me go!" yelled Valeria.

"Hold still," rapped Nelly. Her worried eyes went to Davis. "I didn't think they'd have so good a defense, chick. We'd better get them licked fast."

He nodded. They had only a couple of hours before the tide dropped so far that any ship which remained would be stranded, in mud or the harbor locks, till the next high.

"So we stay," growled Barbara. "Isn't that the idea?"

"Yeh," said Davis. He drew hard on a borrowed pipe. "Only the Doctors must have called in a lot of upland warriors, to patrol between here and Freetoon. Now they'll send for their help. If things go badly, I'd like a way to retreat."

"You would," she agreed, and turned her back on him.

Axes, spears, swords clashed up on the wall, bolts and darts gleamed in the cool early light. The Doctor fighters were rapidly being outnumbered. One of them, in a red cloak of leadership, winded a horn. Her women fought their way toward her.

Davis gulped. It couldn't be that simple! Yes, by all creation, the Doctor forces were streaming down a stairway into their town. A slim young Burke cried triumph, he could hear the hawk-shriek above all the racket and see how her dark hair flew in the wind as she planted the Jolly Roger on the city wall.

Now down the stairs! There was a red flash of axes. The last legate backed out of view, thrusting and slicing at sailor shields.

Nelly grabbed Davis and whirled him in a wild stomp around the dock. "We got 'em, we got 'em, we got 'em!" she caroled. Planks shuddered beneath her.

The man felt sick. His whole culture was conditioned against war, it remembered its past too well. If he could have been in the action, himself, taking his own chances, it wouldn't have been so gruesome. But he was the only one on Atlantis who could bring the Men. He had to hold himself back—

"Scared?" jeered Valeria. "If it looks like you might get hurt after all, we'll take you away where it's safe."

"I'm not going to retreat!" he said in a raw voice.

"Yes, you will, duck, if we got to," said Nelly. "If you get killed, what's for us?" Her seamed face turned grimly inland. "We've got to win . . . no choice . . . if the Doctors win, there'll never be another baby on the islands."

That was what drove them, thought Davis. Below all the old grudges and the glamor of his cause, there was the primeval mother urge. The seafolk had not told it to themselves in so many words, but their instincts knew: a machine was too unsafe a way of bringing life into the world.

The iron harbor doors were flung open. So the west end of town was firmly held by his side. The noise of battle was receding, the

Doctors being driven back . . . So what? A victory where you yourself did nothing was no victory for a man.

Damn! His pipe had gone out.

"I think we'll have the mucking place before ebb," said Nelly. "But then what do we do?"

"We'll have the parthenogenetic apparatus," Davis reminded her. "Not to mention the prestige of victory. We'll own the planet."

"Oh . . . yeh. Keep forgetting. I'm growing old, dearie—huh?"

There was a shriek through the gateway.

Sailors poured out of it, falling over each other, hurling their weapons from them in blind panic. A couple of hundred women made for the ships.

"What's happened?" bawled Nelly. "Avast, you hootinanies! Stop that!" She went into a weeping tirade of profanity.

Barbara snatched her megaphone from the captain. "Pull in!" she cried. "We're going ashore now!"

The helmswoman looked ill, but yanked a signal cord. The ship moved across a narrow stretch of open water and bumped against one of the docked schooners.

"Let's go," snapped Valeria. She leaped onto the schooner deck.

Barbara saw Davis follow. "No!" she yelled.

"Yes," he answered harshly. "I've stood enough." Blind with fury, he dashed to the wharf.

The mob was still coming out of the door and over the quay to mill on the ships. Davis grabbed a Craig and whirled her around.

"What's the matter?" he shouted. She gave him an unseeing look. He slapped her. "What happened in there?"

"We . . . street fighting . . . Doctor troop . . . flame, white flame and it *burned* our forward line—" The Craig collapsed.

"It's Father himself!" gasped a Macklin.

"Shut up!" rapped Davis. He felt sick. "I know what it is. They must have found my blaster up by Freetoon, and the legate took it back here. Maybe records in the Ship describe blasters." He shook his head numbly. "Chilluns, this is not a good thing."

"What are we going to do?" breathed Barbara.

Davis thought, in a remote part of his mind, that later on he would break out in the cold shakes. If he lived! But for now he had to keep calm—

"We're going to get that blaster," he said. "There's nothing supernatural about an ion stream. And there's only one of them."

"You'll be killed," said Valeria. "Wait here, Bert—"

"Follow me," he said. "If you dare!"

They trotted after him, a dozen from the *Fishbird* and as many more from the retreat whose morale had picked up. He went through the doorway and saw an ordered gridiron of paved streets between tall concrete houses. The Ship rose, huge at the end of all avenues. From two other streets came the noise of fighting. The battle had spread out, and few had yet seen the gun fire. They would, though, if he didn't hurry, and that would be the end of the rebellion.

"We went down this way," pointed a Latvala.

Davis jogged between closed doors and broad glass windows. Looking in, he saw that the inhabitants did themselves well, no doubt luxury existed elsewhere on Atlantis. He could understand their reluctance to abandon such a way of life for the untried mythic civilization of Men.

He skidded to a halt. The Doctors were rounding the corner ahead.

There were about twenty. A line of legates, their helmets facelessly blank, spread from wall to wall with interlocked shields. Behind them lifted swords and halberds.

"Get them!" shouted Nelly.

Three girls sprang ahead of Davis. One of them was a Whitley, he thought for a moment she was one of *his* Whitleys and then saw Barbara and Valeria still flanking him.

Over the shield tops lifted a Burke face. It was an old face, toothless and wrinkled below a tall bejeweled crown, and the body was stooped in white robes. But his blaster gleamed in a skinny hand.

Davis flung out his arms and dove to the ground, carrying Barbara and Valeria with him. Blue-white fire sizzled overhead.

The three young girls fell, blasted through. It could have been Val or Barbara lying there dead and mutilated on the pavement, thought Davis wildly. He remembered how he loved them.

He rolled over, into a doorway. His gang were already stampeded. Nelly stood firm in the street, Barbara and Valeria were beside him. Nelly threw her ax, it glanced off a shield, the legate stumbled against the old Doctor. Her next shot missed, and Nelly pumped thick legs across the street.

She hit the door with one massive shoulder. It went down in splinters. Davis sprang into a sybarite's parlor.

Two legates appeared in the doorframe. Barbara's crossbow snapped twice. Valeria and Nelly led the way through another door.

Davis followed and saw a stair. "Uncoil me your lasso, Babs," he said. "I have an idea." They pounded up after him.

A bedroom overlooked the street. Davis shoved up the window. The blaster party was just underneath. Barbara nodded, leaned out— her lariat closed around the chief Doctor.

"Help!" screamed the Burke. "I've been roped!"

Davis sprang into the street. He landed on an armored legate and both went down with a rattle and a gong. She didn't move. Davis jumped up and sent a left hook to the nearest jaw. Valeria's rope snaked from the window, fastened to something. She came sliding down it with her ax busy. Valeria and Nelly followed.

The old Burke snarled. She fought free and reached for the blaster. "Oh, no, you don't!" Davis put his foot on it. A rapier struck his scaly coat and bent upward, raking his cheek. He kicked, and the woman reeled off to trip somebody else.

Nelly had picked up an ax. "Whoopee!" she bawled, and started chopping. Barbara and Valeria stood back to back, their weapons a blur in front of them. Davis was still too inhibited to use whetted steel on women, but every blow his fist dealt shocked loose some of his guiltiness.

The fight was over in a few minutes. Male size and female skill had outweighed numbers. Davis stooped for his blaster. "Let's go," he panted.

They went down the street. There was a narrow passage between the Ship and the wall. On the other side lay a broad open square, lined with impressive temples. . . . No more sound of fighting. Odd!

A sailor troop emerged from behind one of the columned sanctuaries. "It's the Man!" squealed somebody, they ran toward him and drew up, flushed. The leader gave a sketchy salute.

"I think we just about have the town, sir," she puffed. "I was patrolling on the east end. Didn't see anyone."

"Good!" Davis shuddered his relief. He could *not* have used a blaster on women, the memory of the dead Whitley girl was burned too deeply in him.

"Get our people together here," he said. "Post guards. Round up all the Doctors left, herd 'em into one of these chapels . . . and don't use them for target practice! Set up a sickbay for the wounded, and that means enemy wounded too. Nelly, you take charge, I want a look around."

He walked through empty avenues. Behind him he could hear cheers and trumpets, the tramp of feet and triumphal clang of arms, but he was in no mood for it.

Minos was a thin sliver, with Bee sliding close. Nearly eclipse time . . . had all this only taken three hours?

The Whitleys trailed him. He heard: "I take a lot back, Val. You fought pretty good."

"Hell, Babs, you're no slouch yourself. After all, darling, you are identical with me."

The street opened on a narrow space running the length of the east wall. There was a doorway in the center, with wrought-iron gates. Davis looked through the bars to the causeway and the marshes. Mud gleamed on the ridge which the road followed, birds screamed down after stranded fish. The tide was ebbing, the ships already trapped . . . but what the Evil, they had won, hadn't they?

Hold on there!

The highway bent around a clump of saltwater trees three kilometers from the city. Davis saw what approached from the other side and grabbed the bars with both hands.

"An army!" he croaked.

Rank after rank poured into view, with war-cries and haughty banners; now he saw leather corselets, iron morions, boots and spurs and streaming cloaks. They were the hill people and they were riding to the relief of the Doctors.

"A couple of thousand, at least," muttered Barbara. "The legates must have gone after them as soon as we attacked. They've been waiting around to kill you, my dearest—" She whirled on him, her visored face pressed against his side. "And it's too late to retreat, we're boxed in!"

"Not too late to fight!" shouted Valeria. Sea women on the walls lifted horns to lips and wailed an alarm.

Davis looked at the gate. It was locked, but it could be broken apart. His hand went to the blaster. Before Cosmos, that would stop them. No!

The rebel army pelted into the open space. Right and left, arbalesters swarmed up the staircases to the walls. *Hasn't there been enough killing?* thought Davis.

Behind him, Nelly Udall scurried along the ranks, pushing them into a semblance of order. Davis regarded them. Tired faces, hurt faces, lips that tried to be firm and failed; they would fight bravely, but they hadn't a chance against fresh troops.

Up on the parapets, crossbows began to snap. Orspers reared, squawked, went off the road into the mud and flapped atrophied wings. The charge came to a clanging halt, broke up, fought its way back along the road . . . it stopped. Leaders trotted between panicked riders, haranguing them.

Hill women dismounted. Their axes bit at a roadside tree. It wouldn't take them long to make a battering ram. They would slog forward under fire, they would be slaughtered and others take their place, and the gate would come down.

"When they're in range," leered Nelly to Davis, "burn 'em!"

Bee slipped behind Minos. The planet became a circle of blackness ringed with red flame. Of all the moons, only firefly Aegeus was visible. Stars glittered coldly forth. A wind sighed across the draining marshes, dusk lay heavy on the world.

Davis fired into the air. Livid lightning burned across heaven, a small thunder cracked in its wake. Screams came from the shadow army on the road, he fired again and waited for them to flee.

"Hold fast! Stay where you are, Father damn you!" The voices drifted hoarse through the gloom. "If we let the Monster keep the Ship, you'll die with never another child in your arms!"

Davis shook his head. He might have known it.

Someone clattered up the road. Four short trumpet blasts sent the sea birds mewing into the sudden night. "Truce call," muttered Valeria. "Let her come talk. I don't *want* to see them fried alive."

The mounted woman approached. She was an Udall. Barbara squinted through the murk at the painted insignia. "Bess of Greendale!" she hissed. "Kill her!"

Davis could only think that the Doctors' desperation had been measured by their sending clear up to Greendale for help. The swamp and the upper valley must be alive with armies intent on keeping him from his boat.

"No," he said. "It's a parley, remember?"

The Udall rode scornfully up under the walls. "Is the Monster here?" she asked.

"The Man is here," said Barbara.

Davis stepped into view, peering through iron bars and thick twilight. "What do you want?" he asked.

"Your head, and the Ship back before you ruin the life machine."

"I can kill your whole army," said Davis. "Watch!" He blasted at the road before him. Stone bubbled and ran molten.

Bess Udall fought her plunging orsper to a halt. "Do you think that matters?" she panted. "We're fighting for every unborn kid on Atlantis. Without the machine we might as well die."

"But I'm not going to harm the damned machine!"

"So *you* say. You've struck down the Doctors. I wouldn't trust you dead without a stake through your heart."

"Oh, hell," snarled Valeria. "Why bother? Let 'em attack and find out you mean business."

Davis stared at the blaster. "No," he said. "There are decent limits."

He shook himself and looked out at the vague form of the woman. "I'll make terms," he said.

"What?" yelled Barbara and Valeria together.

"Shut up. Bess, here's my offer. You can enter the town. The sea people will go back to their ships and sail away at next high tide. In return, they'll have access to the life machine just as before."

"And you?" grated the Udall. "We won't stop fighting till you're dead."

"I'll come out," said Davis. "Agreed?"

"*No!*" Barbara leaped at him. He swung his arm and knocked her to the ground.

"Stand back!" His voice rattled. "I'm still a man."

Bess Udall stared at him through the darkness. "Agreed," she said. "I swear to your terms by Father."

The rebels shuffled forward, shadow mass in a shadow world. "Don't move," said Davis. "It isn't worth it . . . my life . . . Evil! The men will be here in another generation anyway."

His blaster boomed, eating through the lock on the gate. He pushed it open, the hot iron burned his hands, and trod through. With a convulsive gesture, he tossed the blaster into a mudpool.

"All right," he said. "Let's go."

Bess edged her orsper close to him.

"Move!" she barked. A few women surged from the gateway. She brandished her spear. "Stand back, or the Monster gets this right now!"

Minos was a ring of hellfire in the sky.

"*Wait!*"

It was a Whitley voice. Davis turned. He felt only an infinite weariness, let them kill him and be done with it.

He couldn't see whether it was Barbara or Valeria who spoke: "Hold on there! It's us who make the terms."

"Yes?" growled the rider. Her spear poised over Davis.

"We have the life machine. Turn him back to us or we'll smash it and kill every Doctor in town before you can stop us!" They faced the crowd defiantly.

A sighing went through the rebels. Nelly cursed them into stillness. "That's right, dearie," she cried. "What the blazes is a bloody machine worth when we could have the Men?"

The Whitley walked closer, cat-gaited. "These are our terms," she said flatly. "Lay down your arms. We won't hurt you. By Father, I never knew what it means to be a Man till now! You can keep the town and the machine—yes, the Doctors—if you want. Just let us bring the Man to his ship to bring the Men back for us!"

Bess Udall's spear dropped to the ground.

"You don't know he's a Man," she stammered.

"I sure as hell do, sister. Do you think we'd have stormed the Holy Ship for a Monster?" She waited.

Night and silence lay thick across the land. A salt wind whined around red-stained battlements.

"Almighty Father," choked Bess. "I think you're right."

She whirled her orsper about and dashed down the road to the army.

Davis heard them talking in the orsper host. It seemed to come from very far away. His knees were stiff as he walked slowly back toward the gate.

Several riders hurried after him. They pulled up and jumped to the ground and laid their weapons at his feet.

"Welcome," said a voice. "Welcome, Man."

The sun swung from behind Minos and day burned across watery wastes and the far eastern mountains.

Davis let them cheer around him.

Barbara knelt at his feet, hugging his knees. Valeria pushed her way close to lay her lips on his.

"Bert," she whispered. He tasted tears on her mouth. "Bert, darling."

"Take either of us," sobbed Barbara. "Take us both if you want."

"Well, hooray for the Man!" said Nelly. "Three chee—whoops! Catch him there! I think he's fainted!"

It had been a slow trip up through the valley. They had to stop and be feasted at every town along the way.

Davis Bertram stood in tall grass, under a morning wind, and looked up the beloved length of his spaceship. He whistled, and the airlock opened and the ladder descended for him.

"I'll be back," he said clumsily. "Inside a hundred of your days, the Men will be here."

And what would they say when he walked into Stellamont wearing this garb of kilt, feather cloak, and warbonnet?

The Freetoon army was drawn up in dress parade a few meters off. Sunlight flamed on polished metal and oiled leather, plumes nodded and banners fluttered in the breeze. More of their warriors had survived the invasion than he expected. They came out of the woods to worship him as their deliverer when he ordered the town set free.

Gaping civilians trampled the meadows behind them. Davis wondered how many of their babies he had touched, for good luck. Well, it beat kissing the little apes . . . not that it wouldn't be nice to have a few of his own someday.

Barbara and Valeria stood before him. Under the burnished helmets their faces were drawn tight, waiting for his word.

His cheeks felt hot. He looked away from their steady green eyes and dug at the ground with his sandals.

"You're in charge here," he mumbled. "If you really want to make Freetoon a republic—and it'd be a big help, you folk have a difficult period of adjustment ahead—at least one of you has to stay and see the job is done right. There has to be someone here I can trust."

"I know," said Valeria. Her tone grew wistful. "You'll bring that machine of yours to . . . make her forget you?"

"Not forget," said Davis. "Only to feel differently about it. I'll do better than that, though. I'll bring a hundred young men, and you can take your pick!"

"All right," said Valeria. "I pick you."

"Hoy, there!" said Barbara.

Davis wiped sweat off his brow. What was a chap to do, anyway? He felt trapped.

"It'd be better if you both stayed," he groped. "You'll have a . . . a rough time . . . fitting into civilization—"

"Do you really want that?" asked Barbara coolly.

"No," said Davis. "Good Cosmos, no!"

After all, he was a survey man. He wouldn't be close to civilization for very long at a time, ever. Even a barbarian woman, given spirit and intelligence, could be trained into a spacehand.

And a few gaucheries wouldn't matter. A Whitley in formal dress would be too stunning.

"Well, then," said Valeria. Her knuckles tightened around her spearshaft. "Take your choice."

"I can't," said Davis. "I just can't."

The cousins looked at each other. They nodded. One of them took a pair of dice from her pouch. "One roll," said Barbara.

"High girl gets him," said Valeria.

Davis Bertram stood aside and waited.

He had the grace to blush.

Although Davis caused a small war, the benefits of his incursion far outweighed the drawbacks. For bringing Atlantis into the Stellar Union, history reveres him as a hero.

The same cannot be said of every outside visitor to a primitive world. Interstellar crime did not exist in the days of STL travel, but hyperdrive opened the starlanes to brigands of every sort. Yet those who would profit from the ignorance of others never consider the penalties for ignorance in themselves.

Teucan

SOMETIMES a nuclear-conversion engine develops an ulcer. The containing fields weaken long enough—a few microseconds, perhaps for the machine to start devouring itself. It doesn't happen often, but neither is it unheard of, and it will continue to happen until somebody abolishes the Uncertainty Principle. In the event of an ulcer, the only thing to do is to get out of the neighborhood—fast.

Weber considered himself lucky to be near a planet when his engine broke loose. He had, in fact, been coming in for a landing, and it was a moment's scrambling to get into a spacesuit. He grabbed for the chest where he kept his weapons, and a blue electric bolt sizzled to his hand and limned his insulated suit in ghostly fire. Cursing, he reached again, but the chest was already glowing red-hot and the white-blazing bulkhead aft was slumping into molten ruin. No time—when it went down, he'd get a radiation blast which would finish him. He dove for the airlock, awkward in free fall now that the gravity unit was gone.

Just in time! His impellers whirled him away. The boat was a nova against the bitter stars of space. Alone—weaponless—supplyless save for the suit's little emergency pack—well, that planet had better be habitable!

It was a great cottony ball of cloud below him, blinding in the harsh spatial sunlight. Below him—yes, he was close enough, well within the region of perceptible gravitation. He turned off his impeller and let himself fall. A few hours—

The silence and loneliness oppressed him. As the thunder of his heart and blood eased, he considered the years ahead, a lifetime of separation from humankind and all he had known. The lifetime would be short unless he was lucky. His name would be bandied among the Traders for perhaps a decade, and then his very memory would be dust.

Well—not much he could do about it. At least his instruments had told him the planet was Terra-type: about the same size and mass, pretty similar atmosphere. That meant green plants, which in turn meant animals with high probability, which *might* mean intelligent natives; but of course everything might be poisonous to his metabolism. He didn't think the natives would be very far advanced, technologically; the planet was rather close to its sun, an obscure G6 dwarf, steamy and tropical and perpetually cloudy—so it was unlikely that its dwellers would have much concept of astronomy, the father of the sciences. Still, you never knew.

First there was the problem of getting down. He gave himself a northward velocity—the subarctic regions would be most comfortable for a human. It was necessary to be careful with energy; his powerpack had barely enough to land him and maybe fly around a bit, without wasting any.

The slow hours passed.

When he came below the high permanent clouds it was raining. He swung into the wind, the strong heavy flow of water sluicing over his helmet and blurring vision, lightning savage above him. By the time he was out of the storm, his energy meter was flickering near zero. He slanted groundward, studying the terrain with wary eyes.

It was a rolling land of hills and broad valleys, green with a sweeping stretch of jungle, snaked through by long rivers. But he was on the fringe of the wilds. Beyond were cultivated fields, stone huts scattered like grain seeds over the mighty planetscape, wide highways of beaten earth converging on the distant walls of a city. Quite a sizeable city, too, there in the middle of its huge domain; it might well have twenty or thirty thousand inhabitants if they were humanoid. Weber's brain began to calculate.

You could never tell in advance how primitives were going to react. There were the unpredictable inherent differences, due to climate and ecology and physiology and the very external appearance; and then within the same species you could get fantastic variations of thought and behavior patterns from culture to culture. But his best chances lay in a sort of polite boldness, at least till he knew his way around a little better.

He landed with a jarring thump as his powerpack finally sputtered to extinction. Not far off, behind a grove of trees, stood a hamlet of some ten buildings. Dismissing thoughts of bacteria, molds, and other forms of slow or sudden death, Weber got to his feet, threw back his helmet and breathed deeply.

It was a warm, moist, pleasant air, pungent with the aroma of earth and forest and life, heady after the staleness of his suit. The clouds made a featureless gray sky overhead, and there were no visible shadows in that diffused light, but vision was clear enough. A brilliantly feathered bird flew squawking above him. He crossed the field in which he'd landed, set his boots on the road, and started walking toward the village.

The natives came out of it, and others ran from the distant farm huts, converging on him with shrill whoops. He stopped, folded his arms, and waited.

Humanoid—yes, very. If he survived, his shipwreck might prove quite tolerable. They were a slightly built folk, several centimeters shorter than the average Terran, six fingers to a hand and six toes to a sandaled foot, pointed ears, pale bluish skins, hair and eyes of deep purple, the males beardless as the females—but with handsome features not unlike the Caucasian, wiry and graceful of body. Both sexes wore little more than a loincloth, but the males had all the color and most of the shell, tooth, and hammered copper ornaments, feathers in their long hair, tattooing on their breasts. They brandished obsidian spears and axes, and some had wicked-looking wooden swords saw-toothed with chips of flint. They stood and stared at him.

Weber, who was a big blond man, lifted one arm with all the solemnity he could muster. The natives slowed their prancing approach, women huddling behind the ranked men, children screaming, a pack of lithe, long-bodied, blue-furred animals yowling. The peasants coming near, hoes and spades still clutched in their grimy hands, were almost as gaudily equipped as the villagers. Since it was unlikely that he had arrived precisely at a festival moment, Weber decided that the natives simply liked color. Well—the plain, burnished metal of his spacesuit stood out among them. He waited, taut as a drawn wire, holding his face impassive with a straining effort.

They converged again, closing warily in on all sides, muttering to each other. Weber caught one repeated word. "*Teucan.*" It could mean stranger, god, demon, amazement, metal, or maybe just plain to hell with it—no way of knowing.

An old one finally stood forth—bigger than the rest, his face hard and seamed by ancient wounds. "*Teucan quituhiulat shu?*" he snapped. "*Baldemo azunabriun tzi?*"

"Sorry," said Weber. "No savvy." He read fright and a savage will in the narrowed purple eyes. The other blueskins had fallen silent; they were watching with an enormous anticipation.

Suddenly the native lifted his ax and whirled it down. Weber threw up his metal-clad arm just in time to save his skull. The native screeched and sprang like a wildcat, hacking again, raking the Trader's cheekbone. Weber struck at him, the armored fist glancing off the dodging native's shoulder and sending him spinning.

He stood panting, glaring at the Terran. Another native prodded him with a spear. Before Cosmos—they were egging him on!

He gathered his muscles and leaped again. This time Weber was prepared. He caught the blow once more on his arm, and his other fist slammed into the attacker's nose. He felt bone crunch and saw the blood spurt—red as his own, that blood. The native staggered, and Weber wrenched the ax from him.

Some of the watchers shouted, lifting their weapons to the gray heaven. The assailant looked around him, eyes wild with despair through the blood that masked his broken face. There was no friendliness in the answering stares. With something like a groan, he drew an obsidian knife from his belt and charged afresh. Weber swung the ax, and the keen blade clove his skull.

The Trader stood panting over the body, looking around and raising the bloody weapon. "All right," he said hoarsely. "All right. Who else wants the same treatment?"

There was a long minute's silence, and then the cheers nearly split his eardrums. He was escorted into the village by a crowd that capered and yelled and brought forth flutes and drums to serenade him in. Only the peasants stayed behind, eagerly carving the body of the fallen into chunks, squabbling over the pieces and finally hastening back with their trophies.

Before Cosmos, thought Weber dazedly, *they* expected *a finish fight!*

He was shown to a good-sized hut well furnished with stools, mats, furs, and the other items of primitive wealth. Four nice-looking women came in with him, smiling somewhat timorously. Apparently he had inherited his enemy's possessions along with his rank—whatever that had been.

It might be duplicity, but he doubted it. The attempt to murder him had been honest enough, and the awe which he now received seemed honest, too. It was not the formal and silent respect of more civilized races—these people were whooping things up as much as they could—but it was there nonetheless. In the long blue twilight of the planet's day—he estimated it at thirty hours—they gave him a feast. Meats, vegetables, fruits, and a potent sort of beer—it was fun, and he staggered back to his new wives in the middle-sized hours of morning.

By Sirius, if he couldn't make a good thing out of this he didn't deserve the name of Trader!

Without making claims to brilliance or to any outstanding intellectual interests, beyond the making and spending of as much money as possible, Weber Franz had a sharp brain and knew how to use it. The first thing was to learn the language and find out what the devil he'd gotten himself into.

He held the most intelligent-looking of his wives back from work in his fields and drafted her as his instructor. There was little danger of upsetting his godhead, if any, by asking to be taught something—one very general rule about primitives is that they don't worry about consistency and a god who doesn't know the language is not a contradiction. He wasn't much disturbed in the next few days—his wives did the farming and household chores and except for the gaping children the villagers left him pretty much alone—so he could devote his full time to study. His tutor was only too pleased to be free of manual labor, and the primary trouble was the attempt of a couple of the others, jealous of her privilege, to kill her. Weber knocked a few teeth out and had no difficulties thereafter. He was beginning to realize that brutality was an accepted feature of this society. The men swaggered and fought, the villagers browbeat the peasants, the children abused the animals—and still there seemed to be as much laughter here as anywhere else. *They must like it,* he thought.

Traders generally didn't have too much to do with races as backward as this one. The ideal was a people far enough advanced to have something worth buying or bilking them out of. Thus Weber's knowledge of the present level of society was scant, a fact which caused him considerable grief later on. But he had had mind training, and he understood linguistic principles, so he learned fast now. The names of simple objects and actions—more abstract words derived by indirection or from context—and the language was agglutinative, which helped a lot. It wasn't many days before he could understand and make himself understood.

This, it seemed, was the village of Tubarro, part of the domain of Azunica, to which it paid tribute in the form of foodstuffs and slaves. He—Beber, as they rendered it—was now the Teucan of Tubarro, having killed the old one. He didn't dare ask directly what the Teucan was—that might be going too far—and said merely that he had come from the far land of Terra.

Once a levy of soldiers marched down the road toward Azunica, gay with feathers and shields and flowing cloaks, drums and flutes and gongs, leading a hundred miserable-looking captives roped together. And there was a lot of traffic, runners speeding up and down the highway, porters moving under fantastic loads, nobles borne in litters and commoners trudging with goods bought or to sell. The life of this culture seemed to be in Azunica; Tubarro was only a sleepy fuel station and supply store. Weber decided that he would have to visit the city.

But as it happened, the city came to him.

They arrived toward evening, about two weeks after Weber's arrival—though he had lost count of time in the monotonous round of days. There was quite a procession—a squad of soldiers, a company of slaves, even a group of musicians—and they pushed arrogantly down the one street of Tubarro and halted before Weber's dwelling. The Terran, who was becoming aware of the importance of haughtiness, did not look up. He sat in front of his house, wearing the native dress, which showed his size and blondness to spectacular advantage, playing solitaire with the pack of cards he had had in his pocket at the time of the wreck. "Are you, sir, the Teucan of Tubarro?"

Weber lifted heavy-lidded eyes. A tall old man had gotten from his litter—gaudily painted and ornamented, with a feather cloak swung from his shoulders and an elaborately carved staff in one hand. Weber, whose eyes missed little, noticed that his visitor and everyone in the troop had had the first joint of the little finger removed. He spread his five-fingered hands into plain sight.

"Yes, sir, I am," he replied, with the cold courtesy of formal occasions. Idly, he shuffled the cards and snatched one out of the air. Sleight-of-hand could be useful. "Would you like to come inside and take refreshment?"

"Thank you, sir, I would." The old—priest?—followed him into the house. Was it polite to go in before or after or arm-in-arm with your guest? Weber didn't know. He signaled a wife for food and drink.

"Word of you has come to Azunica, sir," said the visitor after due formalities. "It is said you came from a remote land, and most strangely attired."

"That is true, sir." Weber nodded his head very slightly to the polished spacesuit, standing in a corner. "Weaponless I overcame the old Teucan and gave his body to the earth. I did not choose to use my weapons against a single man."

"I see, sir." The priest made a bridge of his fingers and peered shrewdly at the Terran. "It is plain that you are from far away, and that the *teucans* have placed the holy sign on your hands themselves."

There was that word again—*teucan!* In this context it seemed to mean god; but as used by the villagers, and in view of Weber's daily life, it seemed to mean little more than battle-ax champion. The ins and outs of the primitive mind—they don't *think* like civilized people—

"What I wondered, sir," went on the native, "is why you chose to come to this little wallow, rather than to Azunica the great and sacred. You could, being plainly marked as holy yourself, have had the *teucanno* for the asking now that the old one has returned to the earth."

"I had my reasons, sir."

"So you did, sir, and I do not question them. But I am the Chief Servant of Azunica, and it is my duty to select the next Teucan of the city and the whole domain. I do not know how they do it in your land, sir, but in Azunica we determine the will of the *teucans* by drawing lots among all qualified young men. However, you yourself are so clearly the designated one that when word of you came I hastened to find you. It is past time for the choosing—the *banyaquil* must be planted soon or not at all. The people grow restless."

Weber reflected that most of the fields were still being cultivated, and that the crops in the planted ones were young. He must have arrived just in the sowing time, and apparently they needed someone to preside over fertility ceremonies and whatnot. If the old Teucan had lately died—

Hmmm—this, my boy, looks like the luck of the Webers. If you play it right—

"I am content here, sir," he said. "I have my house and my fields and my wives. Why should I move?"

"But reflect, sir. You will grow old and weak—or perhaps, even before that time, there will be a lucky challenger. There are many restless young men who seek a *teucanno* to make their fortune. You will have to fight many times a year. And all for this little village!"

"But there would be even more challengers in Azunica, would there not?"

For an instant the old man looked astonished, and then the mask clamped down again and the eyes were shrewd. There was a good brain under that grey-streaked purple hair. By betraying his ignorance, Weber had started the brain thinking. The Terran looked nervously at the door, but none of the soldiers shifted from the post of attention.

"You jest, sir," said the priest. "Unless it is indeed that they do matters very differently in your homeland. No, who would dare lift a hand against the Teucan of Azunica? He is—he is the *Teucan!* What he would have is his for the asking. Should he tell a man to slay himself, that man would plunge the knife in his own belly on the instant."

Hmmm—yes, apparently the Teucan of Azunica—which, after all, was the capital of a fair-sized theocratic empire—was something different from the Teucan of a village. The latter were—what? Symbols of some kind, no more. The former might well be an incarnate god.

"The homes of Azunica are stuffed with gold and feathers, sir," said the priest persuasively. "The meats are tender, the fruits are sweet, the beer is a singing in the blood. The maidens are young and lovely. The lords of the realm are glad to wait on the Teucan as his slaves." He sighed. "It is clear to me that you are the intended one, and there will be an evil year if the wrong man should be raised to the golden seat. That, sir, is why I am so anxious to give you all this."

"Hmmm—and what must I do myself?"

"What you will, my lord. There are the ceremonies, of course, and appearances to keep up, but it is not arduous. And every creature in the realm is your chattel."

"I will consider it, sir. You shall have my answer tomorrow."

He'd have to make a few discreet inquiries, confirm what had been said. He couldn't inquire too much, of course, without giving himself away to a dangerous extent—but he could at least find out if the Teucan of Azunica had all that power. And if so—*If so, Weber my boy, you'll take another step to success. From Trader to god—not bad!*

Azunica was a big and well-built city, the heart of a high-level barbarism. Large houses of stone and rammed earth set well back from broad paved streets; rows of painted, fang-mouthed idols leading toward a great central pyramid; parks where flowers were a riot of color and the nobles sailed their barges on artificial lakes to the soft music of slave attendants; crowded, jostling marketplaces, men and women yelling around the booths where everything from rugs and pottery to slave girls bred through many generations for beauty and meekness were sold; workshops and factories—it was a gay and colorful scene, and, as Weber saw it from the litter that bore him to the Temple, he was glad he had come. Whatever happened, life on this planet wasn't going to be dull.

The city, like the villages through which he had passed, was clean, and there seemed to be no beggars, slums, or cripples. It was a culture of priests, warriors, artisans, and slaves, but a healthy vigorous one resting on the sturdy foundation of an independent peasantry and nourished from a rich, deep soil. In centuries to come, its nastier features might die out, it could perhaps accomplish great things, but Weber had to live in its present. He was not an altruist and did not intend to make any changes which wouldn't be of direct personal benefit.

Careful questioning of the Chief Servant, the old high priest Zacalli, had already given him some notion of the social structure. The government was in the hands of the priesthood, who in the various ranks fulfilled not only religious but all important civil and military functions; theoretically, at least, everything was the personal property of the Teucan and everyone his personal slave. A rather moderate tax, as such things go at this level of culture, supported the government and the army. The latter was enormous, every man putting in some time of service and a large cadre of professionals raised to arms from birth. Azunica was in a state of perpetual war with all surrounding nations—which all seemed to have a similar society—and the outer provinces, loosely held, were incessantly rebelling. This yielded slaves and tribute. Pretty rough on the borderland peoples, thought Weber, but it enriched the central domain, and the high soil-fertility and birth rate made it economically feasible. Cripples, the senile, and the hopelessly diseased were killed out of hand, brawls and duels were a casually accepted feature of daily life even among the lower classes; only slaves and low-born women were expected to be humble. The whole setup would have revolted an ordinary Galactic, but Weber had spent most of his life on the frontier and accepted it without too many qualms. The thing to do was to adapt; afterward he could see about steering events in what direction he might choose.

Temple headquarters were in a series of gaudily ornamented one-story palaces sprawling around the great pyramid. Weber was escorted past hundreds of prostrated slaves, servants, priests, and soldiers to a suite which was furnished with a barbaric magnificence that took even his breath away. There were a dozen virgins waiting for him, with the promise of as many more as he desired, and he was left to rest and prepare himself for the inaugural ceremonies.

Those took place that night, an awesome torchlit festival with all the city turned out to watch the dancers and musicians and wildly chanting priests. Weber had little to do but sit under his weight of gold and jewels and furs—until at dawn Zacalli gave him a knife and led him slowly up the stairway to the height of the great pyramid.

There was an interminable line of bound captives coming up the other side, toward the altar and the monstrous idol which loomed in the vague gray light. As Weber stared, four burly priests grabbed the first one and stretched him over the stone. "Now, my lord," said the old priest, "give back to the earth the life that came from it."

"Human sacrifice—no!"

"My lord, the *teucans* stoop low, they are waiting."

Weber looked at the prisoner's tightly drawn face, and back to the knife in his hand, and there was a sickness in his throat. "I can't do it," he whispered. "I can't."

"Hurry, my lord, the light is coming and the earth is hungry."

Weber caught at his sanity with both hands. *If I don't, someone else will—after I'm dead.*

He walked slowly forward. "The liver lies here, my lord," pointed Zacalli.

The knife was sharp, but there were many prisoners. Weber had to stop now and again to vomit. The priests' faces were like carven masks.

It was done—the earth had been fed—and Weber went down again to the orgiastic multitude and slowly back to his dwelling. Even after the blood had been washed off and his concubines had anointed him, he felt it red and wet on his skin, soaking through.

There is a certain type of man, energetic, adaptable, and possessed of a hard common sense rather than any great intellect, who goes where the most money is to be gotten and moves the world to get at it. Afterward he becomes a figure of legend and romance, but in his own time he is merely a practical, if adventurous, businessman, not a brute but not especially tender-minded, willing to take risks but not foolhardy. The glamor is added by others. In the so-called First Dark Age it was the viking. In the Second Dark Age it was the Martian war lord. Now, when man has reached the stars, it is the Trader.

He fulfills little economic purpose—civilization just doesn't need him—but by juggling goods from one planet to another he can often accumulate a tidy fortune for himself. He is, usually, cordially disliked by everyone else, for his practices are sharp at best and piratical at worst. He is apt to break the law and sneak beyond the frontier to find worlds never visited before, and there is little which the Coordination Service can do about it except hope that he doesn't work too much harm. The Galaxy is just too big, and too little of it is known, for control. To the average Sol-bound Terran he is a swashbuckling hero, flitting from planet to wild new planet. To himself, he is merely a hard-working entrepreneur in a business which consists mostly of monotonous waiting, and he dreams only of the big strike and the fortune large enough to retire on—before he can spend it.

Weber was a Trader. He had gone into the uncharted Bucyrus

region to find what he could find. If the Service had known where he was bound, they would have stopped him; if any of his fellows had known, they would have tried to get in ahead of him; so he went off in silence, and now there would be none to look for him and he would remain on this planet for the rest of his life. Wherefore it behooved him, first, to adapt his mind, and second, to make something of his situation.

At least, he thought, he'd been lucky in this planet. The food was nourishing to him, the natives were so humanoid that he wouldn't miss his own species, and he seemed immune to the local diseases. It could be worse. Much worse.

Only—well—he'd almost immediately reached the top. Without effort he'd become the adored god and absolute owner of his environment. It didn't take long for his restless nature to demand action. What to *do?*

The fertility rites attending the planting of the staple *banyaquil* had been exhausting, though—he grinned—fun. His officiation in daily ritual wasn't needed, and there wouldn't be another big ceremony till midsummer. Then another in the mid-rainy season, and then it would be spring again. The planet's year was shorter than Terra's, though not very accurately known in the absence of astronomy, and that swift crop cycle accounted in part for the food surplus which enabled the culture to support its permanent warfare. The prospect of a lifetime of the same round looked boring.

Well—he'd make changes. He could do it, being a god, *the* Teucan. First, though, he'd better learn a few more details.

He summoned Zacalli, who entered and prostrated himself. The old man lay there in silence for a long time before it occurred to Weber that he wouldn't speak or move without being told. "Rise," said the Terran. "Sit down over there." He lowered his own bulk to a cushioned stool. "I want to talk to you."

"As my lord commands."

"I want to ask some questions. Answer me truthfully, but otherwise as you would answer any other man. For I am a man and you know it, in spite of my being Teucan."

"Yes, my lord. The man is the Teucan and the Teucan is the man. The *teucanno* of the old one has entered you, as it will enter your successor, at the time when your own life returns to the earth."

"But a village Teucan is something different. He is but a man among men, and anyone who kills him may have his post. Why?"

Zacalli's eyes rested on Weber with an indrawn thoughtfulness. "My lord has come from far away indeed."

"I know. I admit to being ignorant of much about Azunica. Though—" Weber tried to look faintly ominous— "I know much of which you here have no inkling."

"Yes, my lord. They saw you come from the heavens. I have seen your clothing of unknown metal. I have seen your own self."

"Very well, then. Answer my question. Why may a village Teucan be challenged and *the* Teucan can not?"

"My lord, a Teucan is the life of his people. While he lives, he holds their life and the life of the land within him. Yet he must not sicken or die alone, for then the life of the land would die with him, the crops would fail and the women would grow barren. So he is slain by someone else, someone younger and stronger who can better hold the life. And the man-life of the old Teucan goes back to the earth."

Hmmm—a fertility cult, yes. Sympathetic magic—as the Teucan went, so went the village, and to avoid his wasting away the people had hit on the not unintelligent idea of cutting him off in his prime. And the body, the life of the body, went back to the soil—magic again— yes, that was why those peasants had divided up the corpse . . . In similar manner, the human sacrifices were made for the whole realm, to give the life of the captives to the land of the empire.

"But what then of me? What is the function of *the* Teucan?"

"My lord, you hold the life not of one small village but of the world. Yours is not the chance flux of rain or wind or drought or heat at one place, it is the great cycle of the seasons all over the lands of man. The little Teucans are chance; you are the great overall harmony of the world and the seasons. Thus no one could challenge you; the power is too great to be poured from one vessel to another without due magical ceremony."

"I see. Yet you speak of the *teucans* sometimes as if they were— well—not men. Beings higher than men."

"Certainly, my lord. Are they not the *teucans*? You yourself are now one of them, the *teucan* of the earth and of growth, rainy Mazotuca."

Weber shook his yellow head and gave up trying to follow a thought-pattern which, by civilized standards, just didn't make sense.

It would have been well for him had he known more about primitive peoples; he would have realized that while their logic has a different basis it is quite rigorous, often fantastically so. A civilized man usually compromises with his postulates; a primitive does not, but carries them through to their ultimate logical conclusions.

And because the logic was not his own, he was also led to the assumption that the Azunicans, if not inherently stupid, were at least effectually so. That was another mistake. Zacalli and his cohorts could not have been the real rulers of a large and complex empire for the better part of a lifetime without developing a very practical intelligence.

Their new god was strange, he undoubtedly had remarkable powers and there was no guessing the extent of these. He was ignorant, and one could not tell how he would react to sudden new knowledge—he had certainly been revolted enough by the absolute necessities of the sacrifice. So the thing to do was to keep him in ignorance, and play on him as one plays on a powerful instrument, until—

Previous Teucans had been easy to handle. Sate them with every kind of luxury and it was enough. This one seemed to desire something more. Well, it might be possible to obtain it for him. The law was that the Teucan must have everything he wanted.

Weber was discovering that a god can be very lonely. His associates could not speak to him except in the most elaborately unctuous terms of flattery. A few times he summoned others to him, soldiers, artisans, commoners hailed in the streets as he went by, but they were too awed for coherence. With his harem he could relax, they laughed and frolicked with their master, but they were all featherheads who had never seen the real life of the world, born and bred merely to please a man's body. When he complained of this latter fact once to Zacalli, the Chief Servant hurried off and brought him the most intelligent woman in Azunica, wife of a petty noble, and she proved as evasive in her talk as the high priest himself. Coached in advance?

Yes—a conspiracy of some kind. Weber investigated, making surprise visits to all sections of the palaces, snapping questions at underlings who were too frightened to do more than stammer the truth. Such as it was—they weren't aware of a plot, they merely did their jobs, but the fact emerged and when he had it Weber laughed. This, at least, was something he could understand. And it was merely that the Teucan was an elaborate figurehead and the Temple bureaucracy did everything which counted.

Well—he'd see about that!

Easy, though, easy. He'd been thinking of a way to eliminate the human sacrifices, but it would be a long, difficult job. He couldn't merely order them discontinued—most likely the people wouldn't stand for that, and if somehow he did succeed it would be destroying the fertility cult which was the very basis of his power. No, changes would have to be slow, and he'd just have to rid himself of squeamishness.

But he learned there was to be a staff meeting to plan the summer campaign, and insisted on being there. It was an odd conference, the feathered and painted priest-officers discussing strategy and tactics with a cool calculation that would not have been amiss in the Coordination Patrol. He kept himself in the background at first, giving the men a chance to forget their awkwardness in his presence.

There was to be a battle with the neighbor state of Culacanni, and it was thought that a successful raid could be made far into their territory, stealing much treasure and taking many prisoners. Then the army would swing homeward through Azunica's own province of Onegar. "By then, sirs," promised Zacalli, "the revolt will be well under way, but not far enough so that their armies can stand us off."

"The revolt!" exploded Weber. "I never heard of a revolt there."

The impassive blue faces swung around to look at him. "Certainly not, my lord," said Zacalli. "It has not begun yet."

"But how do you know—"

"Why, our agents will start it themselves, of course, my lord. The Onegarans will expect help from Culacanni, but we will already have put those to flight and can crush the uprising without too much trouble."

"But—start a revolt—*why?*"

"My lord jests. We need prisoners for the harvest sacrifice. How could we get them save through war or the suppression of rebels?"

"Hm." Weber relapsed, grunting. The very basis of this culture seemed to be human sacrifice, and everything else followed logically from that. No sacrifices, no crops next year.

Well, he'd heard of stranger basics, here and there throughout the Galaxy. Even Terra's history would supply plenty of odd ones—there had, for instance, been the fantastic statist arrangements previously to the Second Dark Age, where everything was subordinated to the aggrandizement of the nation, which was somehow thought of as having a real and independent existence—

"I'll go along," he said.

"My lord!" gasped an officer. "You cannot—it is unheard of—"

Weber got up and hit the man in the face, hard. As he fell from his seat, Weber kicked him in the belly. "I go," he said.

He thought there was approval in the eyes of the rest. If their own society was brutal, their god, their ideal, ought to be a perfect bastard. Well, he'd give them their wish!

The campaign lasted through the whole short summer. Weber found himself enjoying most of it, since physical action could veil the fact that he was set apart and lonely. There was little danger to him personally; he could not risk his priceless life in battle and a large cordon of guards was assigned him. The bloodshed didn't worry him anymore. His environment was making him calloused.

They marched down the roads of the empire and up into hill country, through rain and heat, quiet fields and tangled colorful jungles and bare windy heights, hunting or stealing for their provisions, chanting as they went. In the long lightless dark there were rings of flickering campfires, wailing songs, harsh barking laughter. When they took an enemy village, they sacked it thoroughly, and Weber could have his pick of loot and captives. There were pitched battles, but no guerrilla harassment—after all, the war was fought not for possession of the country but of its inhabitants. He'd change that, thought Weber—he'd make something out of this drive to war and turn Azunica into the seat of a real empire. Since there was nothing else for him to do, he'd turn conqueror—next year, maybe, or the year after. It no longer occurred to him to worry about the need or justice of it. Sufficient that he, the Teucan, wanted it so.

They came back through Onegar and scattered the rebels and took prisoners by the hundreds. It was a triumphant return for them.

The harvest ceremonies came, and the grain was stored, and the long rains began.

Weber sat moodily in his palace, looking out at the endless flow of water from a lowering sky, drinking deep of the bowl which a slave kept filled for him. It wasn't right, he thought self-pityingly, that he should be so cut off from the life of the people, that they should all be obsequious masks. He suspected the hand of Zacalli in the constant frustration of his attempts to learn more. He'd have the Chief Servant killed soon. But right now he needed the old thus-and-so, and Zacalli was the only one who did talk intelligently with him. He realized that he was being drawn out—but what of that? Zacalli couldn't use the knowledge.

It was like trying to grasp a smooth sphere too big for the hand. He slipped away, unable to get a grip, unable to penetrate and understand. Damn! If only he'd known some primitive psychology—but he'd always despised the xenologists, it was their influence in Coordination, their eternal jabber about culture traits and the preservation of autochthonous developments, which had made so much grief for the Traders. Cosmos! Would not it ever stop raining?

He gulped down another mouthful of beer. Wasn't much he could do now. Azunica was huddled into itself, waiting for spring, and the world lay dark and sodden beyond. His energy, baffled by its initial attempts, gave up the fight and turned to the pleasures which were given him in such unceasing abundance and variety. Now and then he thought dimly that it was bad to stop thinking, that there were implications which he should reason out for his own safety, but the very air seemed to cloud his brain. Some other time. There was time enough; he'd be here till he died.

A drum was beating, somewhere far off, it had been going every day for quite a while now. Zacalli said that it was the first faint rite of spring. When they had three clear days in a row, then it was time for the *banyaquil*.

Weber looked out again. By Cosmos, the rain was slackening. Night swirled slowly out of the streets, up toward the hidden sky, and a thick white mist rose with it. The rain grew thinner. Maybe there wouldn't be any tomorrow.

There wasn't, except for a brief shower which didn't count. Nor the next day. The drums were loud now, thuttering an insistent summons, and the Temple buildings were suddenly alive with soft-footed priests hurrying on their errands. From the top of the pyramid, Weber could see that the peasants were already out, scratching up their fields, sowing grain. He'd have to give them a proper plow this year.

This year! Had it been a year? Well, the cycle was shorter on this planet. He wondered if it was springtime on Terra.

There was a feast that night—orgy might better describe it—over which he was expected to preside. Which he did, hilariously. The rains were ending! He slept most of the following day, which was quiet and sultry, and did not see the preparations that were made and the slow gathering of the throngs.

"Tonight, my lord," said Zacalli at dusk, "is yours to do as you will."

"Certainly it is," said Weber. "I'm the Teucan, am I not?" He threw another party.

Morning came with fresh rain clouds, sweeping low and black over the land on a hot wet wind. But that didn't matter. The rainy season was officially over.

Weber was shaken gently awake. It was Zacalli, robed and feathered and painted as never before, and a train of priests no less gaudy stood behind him. "Go away," mumbled the Terran.

"My lord, you must arise. It is the time of the festival's beginning."

"I said go away!" Weber sat up on his couch, holding one hand to his throbbing head. "It is my order. I am the Teucan."

"Hail the Teucan," murmured the deep voices. Thunder growled in the sky.

"My lord, you must. It is the law of the *teucans*."

Weber was half lifted to his feet. His mouth tasted vile. Well, if he must, then he must—couldn't be too unconventional at this stage of the game. What ceremony was it? Not the sacrifice—he knew it wasn't scheduled for several days yet. Odd that Zacalli hadn't coached him on the details of this performance, as he had of all others. *I suppose I just have to sit and look divine. Maybe I can catch a nap there.*

"Very well, I am coming, I am coming."

Slaves were there, bathing him, anointing him, painting his body and adorning it with the most gorgeous finery in the empire. He was so used to thinking of the attendants as faceless nonentities that he didn't notice anything special in their manner. He ate a large breakfast to the accompaniment of a wild religious chant whose words he only half caught. "*Now the Teucan, rainy Mazotuca, sinks into the earth and gives it his life, to arise gloriously renewed. . . . Hail the Teucan, dead and yet arisen, hail Mazotuca, who makes the earth to flower. . . .*"

Some kind of symbolism, he thought fuzzily. Hadn't that xenologist once said something about the death and resurrection of the fertility god in many primitive cultures throughout the Galaxy? Symbol of the grain, buried and rising anew, of old generations dying and the young springing from their loins, of summer which dies and is buried under winter and rises again in spring. . . . *So I am to be resurrected today, eh? Cosmos, I need it—ouch, my head—*

The priests had waited unmoving for him to finish. As he rose, they bowed to the floor, and Zacalli took his arm and led him into the hall.

There was a sudden curious, almost wistful note in the old priest's voice as he murmured: "My lord, you came from very far away indeed. I would I might have learned more of your country." And with a flicker of malice, "Perhaps you should have learned more of ours."

"Hm?" asked Weber.

They came out on the palace stairs at that moment, and the throng in the streets, surging and roaring behind the lines of guardsmen like a rainbow maelstrom, began to cheer, thunder of noise lifting into the thick dark sky and drowning the whine of wind. Weber shuddered as his head thumped.

Slowly down the avenue between the lines of the army, leading the chanting priests and the skirling music, past the massive stone buildings to the pyramid. It loomed mountainous overhead, gray in the sulfurous storm-light, lightnings flickering about the idol on its summit. Thunder boomed and crashed; the gods were drumming up there.

Slowly they mounted the steps, up and up while the people of Azunica yelled at the base. The wind was strong, whipping cloaks, throwing the first heavy raindrops stingingly into Weber's face. Black overhead, streaked with an incessant fire of lightning, a hazy wall of rain marching down from the north, thunder and darkness and the idol grinning above him. Weber looked back, down the long slope and the barbaric procession winding at his heels, over the human sea and the heavy old buildings and out to the whole vast sweep of land.

His land, by Cosmos, his earth lying rich and open for the rain's divine embrace, his valleys and rivers and sky-storming mountains, brawling, pulsing fury of life—standing here with the air blowing wild and the thunder a steady salute, crowned with lightnings, he *was* the

Teucan and a sudden drunkenness of power sang in his blood. To be a god—

The priests formed a half-circle about the great idol, and their chants rose loud against the hooting wind. Zacalli prostrated himself once more in front of Weber. Then he stood up, and the knife gleamed in his hand, and four huge priests grabbed the Terran and threw him across the altar stone.

The god of life is reborn each year—but first, he must die.

Luckily, the damage done by Weber was petty and short-lived. Some Traders ravaged entire societies to satisfy their greed, driving some nameless victim to remark: "Commerce is piracy by other means."

Restraining interstellar predators was one responsibility of the Stellar Union's Co-ordination Service. The Cordys' goal was to maximize harmony and minimize discord among the stars. Like the Psychotechnic Institute before it, the Service trusted in the power of reason to create order.

But the cosmos is a chaotic place.

The Pirate

WE GUARD THE GREAT PACT: but the young generations, the folk of the star frontier, so often do not understand.

They avail themselves of our ordinary work. (*Ship* Harpsong *of Nerthus, out of Highsky for David's Landing, is long overdue . . . Please forecast the competition which a cybernation venture on Oasis would probably face after the older firms elsewhere learned that a market had been established. . . . Bandits reported. . . . How shall we deal with this wholly strange race of beings we have come upon?*) But then we step in their own paths and say, "Thou shalt not." And suddenly we are the Cordys, the enemy.

The case of the slain world named Good Luck is typical. Now that the Service is ready, after a generation, to let the truth be known, I can tell you about Trevelyan Micah, Murdoch Juan, Smokesmith, red Faustina, and the rest, that you may judge the rights or wrongs for yourself.

In those days Trevelyan spent his furloughs on Earth. He said its quiet, its intellectuality, were downright refreshing, and he could get all the rowdiness he wanted elsewhere. But of course his custom put him at the nerve center of the Service, insofar as an organization operating across a fraction of the galaxy can have one. He got a larger picture than most of his colleagues of how it fared with the Pact. This made him more effective. He was a dedicated man.

I suspect he also wanted to renew his humanity at the wellspring of humankind, he who spent most of his life amidst otherness. Thus he was strengthened in his will to be a faithful guardian.

Not that he was a prig. He was large and dark, with aquiline features and hard aquamarine eyes. But his smile was ready, his humor was dry, his tunic and culottes were always in the latest mode, he enjoyed every aspect of life from Bach to beer.

When the machine summoned him to the Good Luck affair, he had been living for a while at Laugerie Haute, which is in the heart of the steep, green, altogether beautiful Dordogne country. His girl of the moment had a stone house that was built in the Middle Ages against an overhanging cliff. Its interior renovation did not change its exterior ancientness, which made it seem a part of the hills or they a part of it. But in front grew bushes, covering a site excavated centuries ago, where flint-working reindeer hunters lived for millennia while the glacier covered North Europe. And daily overhead through the bright sky glided a spear that was the Greenland-Algeria carrier; and at night, across the stars where men now traveled, moved sparks that were spaceships lifting out of Earth's shadow. In few other parts of the planet could you be more fully in the oneness of time.

"You don't have to go, not yet," Braganza Diane said, a little desperately because she cared for him and our trumpeter blows too many Farewells each year.

" 'Fraid I do," he said. "The computer didn't ring me up for fun. In fact, it's a notoriously sober-sided machine." When she didn't answer his grin, he explained: "The data banks show I'm the only person available who's dealt with, uh, a certain individual before. He's a slippery beast, with sharp teeth, and experience might make the critical quantum of difference."

"It better!" She curbed the tears that could have caused him to think her immature and bent her lips upward. "You will add . . . the rest of this leave . . . to your next, and spend it with me. Won't you?"

"I'd love to," he said, carefully making no promises. He kissed her, where they stood in the hay scent of summer. They went back to the house for a while.

After he packed his kit and phoned good-bye to some neighbors—landholders, friendly folk whose ancestors had dwelt here for generations beyond counting—she flew him to Aerogare Bordeaux. Thence he took a carrier to Port Nevada. The computer had briefed him so well that he could go straight to work, and he wanted to catch Murdoch Juan at ease if possible.

His timing was good. Sunset was slanting across western North America and turning the mountains purple when he arrived. The city walled him off from that serenity as he entered. It shouldered big square buildings above streets in which traffic clamored; the growl of machines perpetually underlay the shrill of voices; frantically flickering signs drowned out the stars; humans and nonhumans hustled, jostled, chiseled, brawled, clashed, stole, evangelized, grew rich, grew poor, came, went, and were forgotten, beneath a tawdry front was that heedless vigor which the cargo ships bring from their homes to enclaves like this. Trevelyan allowed himself a brief "Phew!" when the stinks rolled around him.

He knew this town, on a hundred different worlds. He knew how to make inquiries of chance-met drinking companions. Eventually he found one of Murdoch's crew who could tell him where the boss was this evening. It turned out to be no dive, with the smoke of a dozen drugs stinging the eyes, but the discreet and expensive Altair House.

There a headwaiter, live though extraterrestrial, would not conduct him to his man. Captain Murdoch had requested privacy for a conference. Captain Murdoch was entitled to—Trevelyan showed his identification. It gave no legal prerogative; but a while ago the Service had forestalled a war on the headwaiter's native planet.

Upstairs, he chimed for admittance to the room. He had been told that Captain Murdoch's dinner guest had left, seemingly well pleased, while Captain Murdoch and his female companion stayed behind with a fresh order of champagne, vigorator, and other aids to celebration. "Come in, come in!" boomed the remembered hearty voice. The door dilated and Trevelyan trod through.

"Huh? I thought you were—Sunblaze! You again!" Murdoch surged to his feet. Briefly he stood motionless, among drapes and paintings, sparkling glassware, drift of music and incense. Then, tiger softly, he came around the table to a fist's reach of Trevelyan.

He was as tall, and broader in the shoulders. His features were rugged, deeply weathered, blond hair and a sweeping blond moustache. His clothes were too colorful to be stylish on Earth, but he wore them with such panache that you didn't notice.

The woman remained seated. She was as vivid in her way as he in his, superbly formed, the classicism of her face brought to life by the nearly Asian cheekbones; and she owned the rare combination of pure white skin and fox-red hair. Yet she was no toy. When she saw Murdoch thus taken aback, Trevelyan read shock upon her. It was followed by unflinching enmity.

He bowed to her. "Forgive me if I intrude," he said.

Murdoch relaxed in a gust of laughter. "Oh, sure, sure, Mike, you're forgiven. If you don't stay too mugthundering long." He clapped hands on the agent's shoulders. "How've you been, anyway? How many years since last?"

"Five or six." Trevelyan tried to smile back. "I'm sorry to bother you, but I understand you're shipping out day after tomorrow, which no doubt means you'll be busy for the prior twenty-four hours."

"Right, buck," Murdoch said. "This here tonight is our lift-off party. However, it began with business—lining up a financial backer for later on—so it may as well continue that way a few microseconds." The tone stayed genial, but the gaze was pale and very steady. "Got to be business, don't it? You didn't track me down just to wish an old sparring partner a bony voyage."

"Not really," Trevelyan admitted.

Murdoch took his arm and led him to the table. "Well, sit yourself and have a glug with us. Faustina, meet Trevelyan Micah of the Stellar Union Coordination Service."

"Juan has spoken of you," the woman said distantly.

Trevelyan eased into a chair. His muscles relaxed, one by one, that his brain might be undistracted in the coming duel. "I hope he used language suitable to a lady," he said.

"I'm from New Mars," she snapped. "We don't have time for sex distinctions in our manners."

I might have guessed, he thought. There aren't as many unclaimed planets habitable by man as is popularly believed; so the marginal ones get settled too. He could imagine scarring poverty in her background, and Murdoch Juan as the great merry beloved knight who took her from it and would bear her on his saddlebow to the castle he meant to conquer for them.

"I did my duty as I saw it, which happened to conflict with Captain Murdoch's rights as he saw them," Trevelyan said.

"I was making a fortune off fur and lumber on Vanaheim," the other man said.

"And disrupting the ecology of a continent," Trevelyan replied.

"You didn't have to come in and talk them into changing the laws on me," Murdoch said without rancor. He rinsed a glass from the water carafe and filled it with champagne. "Hope you don't mind this being used first by a financier."

"No. Thank you." Trevelyan accepted.

"And then, when he was honorably engaged as a mercenary—" Faustina's tone held venom.

"Bringing modern weapons in against primitives who were no menace," Trevelyan said. "That's universally illegal. Almost as illegal as dispossessing autochthons or prior colonists."

"Does your precious Union actually claim jurisdiction over the entire cosmos?"

"Ease off, Faustina," Murdoch said.

"The Union is not a government, although many governments support it," Trevelyan said to the woman. "This galaxy alone is too big for any power to control. But we do claim the right to prevent matters from getting out of hand, as far as we're able. That includes wrongdoing by our own citizens anywhere."

"The Cordys never jailed me," Murdoch said. "They only scuppered my operation. I got away in time and left no usable evidence. No hard feelings." He raised his glass. Unwillingly, Trevelyan clinked rims with him and drank. "In fact," Murdoch added, "I'm grateful to you, friend. You showed me the error of my ways. Now I've organized a thing that'll not only make me rich, but so respectable that nobody can belch in my presence without a permit."

Faustina ignited a cigarette and smoked in hard puffs.

"I've been asked to verify that," Trevelyan said.

"Why, everything's open and honest," Murdoch said. "You know it already. I got me a ship, never mind how, and went exploring out Eridanus way. I found a planet, uninhabited but colonizable, and filed for a discoverer's patent. The Service inspection team verified that Good Luck, as I'm calling it, is a lawfully exploitable world. Here I am on Earth, collecting men and equipment for the preliminary work of making a defined area safe for humans. You remember." His manner grew deliberately patronizing. "Check for dangerous organisms and substances in the environment, establish the weather and seismic patterns, et cetera. When we're finished, I'll advertise my real estate and my ferry service to it. For the duration of my patent, I can set the terms of immigration, within limits. Most discoverers just charge a fee. But I aim to supply everything—transportation there, a functioning physical community built in advance, whatever people need to make a good start. That's why I've been discussing financial backing."

"Your approach has been tried," Trevelyan warned, "but never paid off. The cost per capita of a prefabricated settlement is more than the average would-be immigrant can afford. So he stays home, and puff goes the profit. Eventually, the entrepreneur is glad to sell out for a millo on the credit."

"Not this one," Murdoch said. "I'll be charging irresistibly little— about half what it'd cost 'em to buy unimproved land and make their own homes and highways and such out of local materials. They'll come." He tossed off the rest of his glass and refilled it. "But why are you curious, you Cordys? I haven't told you anything that isn't on file. If you wanted to snoop, why didn't you come see me earlier?"

"Because we have too much else on file," Trevelyan said bitterly. "Our computer didn't get around to correlating certain facts until yesterday. We're trying to keep the galaxy livable, but it's too much for us, too diverse—"

"Good!" Faustina said.

He gave her a grave look. "Be careful, my lady," he said, "or one day a piece of that diversity may kill you."

Murdoch scowled. "That'll do," he said. "I've been nice, but this is my evening out with my girl and you're obviously on a fishing expedition. You haven't got a thing against me, legally, have you? Very well, get out."

Trevelyan tensed where he sat.

"Or good night, if you prefer," Murdoch said in friendlier wise.

Trevelyan rose, bowed, murmured the polite formulas, and left. Inwardly he felt cold. There had been more than a gloat in his enemy's manner; there had been the expectation of revenge.

It looks as if I'd better take direct action, he thought.

The *Campesino* cleared from orbit, ran out of the Solar System on gravs, and went into hyperdrive in the usual fashion. She was a long-range cruiser with boats and gear for a variety of conditions. Aboard were Murdoch, Faustina, half a dozen spacemen, and a score of technicians.

The service speedster *Genji* followed, manned by Trevelyan and that being whose humanly unpronounceable name was believed to mean something like Smokesmith. To shadow another vessel is more art than science and more witchcraft than either. *Campesino* could easily be tracked while in the normal mode—by amplified sight, thermal radiation, radar, neutrinos from the power plant. But once she went over to the tachyon mode, only a weak emission of superlight particles was available. And Murdoch also had detectors, surely kept wide open.

With skill and luck, *Genji* could stay at the effective edge of the field she was observing, while it masked her own. For this to be possible, however, she must be much smaller as well as much faster than the other craft. Therefore nothing more formidable than her could be used. She did have a blast cannon, a couple of heavy slugthrowers, and several one-meter dirigible missiles with low-yield nuclear warheads. But Trevelyan would have been surprised if Murdoch's people didn't build themselves huskier weapons en route.

He sat for hours at the conn, staring into the jeweled blackness of its star simulacrum, while the ship murmured around him and the subliminal beat of drive energies wove into his bones. At last he said, "I think we've done it." He pointed to the instruments. A hunter's exultation lifted within him. "They are definitely sheering off the Eridanus course."

"They may have become aware of us, or they may do so later, and attack," replied the flat artificial voice of Smokesmith.

"We take that chance," Trevelyan agreed. "I can't quite believe it of Murdoch, though. He plays rough, but I don't know about any cold-blooded murders he's done."

"Our information concerning his world line is fragmentary, and zero about its future segment. Furthermore, available data indicate that his companions are quite unintegrate."

"M-m-m, yes, hard cases, none Earth-born, several nonhumans from raptor cultures among them. That was one fact which alerted us."

"What else? We departed too hurriedly for me to obtain entire background, I being ignorant of the biological and social nuances among your species."

Trevelyan considered his shipmate. Chief Rodionov had had to assign the first and presumably best agent he could, and there were never many nonhumans at Australia Center. Homo Sapiens is a wolfish creature; two of him can end with ripping each other apart, on an indefinitely long voyage in as cramped a shell as this. But even when our agents have gentler instincts, we try to make up teams out of diverse breeds. The members must be compatible in their physical requirements but, preferably, different enough in psychologies and abilities that they form a whole which is more than its parts.

The trouble was, Trevelyan had never before encountered a being from the planet men called Reardon's. He had heard of them, but space is too full of life for us to remember it all, let alone meet it.

Smokesmith's barrel-like body stood about 140 centimeters high on four stumpy, claw-footed legs. Four tentacles ringed the top of it, each ending in three boneless fingers whose grip was astonishing. The head was more like a clump of fleshy blue petals than anything else; patterns upon them were the outward signs of sense organs, though Trevelyan didn't know how these worked. Withal, Smokesmith was handsome in his (?) fashion. Indeed, the mother-of-pearl iridescence on his rugose torso was lovely to watch.

The man decided on a straightforward approach. "Well," he said, "the fact that Murdoch is involved was in itself suspicious. He probably came to Earth to outfit, rather than some colonial world where he isn't known, because he wouldn't attract attention."

"I should extrapolate otherwise, when few commercial ventures originate on Earth."

"But the average Terrestrial hasn't got the average colonist's lively interest in such matters. The port cities are mostly ignored by the rest of the planet, a regrettable necessity to be kept within proper bounds. Then, too, Murdoch would have a better chance of getting substantial but closemouthed—uh, that means secretive—money help on Earth, which is still the primary banker of the human species. And finally, though it's true that Service reports from everywhere go to the molecular file at Center . . . that fact makes the data flow so huge that Murdoch might well have completed his business and departed before the continuous search-and-correlation noticed him."

"What was smelled, then, to excite suspicion? I do not hypothesize that the initial stimulus was the composition of his crew."

"No. We checked that out later. Nor did the economics of his project look especially interesting. Doubtless his ready-built community will be a wretched clutter of hovels; but *caveat emptor,* he'll be within the law, and word will soon get around not to buy from him.

"No, the real anomaly is the equipment he ordered. The report on this Good Luck of his is complete enough that you can fairly well predict what a ground-preparation gang will need. The planet's smaller than Earth, relatively cold and arid, relatively thin atmosphere. But it has a magnetic field and a weak sun; hence the radiation background is low."

"What is required would depend on what race is to colonize."

"Sure. Murdoch will sell to humans. Not Earth humans, naturally. Colonial ones, from all over. We won't be able to monitor every embarkation and debarkation, any except a tiny fraction. Not when we are as few as we are, with so much else to do. And local authorities won't care. They'll be too glad to get rid of excess population. Besides, most colonials are anarchic oriented; they won't stand for official inquiries into their business." Trevelyan blinked in surprise. "What started me off on that?"

"Conceivably an element of your mentation has sensed a thought."

"If so, it's a hunch too faint to identify. Well. Why doesn't he have water-finding gear with him, drills and explosives to start forming lakes, that kind of stuff? Why does he have a full line of radiation spotters and protective suits? The biological laboratory he's assembled isn't right for Good Luck either; it's meant to study life forms a lot more terrestroid. I could go on, but you get the idea."

"And now he has changed course." Smokesmith considered the indicators with whatever he used to see. "A geodesic, which will bring him in the direction of Scorpius."

"Huh? You don't have to ask the computer? . . . Trouble is, no law says he must go to his announced destination, or tell us why he didn't." Trevelyan smiled with shut lips. "Nor does any law say we can't tail along."

A keening broke from Smokesmith, made not with his vocoder but with his own tympani. It wavered up and down the scale; a brief shakenness in his nerves told Trevelyan it entered the subsonic. Odors rolled upon the air, pungencies like blood and burnt sulfur and others men do not know.

"Good Cosmos, what're you doing?" he exclaimed.

"It is an old communication of my infraculture. Of whetted winds, frost, a mountain that is a torch, beneath iron moons, a broken night, and the will to pursue that which has poison fangs. . . . Enough."

Five hundred and twenty-eight light-years from Sol, the sky ahead suddenly blazed.

Trevelyan had been meditating upon his philosophy. That, and reading, and listening to music tapes, and tinkering with handicrafts, and physical exercises, had been his refuge from the weary weeks. Smokesmith was a decent being in his way, but too alien for games or conversation. When asked how he passed the time, with no apparent motion save of his endlessly interweaving arms, he replied: "I make my alternate life. Your language lacks the necessary concepts."

The blossoming of what had been merely another, slowly waxing blue star, jerked Trevelyan to alertness. He sat up, clenched hands on chair arms, and stared at the simulacrum until his vision seemed to drown in those glittering dark depths. The star climbed in brilliance even as he watched, for *Genji* passed the wave front of the initial explosion and entered that which had come later. It dominated the whole sky before Trevelyan could shout:

"Supernova!"

And still it flamed higher, until its one searing point gave fifty times the light that full Luna does to Earth, ten million times the light of the next most luminous—and nearby—sun. Although the screens throttled down that terrible whiteness, Trevelyan could not look close to it, and his vision was fogged with shining spots for minutes after the glimpse he had first gotten.

Smokesmith's claws clicked on the deck of the conn section as the Reardonite entered. Trevelyan caught a hackle-raising whiff from him and knew he was equally awed. Perhaps his expressionless phrasing was a defense:

"Yes, a supernova of Type II, if the theoretical accounts I have witnessed are correct. They are estimated to occur at the rate of one every fifty-odd years in the galaxy. The remnants of some have been investigated, but to date no outburst has been observed within the range of recorded explorations."

"We've gone beyond that range already," the man whispered. He shook himself. "Is Murdoch headed toward it?"

"Approximately. No change in course."

"Can't be coincidence. He must have traveled far, looking for game the Cordys wouldn't take from him, and—" Roughly: "Let's get some readings."

Instruments, astrophysical files carried on every Service vessel, and computation produced a few answers. The star was about 150 parsecs away, which meant it had died five centuries ago. It had been a blue giant, with a mass of some ten Sols, an intrinsic luminosity of perhaps 50,000; but the Scorpian clouds had hidden it from early Terrestrial astronomers, and modern scientists were as yet too busy to come this far afield.

So wild a burning could not go on for many million years. Instabilities built up until the great star shattered itself. At the peak of its explosion, it flooded forth energy equal to the output of the rest of the galaxy.

That could last for no more than days, of course. Racing down the light-years, Trevelyan saw the lurid splendor fade. A mistiness began to grow, a nebula born of escaped gases, rich in new nuclei of the heavier elements, destined at last to enter into the formation of new suns and planets. Instruments picked out the core of the star: whitely shining, fiercer still in the X-ray spectrum, lethal to come near. But it collapsed rapidly beneath its own monstrous gravitation, to the size of a dwarf, a Jupiter, an Earth. At the end it would be so dense that nothing, not even light, could leave; and it would have vanished from the universe.

Trevelyan said with bleak anger: "He didn't report it. The information that's already been lost as the wave front swelled—"

"Shall we return at once?" the Reardonite asked.

"Well . . . no, I suppose not. If we let Murdoch go, Cosmos knows what deviltry might happen. There'll be other supernovas, but a dead sentience doesn't come back."

"We have a strong indication of his goal."

"What?" Trevelyan set down the pipe he had been nervously loading.

"Examine the photomultiplier screen, and next these." Fingertendrils snaked across dial faces. "The star to which I point is an ordinary G3 sun within a hundred light-years of the supernova. Proper motions show that it was somewhat closer at the time of the eruption.

Our study object is on an unmistakable intercept track. It is plausible that this is meant to terminate there."

"But— No!" Trevelyan protested. "What can he want?"

"The dosage received by any planet of the lesser sun, through the cosmic rays given off by the larger at its maximum, was in the thousands of roentgens, delivered in a period of days. Atmosphere and magnetic field would have provided some shielding, but the effect must nonetheless have been biologically catastrophic. Presumably, though, most lower forms of life would survive, especially vegetable and marine species. A new ecological balance would soon be struck, doubtless unstable and plagued by a high mutation rate but converging upon stability. Probably the infall of radionuclides, concentrated in certain areas by natural processes, would make caution advisable to the present time. But on the whole, this hypothetical planet could now be salubrious for your race or mine, if it otherwise resembles our homes sufficiently. I might add that it has been conjectured that accidents of this sort were responsible for periods of massive extinction on numerous worlds, including, I have absorbed, your own home sphere."

Trevelyan scarcely heard the flat words. All at once he was confronting horror.

When the yellow sun was a disk, too lightful for bare eyes but softly winged with corona and zodiacal glow in a step-down screen: then the supernova nebula, thirty parsecs off, was only an irregular blur, a few minutes across, among the constellations opposite, as if a bit of the Milky Way had drifted free. One had trouble imagining how it had raged in these skies four hundred years ago. Nor did interplanetary space any longer have an unusual background count; nor did the seven attendant worlds that *Genji's* cameras identified seem in any way extraordinary.

That was a false impression, Trevelyan knew. Every world is a wilderness of uncountably many uniquenesses. But the third one out, on which his attention focused, resembled Earth.

He was confined to optical means of study. Beams and probes might be detected aboard *Campesino*. Murdoch had gone out of hyper into normal mode several millions of kilometers back. His shadowers necessarily followed suit. Then—lest he spot their neutrino emission, as they were now tracking him by his—they stopped the fusion generators and orbited free at their considerable distance, drawing power from the accumulators.

"The study object is in the final phase of approach to atmosphere of the terrestroid planet," Smokesmith announced.

"I'm scarcely surprised," Trevelyan answered. He looked up from his meters and notes. "Apparently it is as terrestroid as any you'll ever find, too. Air, irradiation, size, mass as gotten from the satellites— nearly identical. Those are two small, fairly close-in moons, by the way; so the tide patterns must be complicated, but the oceans will be kept from stagnation. Twenty-eight-hour spin, twelve-degree tilt. Mean temperature a touch higher than Earth's, no polar caps, somewhat less land area . . . an interglacial macroclimate, I'd guess. In short, aside from pockets of leftover radioactivity, idyllic."

"And possible ecological difficulties," the Reardonite said.

Trevelyan winced. "Damn, did you have to remind me?" He left off peering, leaned back in his chair, held his chin, and scowled. "Question is, what do we do about Murdoch? He doesn't seem to have committed any violation except failure to register a discovery. And we probably couldn't prove this isn't his own first time here, that he didn't come this way on impulse. Besides, the offense is trivial."

"Do methods not exist of compelling humans to speak truth?"

"Yes. Electronic brainphasing. Quite harmless. But our species has rules against involuntary self-incrimination. So it's mainly used to prove the honesty of prosecution witnesses. And as I said, I've no real case against him."

"Need we do more than report back? Authorized expeditions could then be dispatched."

"'Back'" is a mighty long ways. What might he do here meanwhile? Of course—hm—if Murdoch doesn't suspect we're on to him, he may proceed leisurely with his preparations, giving us a chance to—"

"The study object has ceased to emit."

"What?" Trevelyan surged from his chair. He abraded his arm on his companion's integument, so fast did he brush by to look for himself. The indications were subtle, because the normal neutrino count is always high. But this tracer included a computer which identified engine sign amidst noise and put its volume on a single dial. That needle had fallen to zero.

Chilled, Trevelyan said: "He's going down on accumulators and aerodynamics. By the time we come in range for a different tracking method, he can be wherever on the surface."

Smokesmith's tone was unchanging, but an acrid odor jetted from him and the petals of his face stirred. "Apparently he does not fear detection from the ground. We observe no trace of atomic energy, hence doubtless no one capable of locating it. The probability is that he desires to remove us and none else from his trail."

"Yeh." Trevelyan began to pace, back and forth between the caging bulkheads. "We half expected he'd tag us somewhere along the line, when I'd already put him on the *qui vive* in Port Nevada. But why's he telling us unequivocally that he has?"

"In my race, messages are always intended as vectors on the world line of the percipient."

"In mine too, sort of." Trevelyan's strides lengthened. "What does Murdoch hope to get us to do by thumbing his nose at us? We have two alternatives. We can go straight back, or we can land first for a closer look."

"The latter would not add significantly to the interval before we can have returned."

"That's the black deuce of it, my friend. The very nearest Service base where we could originate any kind of investigatory expedition is, um, Lir, I suppose, if they aren't still too busy with the Storm Queen affair. There are frontier planets closer than that, full of men who'll gladly swarm here for a chance of striking it rich. And if they can also do the Cordys one in the eye, why, fine."

"Furthermore," Smokesmith pointed out, "we have no clear proof that anything is involved sufficiently important to justify a long-range mission. The supernova, yes. That is a scientific treasure. But here we have merely a seemingly uninhabited planet. Why should a base commander who does not know Murdoch's past—especially a nonhuman base commander who cannot ingest its significance— assume he has an unlawful purpose? Will he not expect Murdoch to request an inspection team, that a patent of discovery may be issued?"

Trevelyan nodded. We are scattered so thinly, we who guard the great Pact. Often we must pass by tracks that may well lead toward a hidden evil, because we *know* about another beast elsewhere. Or we learn of something that was wrong at the beginning and should have been stopped, but whose amendment now would be a worse wrong. We have Nerthus, for example, always before us: a human colony founded and flourishing, then learning that native intelligent life did exist. We are fortunate that in that case the interests of the two species are reconcilable, with endless difficulty.

"Does Murdoch wish us to return in alarm bearing data inadequate to provoke prompt official action?" Smokesmith queried. "That seems plausible. Coming as he lately did from the Union's Scorpian march, he must be better informed than we about current situations there. Thus, he might know we can get no help at Lir."

"We can—we can even commandeer civilian ships and personnel— if yonder planet has sentient beings on it. Clear and present danger of territorial conquest. Or Murdoch might simply be plundering them."

"It is improbable that such are alive."

"True. But if dead—"

Trevelyan stopped. He looked long outward. Unmagnified, the world was a point of light, a clear and lovely blue. But close in would be mapless immensity. The other crew would have had ample chance to conceal their vessel. They could be anywhere, preparing anything. They surely outnumbered and outgunned him. He hated to imagine big, bluff Murdoch Juan as planning murder. On the other hand, Faustina might, and she had had this entire voyage in which to be the only human female. . . .

Resolution crystallized. "We're going in," he said.

They approached slowly, both to observe in detail and to make certain preparations. Circling in the fringes of atmosphere, they confirmed the thing they had guessed at.

This had been a peopled world. The people had been slain.

Were there survivors, there would be evidence of them. Civilization might well have gone under in mass death, panic, anarchy, and famine after crops perished in fields now brushland or desert. But savage descendants of a city-building race would live in villages. *Genji's* sensors would register their very campfires. Besides, it was more reasonable that some comeback would have been made, however weak. For the sleet of cosmic radiation harmed no buildings, no tools or machines, no books, little, indeed, except what was alive.

Gazing into a viewscreen, where clouds parted briefly to show high towers by a lake, Trevelyan said: "Populous, which means they had efficient agriculture and transportation, at least in their most advanced regions. I can identify railway lines and the traces of roads. Early industrial, I'd guess, combustion engines, possible limited use of electricity. . . . But they had more aesthetic sense, or something, than most cultures at that technological level. They kept beauty around them." He hauled his thoughts away from what that implied. If he did not stay impersonal he must weep.

"Did they succumb to radiation effects alone?" Smokesmith wondered. He appeared to have no trouble maintaining detachment. But then, he did not feel humanlike emotions, as Trevelyan judged the dead beings had. "Shelter was available."

"Maybe they didn't know about radioactivity. Or maybe the escapers were too few, too scattered, too badly mutated. Anyhow, they're gone—Hold!"

Trevelyan's hands danced over the board. *Genji* swung about, backtracked, and came to hover.

Atmosphere blurred the magnified view, but beams, detectors, and computer analysis helped. A town stood on an island in a wide river. Thus, despite the bridges that soared from bank to bank, it was not thickly begrown by vegetation. What had entered was largely cleared away: recent work, the rawness identifiable. The job had been done by machines, a couple of which stood openly in a central plaza. Trevelyan couldn't spot details, but never doubted they were Earth-made robotic types. Several buildings had been blasted, either as too ruinous or as being in the way, and the rubble shoved aside. He got no indications of current activity, but strong electronic resonance suggested that a modern power network was partly completed.

"Murdoch," Trevelyan said like a curse.

"Can you obtain indications of his ship?" the Reardonite asked.

"No. When he detected us approaching, he must have moved her, and screened as well as camouflaged the hull. Maybe he hoped we wouldn't chance to notice what he's been up to, or maybe this is another gibe. Certainly he must've gotten busy here the instant he landed, after choosing the site on his first visit."

Trevelyan put the speedster back into orbit. For a while the conn held only a humming silence. The planet filled half the sky with clouds, seas, sunrises and sunsets; the other half was stars.

"No autochthons left," Smokesmith mused at last. "Their relics are of limited scientific interest. Will this be adjudged grounds for sending armed craft, that are badly needed elsewhere, to make him stop?"

"Supposing it is—that's uncertain, as you say, but supposing it is— *can* they stop him?" Trevelyan seized the controls again. The power hum deepened. "Prepare for descent."

He chose a city near the edge of morning, that he might have a long daylight. A mole jutted from the waterfront into an emerald-and-sapphire bay. Sonic beams declared it to be of reinforced concrete, as firm as the day it was dedicated. He landed there, and presently walked forth. A grav sled would have taken him faster and easier, but part of his aim was to get to know somewhat about those who were departed. His ship, all systems on standby, fell behind him like a coppery cenotaph.

He didn't worry about the safety of the environment. Murdoch had proven that for him. What had still to be learned was mere detail: for instance, what imported crops would do well?

Any number, Trevelyan felt sure. It was a rich and generous planet. No doubt it had been more so before the catastrophe, but it remained wonderful enough, and nature was fast healing the wounds.

The bay glittered and chuckled between golden-green hills. At its entrance began an ocean; coming down, he had identified fantastically big shoals of marine plants and animals. No wings rode the wind that rumpled his hair. Most, perhaps all vertebrates were extinct. But lower forms had survived the disaster. Insects, or their equivalent, swarmed on delicate membranes that often threw back the sunlight in rainbows. Silvery forms leaped from the water. The wind smelled of salt, iodine, and life.

Overhead wandered some clouds, blue-shadowed in a dazzlingly blue heaven. At this season, the supernova was aloft by day, invisible. Disaster, Trevelyan thought with a shudder. How little had Earth's ancient astrologers known of how terrible a word they were shaping!

But the day was sunny, cool, and peaceful. He walked shoreward, looking.

The watercraft had sunk or drifted free of their rotted lines. However, the shallower water inshore was so clear that he could see a few where they lay, somewhat preserved. The gracious outlines of the sailboats did not astonish him; that demand was imposed by natural law. But his eyes stung to think that the dead had loved sloops and yawls as much as he did. And they had put bronze figureheads on many, whose green-corroded remnants hinted at flowers, wings, flames, anything fair and free. A large ship had drifted aground. It had been iron-hulled and, judging from the stacks, steam-propelled. But it, no, she had also been designed to look like a dancer on the waves.

He neared the quay. A row of wooden warehouses (?) was partly moldered away, partly buried under vines. Nevertheless he could make out how roofs once swept in high curves that the doorways matched. A rusting machine, probably a crane, was decorated at the end of its lifting arm with a merry animal face.

He stood for some while before an arch at the head of the mole. Here the dwellers had represented themselves.

Their art was not photographic. It had a swing of line and mass that woke a pulse in Trevelyan, it was not quite like anything he had ever seen before. But the bipeds with their long slim six-fingered hands, long necks, and long-beaked heads, came through to him as if still alive. He almost thought he could hear their stone cloaks flap in the wind.

Walking farther into the city, he began to find their bones.

Carrion eaters had seldom or never disturbed them. Dust blew in, settled on pavement, became soil; seeds followed, struck frail roots that gradually crumbled brick and concrete; bushes and vines grew over that first carpet and up the walls; those kinds of trees that survived extended their range into the domains of trees that had not, and beyond into farm and town. But the invasion was slow. The wilderness had all the time in the world. It was in full occupation of the shoreward edges of this city, and reducing the next line, but as yet just a few forerunners and (Trevelyan thought with a hurtful smile) sappers had won this near the waterfront.

The buildings of granite, marble, and masonry rose tall, washed by rain and sunlight, little damaged by weather, only occasional creepers blurring their outlines. Like the relief sculpture on their walls, they leaped and soared, not as man-built skyscrapers do but in that peculiar rhythm which made their heights seem to fly. They were colonnaded, balustraded, many-windowed, and kept some of the coloring that once softened their austerity.

Trevelyan wondered at the absence of parks or gardens. His observations from altitude had suggested a deep-reaching love of landscape and care for it. And floral motifs were about the commonest decorations. Well, the dwellers had not been human; it would take long to get some insight to what their race psyche might have been. Maybe they enjoyed the contrast of art and openness. If this place was typical, every city was a delight to live in. At some economic sacrifice, the dwellers had avoided filling their air and water with noise, dirt, and poison. To be sure, they were lucky that no heating was required. But as far as Trevelyan had been able to ascertain, industrial plants were widely scattered outside urban limits, connected by railways. There were no automobiles, though that was probably within the technological capabilities. Instead, he found the depictions, and some bones, of large quadrupeds that served like horses; he also identified the hulks of what appeared to have been public vehicles with primitive electric motors. It was hard to tell after four hundred years, but he at least got the impression that, while theirs was a productive and prosperous civilization, the dwellers had not created overly much trash either. They could have foreseen the problem and taken steps. He'd like to know.

Not that they were saints. He came upon statues and dimmed murals which showed combat. Twice, above inscriptions he would never interpret, he saw a being dressed in rags bursting chains off himself; no doubt somebody put those chains on in the first place. But oftenest he found imagery which he read as of affection, gentleness, work, teaching, discovery, or the sheer splendor of being alive.

He entered courtyards, walked past dried pools and fountains, on into the buildings. Few had elevators, which was suggestive since the culture could have supplied them. He noted that the shafts of the wide circular staircases would easily accommodate grav lifts. The murals indoors were scarcely faded; their vividness took some of the grief off him. Nevertheless, and although he was not superstitious or even especially religious, he knocked on the first door he came to.

Every door was sliding or folding, none bore locks or latches, which again implied unusual traits. The majority of apartments had been deserted. Cloth had decayed, metal tarnished, plaster cracked, and dust fallen centimeters thick. But the furnishings remained usable by humans, who were formed quite like the dwellers. Clean and patch up;

restore the water supply; make do with the airily shaped oil lanterns, if need be, and a camp stove since the original owners didn't seem to have cooked anything; throw padding over chairs, divans, beds, intricately grained floors: and you would be altogether comfortable. Soon power would become available, and you could change the place around at your leisure until it was ideal.

Early in the game, though, you'd better get rid of those pictures, papers, enigmatic tools, and shelves full of books. They could be disturbing to live with.

As the hours passed, Trevelyan did find skeletons in a few apartments. Either these individuals had died by surprise, like those he infrequently noticed in the streets, or they desired privacy for their final day. One lay in a kind of chaise lounge, with a book upon what had been the lap. Twice he found small skeletons covered by a large one. Did the mother understand that death was coming from the sky? Yes, she could see it up there, a point of radiance too brilliant to look near, surrounded by the auroras it evoked in this atmosphere. Probably she knew the death was everywhere. But she was driven by the instinct of Niobe.

When he discovered the ossuary, Trevelyan decided there must be several, and this was how the average dweller had elected to go. It was in a large hall—theater? auditorium? temple? The most susceptible must already have died, and radiation sickness be upon the rest. In man it approaches its terminus with nausea, vomiting, hair coming out, internal bleeding, blood from the orifices and eyes, strengthlessness, fever, and delirium. Doubtless it was similar for the dwellers.

Outside were the remnants of several improvised coal furnaces. Their pipes fed into the sealed hall, carbon monoxide generators. Bones and rusted weapons nearby suggested the operators had finished their task and then themselves. The door was the single tightly fastened one Trevelyan had encountered, but being wooden it yielded to his boot in a cloud of punk. Beyond lay the skeletons of adults, hundreds of them, and many more young, and toys, games, cups, banners, musical instruments—*I don't know what they did at that party,* Trevelyan thought, *but if we humans had the same guts, we'd tell the children that Carnival came early this year.*

He walked back out into the bright quiet. Something like a butterfly went past, though its wings were fairer than anything evolved on Earth. Being a little of an antiquarian, he said aloud: "The Lord giveth and the Lord taketh away; I will not bless the name of the Lord. But I will remember. Oh, yes, I will remember."

He had not gone much farther toward the middle of town when he heard a thunder rumble. Looking up past the towertops, he saw the great shining form of *Campesino* descend. She came between him and the sun and covered him with her shadow.

Reflexively, he took shelter in a doorway. One hand dropped to his pistol. With a sour grin at himself, he activated the tiny radio transceiver in his tunic pocket. On the standard band, he heard Murdoch's voice: "Cordy ahoy! Respond!"

The empty speedster made no reply. A drone and a quivering went through the air as *Campesino* balanced on her gravs. "You!" Murdoch barked. "We picked up your tachyons halfway to here. We followed you down by your neutrinos. Don't try bluffing us about having a friend in reserve. You're alone, and we've got a cyclic blast zeroed in, and I want to speak with you."

More silence in the receivers. Trevelyan felt the sweat on his ribs, under his arms, and smelled it. He could not foretell what would happen. At best, he had sketched behavior patterns Murdoch might adopt and responses he might make. His plan amounted to creating a situation where he could improvise . . . whether successfully or not.

A barely distinguishable background growl: "No one inside, I'd guess. Exploring the city?"

"Could be," Murdoch said. "Odd they'd leave their boat unguarded."

"A trap?"

"Well—maybe. Don't seem Cordy style, but maybe we better keep clear."

Trevelyan did in fact wish *Campesino* to set down elsewhere, making *Genji* less of a hostage. He decided to push matters, trod forth, and shot a flash from his gun into the air. It crackled. Ozone touched his nostrils.

"Look! Below! You, d'you read us?"

Trevelyan saw no sense in giving away the fact that he could listen. He might gain some slight advantage thereby; and Cosmos knew, with that metal storm cloud hanging above him, he needed whatever help he could get. He waved and jogged off toward the city center, where he had noticed a plaza from above.

After a conference he couldn't make out, the others did what he would have done in their place. *Campesino* opened a hatch and discharged a grav sled with a man or two aboard. Not carrying missiles, she could give them no effective armament. But they would hover near *Genji* and cry warning of anything suspicious. The ship herself dropped behind the towers. When she landed, the ground trembled and echoes boomed slowly from wall to wall.

Trevelyan switched off his radio speaker, turned on the transmitter, and hastened his trot. Once he accidentally kicked a skull. It rolled aside with a dry clatter. *I'm sorry,* he thought to it. That being not altogether alien to him had felt this street underfoot, sunwarmth reflected off cataract-like façades, muscle movement, heartbeat, breath. The city had lived around the being, with friends, loves, traffic, music, pleasure . . . did the race laugh? *I may be joining you soon,* he added, and scorned himself for the juvenilism.

He emerged not on a square but a golden rectangle. Grassy growth was thrusting up and apart those blocks which had paved it, but the rains of four centuries had not quite washed out the grooves worn by generations of feet. The enclosing buildings were lower here. Their lines bespoke tranquility rather than excitement, though three of them held the fragments of dazzling stained-glass windows. Numerous skeletons lay prostrated before one. *Campesino* rose brutal from the plaza center.

Several men and not-men waited, guns at the ready. They were a hard-looking gang. Murdoch stood at ease, Faustina tensed beside him. Both wore black coveralls with silver ornamentation. Her hair glowed in the light. Trevelyan approached at a reduced pace, hands well away from his pistol.

"Mike!" the adventurer bawled. He threw back his head in laughter that made his moustaches vibrate. "Why the chaos didn't I expect you'd be the one?"

"Who else with you?" Faustina said.

Trevelyan shrugged. "Who with you?" he countered.

"You've seen our roster," Murdoch said. "I figured you'd refuse to board, afraid we'd grab you, so I came out." He jerked a thumb at the sheer hull behind. "Got a full complement inside at alert stations."

Trevelyan achieved a smile. "What makes you expect trouble, Juan?" he asked in his mildest voice.

Murdoch blinked. "Why . . . you dogged us clear from Earth—"

"No, think," Trevelyan said. "Space is free. The Coordination Service investigates where it can, but forbids violence to its agents except under extreme necessity. You know that as well as I do."

The guards around shifted stance, muttered among themselves, flicked eyes from side to side. Trevelyan virtually felt the unease in them.

"For example," he drawled, "you're breaking the law here, first by not reporting a discovery—"

"We've only just made it!" Faustina said. Red stained the white cheekbones. Her fists were clenched. He studied her for a moment, thinking with compassion: *She's afraid I'll take away her glory—her chance to rake in money until she can lose the fear of being poor that was ground into her,* and with caution: *In an aggressive human personality, fear begets ruthlessness.*

"Please let me finish," he said. "I'm not interested in lodging charges, nor would my superiors be. The offense probably occurs hundreds of times a year, and seldom matters. Out of necessity, the Service operates on the old principle that the law should not concern itself with trifles."

She stepped back, breathing hard, lips pulled away from teeth, but plainly bemused. Murdoch's massive features had grown immobile. "Continue," he said.

"You've committed a more important breach of law by tampering with and destroying material of scientific value." Trevelyan kept his tone amiable and a faint smile on his mouth. "I refer to that island city. But the planet is such an archaeological and biological Golconda that we'll overlook your indiscretion, we'll put it down to an amateur's forgivable enthusiasm, in exchange for the service you've done to civilization by bringing this world to our knowledge. You'll remember an agent like me has authority to issue pardons in minor cases. I'll write you one today, if you wish, and recommend you for next year's Polaris Medal into the bargain."

He offered his hand. "Stop worrying," he said. "Let's have a drink and go home together."

Murdoch did not take the hand. The big man stood for a while, staring, and the silence of the dead grew and grew. He broke it with a whisper: "Are you serious?"

Trevelyan dropped pretense. He said in a hardened voice, while his nerves felt the surrounding guns: "It's an honest offer. You already have Good Luck to make your living off. Be content with that."

"Good Luck?" Faustina cried. She swept one arm in a taloned arc. "You incredible idiot! *This* is Good Luck!"

"I kept hoping it wasn't," Trevelyan said low.

"What do you figure I had in mind?" Murdoch demanded.

"Obvious," Trevelyan sighed. "Here was your real discovery. But how to exploit it? You couldn't get a patent, because the Union would forbid colonization until the scientists finished their researches. Considering the distance, and the shortage of personnel, and the vast amount there is to study, that would take at least a hundred years, probably longer. In fact, the odds are we'd put a secrecy seal on the coordinates for a decade or two, to keep unqualified visitors away until a big enough enterprise got started that the scientists could do their own guarding."

"Scientists!" Faustina nearly shrieked. Murdoch laid a warning grip on her arm. His predator's gaze stayed on Trevelyan.

"What a means to a fortune, though!" the Coordinator said. "You could offer an utterly desirable home, complete with every facility for hundreds of millions of people, at a price the ordinary colonial can afford. You stood to become one of the wealthiest humans that ever lived.

"Well, you went looking for a world we wouldn't disallow. What you turned up isn't particularly good. But it's no worse than some which have been settled, and at least doesn't have a population already squeezing its meager resources. People would buy your real estate there, if the preliminary work had been done for them and the cost was not beyond their means.

"Some you actually would take to the marginal planet—say when an agent like me happened to be around. You'd lose money on them. But it wouldn't matter, because most would be shipped here, where entire cities cost you practically nothing. They'd write home. Your ships would carry the overjoyed mail, maybe censoring it a wee bit to keep us Cordys from getting wind of your enterprise too soon. Not that we'd be likely to, when we're run off our feet with urgent cases, and when few people on those thousands of entire worlds give us any active cooperation. You could carry on for a number of years, I'm sure, before the discrepancies got so glaring that we investigated."

"What'd you do after you learned?" Murdoch asked.

"Nothing," Trevelyan said. "How could we displace tens of thousands, maybe millions of men, women, and children, who'd come in good faith, started a good new life, put down roots, begun bringing forth a new generation? It'd be a political impossibility, a moral one, maybe a physical one. They'd fight for their homes, and we couldn't bomb them, could we?

"You personally would be subject to—in theory, confiscation of your properties and imprisonment of your body. In practice, you'd have put both where we couldn't touch them without more effort and killing than it was worth. You'd have rigged the colonial government and its constitution early in the game to make you something like the Founding Father president of Good Luck. They'd fight for you too. So, rather than violate its own prohibition on conquest—for the sake of scientific and aesthetic values that'd already been ruined—the Union would accept what you'd done to it." Trevelyan closed his mouth. He felt hoarse and tired and wanted a smoke, but didn't dare reach for his pipe under those guns.

Murdoch nodded. "You read me good." He chuckled. "Thanks for the Founding Father title. I hadn't thought of that. Sounds like what I need."

"I can't allow it, you know," Trevelyan said.

"Why not?" Murdoch grew curiously earnest. "What's here, really? A worldful of bones. I'm sorry it happened, but dead's dead. And they were, well, one more race among millions. What can we learn from them that matters? Oh, I suppose you can hope for a new technique or art form or whatever, that'll revolutionize civilization. But you prob'ly understand better than me how small that chance is. Meanwhile, yonder we've got people who're alive, and hurting, now."

"The planet will be opened for settlement, region by region, in due course."

"How long is due course? How many'll die during it, that could've lived happier?"

"Emigrants are always replaced at home by fresh births. In the long run, the exact time of migration makes no difference."

"Forget the long run and think about flesh and blood."

Trevelyan's anger broke his control. "Don't hand me that guff, Murdoch," he snapped. "You're about as altruistic as a blast cannon."

"And you," Faustina spat, "you're a machine. I look forward to killing you—dismantling you!"

"Wait, wait, there," Murdoch said. "Ease off and let's talk sane."

He regarded the ground for a moment before he straightened, faced Trevelyan squarely, and said: "I'll tell you how it lies. When we knew we were being dogged, we decided to lead you on, because once the supernova got reported, this sector would be swarmed and somebody else might find our Good Luck.

"You could've skited for home without landing. If you'd done that, we'd've made for the nearest human planets to here. We'd've rallied a lot of men, transported 'em free, gotten well dug in before you could raise any action at headquarters. It might've been enough to stop you from doing anything."

"I assumed that was your plan," Trevelyan said. "On my way back, I'll visit every Scorpian world and announce, without specifying location too closely, that this planet is interdicted to preserve cultural values. To come here then, knowingly, will justify and require violence by the Service. We do have to maintain the precedent."

"What makes you think you're going back?" asked Faustina. She grinned with hatred.

"Ease off," Murdoch repeated. To Trevelyan: "I did hope you'd land, like you have. Waved a large red flag at you, didn't I? You see, I knew you must have less beef than my ship. Now I've got you."

"What will you do with me?" the Coordinator replied.

"Well, uh, I'll admit some of my mates got a little, uh, vehement," Murdoch said. "But I don't see any point in killing you. I sure don't want to. You're not a bad osco, Mike, for a Cordy. And they can't have any idea on Earth which way we headed. I'm not about to return there; I've done my credit arranging. If they ask me about you later on, why, I never had any notion you were trying to follow me. You must've come to grief somehow, and I'm awful sorry. Maybe I'll use your boat to fake some clues."

His mask of bashfulness fell away. He beamed. "Tell you what, Mike," he said. "Let's find you a nice island out in mid-ocean. We'll leave you tools and supplies and show you what's safe to eat. You Cordys are supposed to be philosophers. You should be glad of a few years for thinking. If you want, I'll try to get you a woman. And soon's I can, I'll flit you to our spaceport we'll've built. How's that for a fair proposition?"

Trevelyan savored the breath he drew, the light he saw, the will rising within him like a physical tide. "Let me be sure I understand you," he said. "Do you seriously intend to maroon me in order that I won't report the facts of this case?"

"Too good for you," Faustina said. "But if Juan's that tender-spirited, yes."

"Do you realize that this involves grave violations of personal integrity?" Trevelyan asked. "Do you realize that it involves direct interference with an officer of the Union in the performance of his duty?"

Murdoch flushed. "Obscenity your duty!"

"I demand you let me go back to my spacecraft and depart unmolested," Trevelyan said.

Faustina snickered.

"You will not?" Trevelyan asked. He waited. A breeze whispered.

"Very well," he said. "I can now testify under brainphasing that you are guilty of attempted crimes sufficient to justify your arrest. Will you come quietly with me?"

"Have you lost your orbit?" Murdoch exclaimed.

"Since you resist arrest in addition," Trevelyan said, "the necessity of applying force becomes incontestable."

The guards jabbered, swore, and brought their weapons to bear. Faustina hissed. Murdoch's hand streaked to his own pistol.

Trevelyan ostentatiously folded his arms and said: "If my Service does not respect your rights, civilization is worthless. But civilization has rights of its own. I admit I led your thoughts away from my partner"—he heard a gasp and an oath—"but that scarcely constitutes entrapment. He's under a roof in this city, on an accumulator-powered grav sled, along with several nuclear missiles. Through a miniradio in my pocket, he's been listening to our conversation. If you don't surrender yourselves, he'll destroy you."

He paid scant attention to the uproar of the guards. His focus was entirely on their leaders.

Murdoch yanked a transceiver from his jacket to speak an order.

"Give them a demonstration, Smokesmith," Trevelyan said.

No one saw the torpedo rise. It went too fast. Momentarily the sky was bedazzled with hell-colored flame. Concussion smote, not unduly hard from that altitude, but it shook men where they stood and bellowed in their ears. The bones before the temple shuddered.

"A bit close," Trevelyan said. He was aware that his own body quivered and went dry in the mouth. A remote part of him decided this was an unintegrate reaction and he needed more training. Speech and reasoning mind, though, were steel cool. "We may want antirad shots. I think you'll agree, Juan, the next can drop right here. Afterward my Reardonite friend won't have trouble picking off your watchmen."

"You'll be dead too," Murdoch groaned.

"I don't want to be," Trevelyan said, "but rather more is at stake than what I want."

Faustina whipped around behind Murdoch. She snatched his gun from the holster, flung herself forward, and rammed the muzzle into Trevelyan's belly. "Oof!" he choked. *I don't exactly cut a heroic figure, do I?* flashed through him. *But the beings here only had what dignity they could make for themselves, after heaven's meaningless anger fell on them.*

"I'll kill you myself!" she raved.

He knew tricks for knocking the weapon aside and taking it from her. But others were trained on him. He met her eyes, from which the tears went flooding, and said: "If you do, why should my partner not destroy you?"

Murdoch wrenched the gun from her. She raked at his face. He knocked her down. Panting, sweat a-river on his skin, he said: "What do you want?"

"If you know something about Reardonites," Trevelyan said, and saw that Murdoch did, "you'll realize it won't bother Smokesmith to annihilate me along with you. But he agrees it's undesirable. So is the destruction of this beautiful plaza. Let's compromise."

"I asked what do you want, you devil?"

"Safe conduct back to my vessel. Smokesmith will monitor me by radio. Your ship will stay put. At the first sign of any ill faith whatsoever, he shoots. At worst, you see, he must eliminate both ships and hope this world gets rediscovered by someone who'll respect it. Once aloft, I'll quickly drop down again and pick him up, too quickly for you to rise. At that point you'll be helpless; but have no fears. With a head start and a faster craft, I'll be on the frontier planets before you, issuing prohibitions. No one's going to follow you when he knows it'll bring warships down on him. I suggest you find an obscure place and lie low."

Murdoch beat fist into palm, again and again. For a minute he looked old and hollowed out.

Then his mirth awoke. "You win this 'un too, Mike," he said. "I'll escort you to your boat personal. Here." He offered his pistol. Trevelyan accepted it.

Faustina sat up. A bruise was spreading on her slim jaw where her lover's fist had smitten. She looked at them both, through tears and matted locks, and was no longer anything except a bewildered beaten child.

"Why?" she pleaded. "Why can't we have a patent—when w-w-we found the supernova for you? You'd do this—wreck everything for . . . two, three hundred s-s-specialists—and their curiosity?"

Trevelyan hunkered down before her. He took both her hands in one of his. The other pointed around, ending at the temple. "No," he said most gently. "For these. Have they no rights? That someone shall come to know them, and they won't be lost from us."

But she did not understand. We guard the great Pact, which is the heart of civilization, of society, and ultimately of life itself: the unspoken Pact between the living, the dead, and the unborn, that to the best of poor mortal abilities they shall all be kept one in the oneness of time. Without it, nothing would have meaning and it may be that nothing would survive. But the young generations so often do not understand.

Although Trevelyan would pass into legend, he was never afterwards content in his work. The uncertainty of life in an uncaring universe mocked his pattern-making rationality. He knew that his civilization—even his species—could perish as completely as those beings that the supernova had exterminated.

A few years later, he resigned from the Coordination Service and married into the star-faring Nomad people. He found shipboard life as a clansman far more satisfying than the lonely cerebral existence considered normal on Earth.

Needless to say, the humans who spread across the galaxy were not always contending with lofty issues of philosophy or society. They also encountered mere technical puzzles that were not so "mere" when lives depended on solving them.

Entity

"WE'D BETTER ALL have a look at it," said Captain Nielsen into his helmet phone. "There doesn't seem to be any life at all here, and this is the only real oddity. But it frankly baffles me."

He stood in the semi-darkness waiting for his crewmen. They were scattered through the abandoned city exploring for signs of the inhabitants of a thousand—a million?—years past. But so far, there had been only the empty shells of buildings, dark and blind under the enormous heavens. Whoever or whatever had built the city had made an orderly withdrawal and left little behind,

Ramachandra, the physicist-chemist, arrived first, swooping on his spacesuit's gravitic impellors through one of the gaping holes in the wall. The keen spatial starlight limned his bulky form in cold radiance as he entered. He stood for a moment letting his vision adjust to the murky room after the dazzling sun outside.

"What is it?" he asked.

"This gadget or idol or piece of furniture or whatever," Nielsen gestured. "So far, the remains of the city have indicated an almost depressing functionalism, as you might expect in a colony—"

"Colony?"

"Certainly. A planet this small must have been airless from the very first. But then any native life—of which so far, we have found not even fossil traces—would he nonbreathing. These structures are gutted, but they were definitely of space-tight construction, with airlocks and the rest. Anyway, what is this gizmo?"

167

Ramachandra peered at the thing which occupied the center of the room. It was simple enough, a black sphere on a pedestal. Only—

Never had he seen anything quite so black!

His eyes seemed to sink into that bottomless dark circle. It took an almost physical effort to wrench his concentration loose and say, "It's peculiar, but I suppose there's no telling what a completely foreign science will produce. Look at that of Alpha Centauri, for instance. And then when you get into the nonrational aspects of a civilization, like its objects of worship, reason quits altogether."

"Not so." Nielsen, who was captain in his capacity of psychotechnologist rather than vice versa, shook his head. "The laws of mentality are quite definite, and despite large superficial differences between intelligent races, they must follow the same basics in order to be intelligent. Since we have found no trace of life anywhere in this system, it is almost certain that the colonists here came from another star. But it is reasonable that a people advanced enough to colonize between the stars would still have josses and mascots? No, I'm convinced it must be part of some device, and the thing that bothers me is, what?"

"Who knows? There are so many ways of doing the same thing that this might be part of anything you care to name. Really, Robert, I don't see anything remarkable about it except its color."

"No?" Nielsen smiled thinly. "Go closer. Try to touch it."

Ramachandra approached the sphere, automatically estimating its dimensions. The pedestal seemed to be some ordinary space-concrete, about one-half meter thick and one and a half high. The sphere, about eighty centimeters in diameter, rested in a cuplike depression on the top of the pillar. He reached out a hand—and jerked it back, gasping. Through the insulated glove and the heating coils, that fang of cold had bitten. His fingers tingled with pain.

Nielsen said: "You're the physicist. Tell me how an object can be so much colder than its surroundings that the best spacesuits made on Earth won't insulate against it?"

"Unreasonable—" Ramachandra stopped, then resumed slowly: "I suppose it's an atomic-powered refrigerator of some kind. But that really doesn't make sense, because even at absolute zero, our spacesuits should protect us. It's as if the sphere sucked heat from—" His voice trailed off.

※　※　※

The other men, save for three left on watch at the ship—a precaution that seemed unnecessary in the death and silence of this world—had arrived by now. Seven human beings, so far from Sol that it was lost to sight, clustered around the black sphere.

Morley, the planetographer, flashed his light on the object. The puddle of undiffused light he expected did not appear on its surface. "Perfect absorber," he muttered.

"Could I have a look over here?" asked Schumacher, one of the three general assistants in a crew otherwise composed of specialists. He held out his hand and Morley gave him the flashlight.

"What did you do to it?" he asked, looking at the dim red glow.

"Eh?" Morley took the light back. "Looks burned out—but I put new cells in a week ago, and Phillips cells just don't wear out that fast."

"Let me see," said Ramachandra quickly. He took a small meter from his capacious bag and deftly, despite the clumsy gloves, took a reading. "Yes, those cells are dead all right."

"Is that thing safe?" Duncan, the biologist, waved the men back. He had seen too many deaths on planets never meant for man.

"Should be, if it only absorbs light," said Ramachandra. "But I never heard of anything like it before. How could a perfect absorber be that cold?"

"It absorbs more than light," pointed out Morley. "That battery went dead as if it had been shorted."

"Um-m-m . . . yes." Ramachandra took another flashlight. "Curious effect. Let's see—"

He pointed the lens at one of the highly polished metal sleeves of his spacesuit, letting the light reflect onto the sphere. This time, there was no evident battery drain.

"Apparently, it absorbs all directly impinging energy," he said. "And if a photon beam with an electrical source is focused on it, there is in effect a short circuit. Of course, that's too general a statement to be made without further tests, but as a guess based on the universal principles of action and reaction, it doesn't seem too unreasonable."

"As reasonable as anything connected with this dingus," added Schumacher wryly.

Nielsen raised a hand. "We're supposed to be getting a sketchy pre-exploration idea of what is to be found in this part of the Galaxy," he said, "but I think this is important enough to justify study. Whatever civilization once existed here may have known things we don't even suspect, simply through its science having taken a different path from ours—you all know the case of Centaurians as one example. I'm no physical scientist, but if this wingding is new to Krishni, it's *new*. I'll turn you boys loose on it."

He paused, then added soberly: "Only for the love of Cosmos and the hope of seeing Earth again, don't take any chances. Our crew is too small already—well, it can't be helped when an expedition takes several years, but that's the way it is. We're each so specialized as to be indispensable. And we're a long way from home."

He turned and walked out into the bitter sunlight.

The city was not large. A cluster of domes gaping open to the sky, it huddled on a valley floor with uneroded mountains shouldering brutally upward from the near horizon on all sides. Remnants of space docks and what seemed to be warehouses were in evidence, and a few scattered pieces of tools, machinery, and the like. But there was really nothing indicative, and everything had suffered from uncounted millennia of meteor bombardment and temperature extremes.

"The size and shape of artifacts indicate a race roughly humanoid, perhaps somewhat taller," said Duncan. "That's really about all I can say. They left almost nothing portable behind, they even removed airlock valves and thermostatic units."

"Are there any signs of colonization elsewhere in this system?" asked Ivanoff, of the general-assistant staff.

"No," said the mate, Chai-Chou. "Of course, you can't tell for sure, but it seems a fairly safe bet. This sun only has five planets, all small and barren like this, and we checked them all, as you know. If our metal detectors found this city for us, they should certainly have located any other of comparable size."

"Anyway," said Nielsen, "a civilization colonizing a system as harsh as this one would hardly care to establish more than one outpost. I suppose the city was a sort of combined refueling station, mining town—there are signs of working in the mountains—and so on. Maybe it was abandoned because of something, say a new fueling technique, that made it obsolete and uneconomic. Maybe the civilization still exists."

"I doubt it," said Duncan. "We discovered the means of interstellar travel only a few decades ago and have already got this far. If they had had the hyperdrive that far back, they would have visited the Sol sector by now."

He looked skyward. The glaring F3 sun had set and the valley lay wrapped in night. Above its mountains, the stars blazed in cruel brilliance, unfamiliar constellations spilling across the sky. "I wonder where they were from—" he murmured.

"Who knows?" Nielsen shrugged. "We came to this star only as part of a random pattern of search. It might take millions of years, even systematically hunting, to find one single system in the Galaxy. And if we found it, we might not even know we had. Space is just too big."

He felt again the weariness of his years on the long hunt. Civilization could not expand blindly into the stars. Someone had to go ahead of even the explorers and give a vague idea of what to expect. Only Earth's finest, the most ultimately sane of all mankind, could endure being cooped in a metal bubble floating through darkness and void for years on end, and even they sometimes broke.

Olga, Olga, it's a long way home to Earth and to you, a long way in space, and a longer way in time. And will you still be waiting, Olga, dearest of all, when I come home?

"Something made the colonists leave this system," he said heavily. "Maybe the answer is in that sphere. Let's see what the boys have found out."

He entered the central building. A lighting system had been rigged which threw an indirect but sufficient illumination on the sphere. It lay on its pedestal, a black enigma surrounded by instruments and technicians.

"Well, you've had a couple of days now, Krishni," said Nielsen. "And I might say that you're on the spot. Because none of us have been able to dig up one piece of real information."

"Well, we have a little, but it's mostly negative," said the scientist. "After some trouble, we got the precise dimensions—"

"How? I should think your calipers would shrink in the cold."

"They do, but we measured the rate of shrinkage, did some fancy extrapolation and other juggling, and came up with a fairly accurate answer. We also know that the surface can't be chipped by any available means and is inert to any reagents we have—some of which are pretty fierce. The base pedestal is just an ordinary concrete post. What the sphere is, nobody knows."

"X rays? Sonic probes?"

"It absorbs every sort of energy that falls on it. We blew an air jet at it and the air froze solid as it struck, all molecular motion-energy sucked out. When we get careless and let a beam of anything fall directly on it . . . well, you saw what happened to that flashlight. Why continue the sad tale?" Ramachandra smiled wryly, "The thing is thermodynamically impossible. It absorbs everything and radiates nothing. I honestly believe it's at absolute zero, though our instruments acquire too much error for me to tell with certainty."

The captain scowled. "There must be some way to get at it. We can't hang around here forever."

"We won't have to," said Ramachandra. "The sphere isn't fastened to its pedestal in any way, so we'll just take it to the ship and I can work on it at my leisure."

"Good," muttered Schumacher. "This planet gives me the creeps— it's *dead*."

He and the third assistant, Rosenstein, left the building and went over to the ship. Her bright torpedo form loomed over the nighted city, challenging the stars. The Afro-Venusian chief engineer, Cetewayo, hailed them as they entered his place of work. "What goes?" he asked.

"It's that thing they found in the city," said Rosenstein. "The skipper wants to bring it aboard so we can get under way again."

"Just what is that gadget, anyway?" inquired Cetewayo, "Themistocles and I have been too busy repairing that burned-out fuel injector to know just what was going on. I heard talk of an impenetrable sphere—"

"That's about all anyone knows," said Schumacher. "But it's too cold to touch, so we want the levi."

Cetewayo helped them load the portable levitator onto its gravity impellors. They floated it out with some effort, for though the applied gravitic force neutralized the weight of the grappling machine, the inertial mass was still there.

When the machine was fixed in front of the sphere, Rosenstein manipulated its controls and closed the grapnel jaws. Had there been air, the metal would have screamed as it touched the ultimately cold object. Only a few special alloys could endure such conditions, and Rosenstein didn't want to overstrain the molecules. He threw the lifting switch.

The motor spun. The levitator seemed to almost arch its back and dig its gravity beams into the floor as it sought to lift the sphere. Rosenstein scowled in puzzlement and raised the power another notch. By the time he had applied several tons' force, the motor was too hot to run and the sphere had not budged.

"Never mind," said Ramachandra. "I have a notion that nothing short of an infinite force will ever raise that beast."

"How so?" asked Duncan. "Work isn't radiation, is it?"

"No, but the sphere gobbles *all* sorts of energy, literally all, including any hypothetical energy of work against gravitation. Actually, of course, no work has really been done on the sphere. The levi motor got hot from an infinite overload." Seeing incomprehension in some faces, he said, "Well, imagine the machine doing a very small amount of work, an infinitesimal amount, on the sphere. The sphere promptly shunts that energy off into the same omnivorous region where all other incident energy goes—and so, of course, the sphere doesn't move."

"Never mind the details," said Nielsen. "The point is that we can't stir the brute. So what will we do with it?"

"I'm for busting it wide open and seeing what makes it tick," proposed Chai-Chou. "If we can't do anything with it, no other ship that could practicably be sent from Earth will be able to. So, if we ruin it, there's no real loss."

"The attitude is not entirely correct," said Ramachandra, "but I agree. The ship's rocket arc welders should be able to do the job—if they can't melt it open, we might as well quit. The thing must have an upper limit to its energy-gobbling capacity."

"All right," said Nielsen. "I'll put some men on it."

Cetewayo handled the huge arc welders. His assistant Kiarios—the two of them, with occasional help from the three general technicians, comprised all the help the robot-run *Diogenes* needed—remained alone in the ship to tend the power source. Thus it was that he heard the whine.

It rose from a low-pitched hum to an unbearably high squeal within a few seconds, and he'd had enough experience with generators to know what a runaway sounded like. Cursing, he dashed for them, knowing already that he would be too late. He was.

The room was not a pretty sight. A generator on the loose literally tears itself to pieces; and the prospect of rewinding the whole batch made Kiarios slightly sick. A few of the plates here and there had buckled in the middle, and smoke still rose from the scorched insulation inside. He dreaded the thought of dismantling the covers and seeing the twisted mess.

He was still cursing when Nielsen came in on the run. The helmet phones were set to a common frequency, and it had been plain that the second engineer was in trouble. Simultaneously, the captain was listening to some potent remarks as Cetewayo's arc welders died.

He threw back his helmet as he entered the engine room and removed his earphones, cutting off the Venusian's words. His face was grim as he asked. "What's the matter, Themistocles?"

Wordlessly, Kiarios gestured.

"Oh, *no*—" Nielsen fought for control. His voice came shakily; "What's the cause of this? If it has anything to do with that sphere, I'll really blow my top."

"You're right, I'm afraid," said Kiarios.

For some seconds, the air was made a deep rich blue. Finally, Nielsen got out in a strangled tone: "How did it happen?"

"I don't know. We powered the rocket arc welders with the generators; they're the only power source husky enough—"

"Say no more," Nielsen threw up his hands and stalked out of the room. Kiarios put on a spacesuit and followed him.

As they went by the radionic lab, Morley hailed indignantly, "What sort of fumblydiddles are going on anyway? Who has burned out my instrument?"

"Eh?" Nielsen stopped, looking dully at the man. Morley gestured at a disorderly heap of apparatus on the bench before him.

"I was trying this out," said the planetographer. "Wasn't much I could do to help about the sphere, and I took the chance to do a little work on this pet project of mine."

Nielsen nodded vaguely, not really listening. He knew Morley was trying to perfect a device to graph stellar energy output in the low frequencies, anomalous for some types of stars. He heard the voice, remote from his own thoughts: "I was trying it out and all at once, just like that—it burned out. Three coils and a good amplifier tube burned out, fusion, completely gone—"

"Never mind," said Nielsen. "We have something else to think about. All crewmen meet by the sphere."

✖ ✖ ✖

He felt a loneliness as he stood facing the men. They were more than his subordinates, they were his friends. Only those with the highest congeniality indexes could ever have survived a survey trip, so rank and formal discipline were unnecessary and unknown. The captain was only the coordinator of a band of specialists.

Still—the captain had the ultimate responsibility. And an admission of failure in that obligation was not only humiliating, it could be disastrous to a morale, which was the only real shield they had against the outer universe.

"It was my fault," he said in a low and toneless voice. "This is an unlucky set of circumstances, but if I'd been alert, we could have forestalled the present situation. As it happened, Matthew and Themistocles had been so busy with a repair job that they hadn't really heard what the sphere did, so they saw no danger in running the arcs off the ship's generators. And those of us who did know were either arguing too much about it or too preoccupied otherwise to stop to think just what the arc power supply was. Certainly, I should have done so. As it was, when the arc was turned on the sphere, it drank all the applied energy and in effect shorted the generators."

"You're no more to blame than the rest of us, Skipper." said Rosenstein awkwardly. "Less, really, because no one else has to think of everything."

"Thinking of everything is my business," said Nielsen bitterly.

"No real harm done," put in Cetewayo. "It'll be hard and tiresome, but we can repair the generators."

"If that sphere doesn't pull another trick," added Schumacher.

"It does seem to be deliberately opposing us—" murmured Chai-Chou.

Duncan snapped his head up in surprise. The others noticed the movement and a pregnant silence descended.

Between his teeth, the biologist said, "Deliberately opposing us—? Life takes some fantastic forms throughout the universe." His eyes steadied on Nielsen. *"Captain, is that sphere alive?"*

Their heads turned slowly, as if dragged by some irresistible force, to the thing. It lay blacker than outer space, a pit of enigma confronting them with a blind negation which was night and mystery and horror. The cold it breathed forth seemed to touch their hearts and run eerily down their spines, a reflex of primitive fear of the unknown carried from Earth's primeval forests out to the far stars.

Morley said: "Nonsense! It has no characteristic of life—"

"Hasn't it?" Duncan stared at the sphere as if hypnotized. "How do we know what characteristics it really has? For that matter, how do we know what universal characteristics life has—if any?" His eyes turned slowly to Ramachandra. "You said this thing was a thermodynamic impossibility. Well, in a way any living organism is, since it brings order out of molecular chaos—it's even been shown that the chemistry of animate matter actually involves a net decrease of entropy. If this . . . thing is an entity, maybe an intelligent one."

"It can't be," protested Nielsen. "It has shown no reaction associated with intelligence—"

"With our kind of intelligence," corrected Duncan softly. "This sphere is certainly not life as we know it—but that's a limited term anyway. If it is alive . . . if it came, say, from elsewhere . . . well, *something* must have expelled the builders from their city!"

Chai-Chou shook his head like a wounded animal. "I might have expected someone without a degree in biology to advance that," he said, "but you, of all people—!"

"And why not?" challenged Duncan. "I've seen enough strange turns and twists of life-forms, and learned of still more, so that I don't feel it's safe to dogmatize about any of them. What do we really *know*?"

"Very little," admitted Nielsen. "However, science must proceed not on certain hypotheses, because there are no such, but on the most reasonable. And postulation of something so utterly different from anything ever observed elsewhere is not reasonable."

Duncan shrugged. "I don't insist on my notion. You explain the facts another way, then."

Ramachandra scowled. "That energy must go somewhere," he said. "I'm almost willing to admit you're right. Some weird form of life, feeding directly on energy and storing it in some peculiar manner—"

He paced rapidly, around and around the sphere. "Just imagine that, for the sake of argument," he muttered. "Suppose there are energy-eating entities, maybe floating in space itself. They might be drawn to a city by its radiations, settle down, and paralyze the place by draining all energy sources. If they were vulnerable to any weapons the city dwellers might be able to apply without destroying the city—why, then, nothing would he left but to abandon the site." His voice rose, "And when no energy source was left, the sphere might go into a sort of spore state till we came along and gave it fresh nourishment!"

The men shrank back from the object in a pure reflex. It lay there, unmoving, black against the lights of the room.

Nielsen's voice was thick: "But—in that case it wouldn't bother with cities. It would go to energy sources immeasurably greater—to suns!"

"Maybe it doesn't like sunlight. Maybe . . . oh, say ionized particles irritate it, or it doesn't like the color of this particular sun, or it just wanted to sleep for a few thousand years and is ready to come outside now."

"Ready to come out—" mumbled Ivanoff. The thought ran on in his mind: *Ready to come out and eat the sun, and all the world will grow dark.*

"It's fantastic." said Nielsen grayly. "But . . . well . . . I still think the hypothesis is unreasonable and improbable. Still, we have no choice but to act on it."

The men looked at him in puzzlement. He went on: "Here is a phenomenon completely new to science, so new that on the surface it looks impossible. Whatever it *is*, it has lain here harmlessly for a long time and would presumably have lain here indefinitely—but we came along. We've tampered with it. We've swollen it with energy. We have, if it really is alive, made it aware of us. I repeat my belief that the thing is simply a scientific oddity, but we dare not assume that. There is always the chance that it really is alive—and that it may decide to do to the present civilization whatever it did to the past one."

His face was taut in the weird illumination of undiffused fluoro-light. "In short," he finished, "until we have either captured, destroyed, or understood this entity, we dare not leave this planet."

The sun rose, and set, and rose again. The constellations wheeled tremendously over the vast dark of the sky. The little dead planet spun rapidly about its obscure sun, a dust-speck lost somewhere in the fringe of the universe.

The incandescent glare of sunlight or the choking shadows of night, the swoop of temperature between insane extremes, the noiseless glare of sparks and swirl of dust when meteorites struck were the only evident changes. Mountains ringed in the rocky valley, walls of shadow and silence. Always there was the silence and the motionlessness and the waiting. It was not good for men who remembered green planets and blue skies and the warm yellow glow of lighted windows.

It was, thought Nielsen bleakly, just as well that the generators had burned out. The work of repair was heartbreaking, but it gave those of the crew not occupied with the sphere something to do. Sweating and cursing was better than thinking of the thing that squatted in the dead city.

There seemed to be no penetration of the sheer negativeness, which was the sphere. It made no response to any attempt at communication, and Duncan tried everything from in wig-wagging to a hypothetical telepathy. No instrument could lift it, or look beyond the blackness of its surface. Any energy source focused on it was savagely drained, otherwise there was no sign of activity.

"It . . . why not admit it, the thing scares me," said Ramachandra. "It scares all of us."

"Certainly!" Nielsen bit out the word. "A tendency toward xenophobia is inherent in humanity, probably a hangover from pre-human ancestors who had reason to fear everything strange. The way to overcome that fear, as man has finally learned, is to face the unknown boldly and come to understand it—thereafter, of course, it is no longer unknown. But when we are faced with something that resists all our efforts at understanding, the initial slight fear is bound to grow."

"You make it sound reasonable."

"It is." Nielsen's haggard face twisted in a smile. "Only knowing what makes us tick psychologically doesn't really change anything. Knowing why we fear the unknown will alleviate the fear only temporarily. If the problem remains insoluble . . . well, that's a good way to go insane. Or else take the refuge of deliberately forgetting that there ever was a problem—which, if Duncan is right, may he just what the sphere wants!"

He took a restless turn about the cabin. "Man isn't really meant for space," he said. "It's too unlike his whole evolutionary heritage. Oh, he can learn; most spacemen do, but the incidence of neurosis and insanity is high. You know, Krishni, I think we're all worn down by too long a time in completely strange environments. We're teetering on the edge of neurosis. I think this whole problem is basically of childish simplicity, but with our mental efficiency at its present low ebb, we've got onto a wrong track and now get farther and farther from the solution."

"Not farther," Ramachandra smiled grimly, "just—nowhere."

"If we could solve the problem, it would be a terrific moral shot in the arm. But if we can't—well, Earth is a long and dangerous way off and I hate to think what might happen to us before we ever get there."

"Aren't you exaggerating?"

"Maybe. Maybe not." Nielsen passed a hand over his weary eyes. "I think we're all exaggerating the trouble, like a scientist who starts out with a too complicated hypothesis and has to build ever more elaborate and fantastic theories to explain facts which are really very simple." He stopped his pacing, "As captain and psychologist, I order us all to take the evening off and get drunk."

It was quite a party. The men were depressed at first, but presently an almost hysterical gaiety came. They began singing songs, the old space ballads, the barroom ditties of Earth, the ribald lays of frontiers where women were few and far between. The *Diogenes* had started out with a generous liquor ration, and had since stopped at two terrestrial-type worlds whose inhabitants were familiar with alcohol. A good time was had by all.

Nielsen sat back in a pleasant haze and watched his men. Good boys, fine boys, the bravest and best old Earth had ever sent out. No black sphere was going to stop them, no sir, not when the beer supplies were running low and Earth's girls waited with the sun bright in their hair.

"Roll me over, in the clover—"

"I still think that shere . . . sphere did it," insisted Morley. "Who else would do that to me? After I worked so hard on my set—You wouldn' do that, would you, Themy?"

"Never," affirmed Kiarios.

"Burn out my set," mumbled Morley aggrievedly. "Shoot out a long hairy arm and grab my set and burn it out—"

"Now this is number six—"

Nielsen leaned forward. He had a sudden wobbly feeling of revelation, as if someone had rolled back a curtain he hadn't even known was there. "What—" His tongue twisted and he had to back up. "Hey! What was that?"

"What was what?" Morley blinked at him.

"What you just said."

"What'd I jus' say?"

"About the sphere."

"I don't like it," Morley drained his glass and looked around for a refill.

"Neither do I, but—" Nielsen could feel his heartbeat accelerating. He struggled for calmness. Slowly, then he said, "Your receiver set burned out just when the generators did—"

"Uh-huh. That is, the antenna coil, RF grid coil and plate coil, also the RF amplifier tube. It was set for about 30 KC. So what?"

Nielsen turned to Ramachandra, who had his arms about Ivanoff's and Cetewayo's shoulders. The three were making an ineffective attempt to harmonize, and it took a bit of shaking and pommeling to attract the physicist's attention.

"I think I've got it," said Nielsen. "I think I have the answer."

"What answer?"

"The answer to our problem—the simple elementary answer we were too tired and tense to think of." Nielsen beamed. "Isn't alcohol wonderful?"

"I hate to do this to your beautiful theory," said Ramachandra to Duncan. "It was much more picturesque than the truth."

"You are forgiven," replied the biologist. "But please tell me what the real answer is."

"The sphere is just about at absolute zero *in most wavelengths*," stated Nielsen. He felt a deep inward satisfaction that it was he who had hit on the answer. It restored his damaged ego, which is necessary compensation for the load of responsibility. "But all incident energy is reradiated on a radio hand, about thirty kilocycles to be exact. How it's done we don't yet know—but we'll find out. We just made quantitative measurements which confirm it."

"Then the sphere is just a . . . a radio wave generator?"

"A nearly perfect one," said Ramachandra. "It turns every kind of energy into this one type, with a negligibly small loss. Solar heat, molecular motion, waste heat for a less efficient device—*anything*. I rather imagine the second law of thermodynamics will have to be amended to cover this case—but since it's already been amended for certain biochemical processes, I daresay it'll stand the strain."

"But what's the purpose?" asked Chai-Chou.

Nielsen smiled fondly at the sphere. It was, really, rather a nice friendly thing to look at. "Power," he said. "At 30 KC, this one unit could probably cover the planet, or at least a sufficient area for the purposes of the colony. It could transform any energy into useful power, so that there was no waste really in broadcasting. It's that waste which had held Earth back from using central power-casting units—now, once they find how this machine works, we can have free power out of the air."

"Sounds nice," said Kiarios dubiously, "except that we can't get the thing off this planet."

"Sure we can," Nielsen grinned. "That, too, came to me in a moment of bacchantic inspiration. If you stop to think about the principles of relative motion, you'll see that the sphere can be moved either in free space or perpendicularly to the local forcefield without effect on its energy-conversion mechanism; it's changes in the kinetic energy of its own structure relative to its center, that is, temperature changes, and changes in the potential energy of the sphere as a whole that are resisted. Therefore, all we have to do is cut away the concrete pedestal and have the levi lift the sphere. We can't raise it against gravity that way, no, but we can keep it from falling by pushing it, so to speak, against the equipotential line of the gravitational field. And when we move it over to the ship along such a perfect equipotential, we are doing no work on it!"

"Then how do we get the ship off the ground?"

"Again, simple," smiled Ramachandra. "Instead of letting its radiated energy dissipate uselessly, we should have no great trouble rigging up a system of reflectors and receivers which will feed all that power right back into the engines. Hey, I think we can fix it up so that the sphere will replace the generators and save us the trouble of rewinding them!"

"Well, so much for that," Duncan frowned. "But I'd still like to know just what happened to the builders."

"Who can tell?" Nielsen shrugged. "I can think of a number of adequate—and unspectacular—reasons why their culture should have declined. Somehow, I don't think it'll take too long to find out, not when we have electronic spaceships."

He went out of the building toward the *Diogenes*, shining under the stars.

In another part of the galaxy, that ancient maxim "a house divided against itself cannot stand" was being tested to destruction.

Symmetry

AT ONE MOMENT he stood under heaven and the eyeless gaze of machines he did not understand; the next instant he was in a room of steel and another man with him. The sheer swiftness of the change was like a blow to the head. He swayed on his feet, while the afterimages from daylight faded away and the knowledge seeped through him that he was elsewhere.

Almost, he fell. The need to catch his balance jarred him back toward alertness. He swore, the oath seemed to echo, and stared.

The stranger stared back across the width of the room. His mouth also snapped shut. Dunham's glance went over him, centimeter by centimeter, in a single sweep. He was a big fellow, likewise clad in a gray coverall and gripsole boots. Hair bristled short, reddish-brown, above a wide face with a scar on the right cheek.

They spoke together:

"WWhhoo tthhee hheellll aarree yyoouu??"

Real echoes rang off the polished steel that enclosed them. Dunham's hand dropped to his hip before he remembered he'd left his sidearm in the spaceship. The stranger's hand dropped too, and his second curse was the same and exploded at the same time.

Slowly, the truth grew on Dunham. Two mouths sagged and two pairs of eyes opened till white ringed the gray. It was like standing before a mirror—a mirror that did not reverse.

The stranger was himself.

"AAllmmiigghhttyy CCoossmmooss,, wwhhaatt iiss tthhiiss??"

183

Step by step they approached each other. Their right hands they held out at arm's length as if they were blind; their left made fists and drew back. Dunham felt sweat trickle down his ribs. It reeked. Nightmare, nightmare. He tried to wake up and couldn't.

The room had gone quiet. Only the soft thud of boots and the louder breathing sounded within it. A wave of loneliness such as he had not felt since childhood washed over Dunham. The fact that he was the only man on the whole planet, and it fifty light-years from the nearest human base, was no longer cause for joy but for horror, now that he was not. He stamped the feeling down. It struggled.

In the exact center of the room, the men met. They touched fingertips together and jerked them back. For heartbeats more, they again merely stared.

Then two breaths shuddered inward and two voices nearly whispered: "LLeett'ss kkeeeepp oouurr hheeaaddss. WWee'vvee ggoott ttoo ffiigguurree tthhiiss oouutt—"

Panic flared into rage. "FFoorr CCoossmmooss'' ssaakkee,, wwiillll yyoouu ssttoopp tthhaatt ppaarrrroottiinngg??"

Echoes gibed. They took each a step backward. The gray cloth wrinkled identically with every movement.

Silence anew. Dunham's mind grabbed after reality. It closed on what was around him. That was the truth which it would be insane to deny. This thing was actually happening to him.

To them.

Acceptance brought a measure of steadiness. He'd been in wicked situations before, after all. The problem now was to fathom what had caught him and work out how to get free of it.

He looked about the chamber. It must be the inside of the metal box he had been investigating (or, rather, he thought with brief wryness, had been gawking at). About five meters square and two high, it was strictly right-angled at the corners and featureless except for the door. That door made a one-meter circle at the exact center of the ceiling. He had climbed up one of the metal-encased machines— if machines they were—that surrounded the box, gotten onto its flat top, and found the door at the middle. Precisely at the middle of the door was a knob, as might have been on some museum-piece house on Earth. When he leaned over, grasped the knob, twisted and tugged, the door began to swing open.

And all at once he was here.

The door must have fallen shut, but there was a knob on this side too, likewise at the center. He saw it through a transparent hollow cylinder that ringed it. The cylinder was about thirty centimeters long and fifteen interior diameter. Dunham judged that he could get one of his thick forearms up it to turn the knob. Push the door aside, grab the rim, chin himself and scramble out; yes, he had the strength to do that, one-handed if necessary. Weight on this planet was about nine-tenths standard.

Otherwise he saw blankness. The metal radiated white light. It was not too bright for human vision, but the absence of any demarkable source, of any shadows or shadings, might well be the eeriest thing about the room.

He grew aware that it was hot, and had a feeling that temperature had risen in the short while he had been captive. The sun was passing midday outside—both Dunhams glanced at their chronos—and could well turn this into a Dutch oven.

What he'd give for a cold beer! Well, the spacecraft held an ample supply, just a few kilometers' hike away.

The other Dunham licked his own lips.

They gaped. At the back of his head flickered half-remembrances, legends he'd heard as a boy from a kinsman who was interested in antiquities, the *Doppelgänger*, the *fylgja*, the fetch, if you see yourself you will soon die. . . . He thrust them off. He was no damned romantic, he was a practical man with a practical problem to solve.

"WWhhaatt aarree yyoouu,, aannyywwaayy?? WWhhaatt''ss ccooppiieedd mmee—hhooww—SShhuutt uupp,, ddaammnn yyoouu,, II'mm ttaallkkiinngg!!"

They stopped. Their eyes narrowed. Dunham summoned patience and tried, slowly:

"LLoooookk,, wwee ccaann sseetttllee iitt llaatteerr—"

Silence clapped back down. He saw how he must be tensed and glowering. But this was crazy. They had to get out. Once free, they could confer or fight or whatever they wanted. Somebody had to take action. Fast.

Dunham jumped back to the middle of the room. So did his double. Two right hands reached up for the sleeve around the doorknob.

They collided at the lip. It had only space for one arm.

"GGeett oouutt ooff mmyy wwaayy,, II'lll ooppeenn iitt—"

The hands fell. In the face that confronted his, Dunham saw grimness take hold.

His kind has been born, and died, and been reborn, throughout human history. Frontier scout, mountain man, voortrekker, names in many languages have bespoken him who always fares ahead of his race, driven by longings for which he has no name. Not that he expresses it thus. He leaves fancy words to the effete who stay behind. In his own mind, he doesn't like being one more interchangeable part of society, but he does like the fun and luxury civilization has to offer. Therefore he goes out beyond the edge of the known, and brings back what he can find that will command a goodly price. He believes his hope is that he will gain such a fortune that he can do anything he wants after he retires. It hardly ever befalls him. Likeliest he ends his days in poverty, though if he is somewhat luckier he leaves his bones in a strange land before he has grown very old.

Dunham was typical; he expected to become rich. Thus far, his gains had won him a half share in an aged, barely spaceworthy scoutcraft, mortgaged to buy supplies. He lost his partner to an oxygen recycler that failed in a human-poisonous atmosphere. Having buried the man as decently as he was able and brought under control a sorrow whose sharpness surprised him, Dunham resolved not to head straight back. Nothing awaited him on Nerthus but the loss of his ship to his debts. Being already well beyond every region mapped into the databases, he'd continue casting about as long as the deuterium tanks allowed. Solitary exploration was appallingly risky, of course, but at worst he would die and at best—at best, anything was imaginable.

In point of fact, he was not altogether reckless. The interstellar voortrekker is by no means the half-educated hotspur whom our more hackneyed dramas depict. The Co-ordination Service would never license any such person to operate anything as powerful as a spacecraft; nor could he survive long, no matter what its robotics did to help him. He needs a substantial knowledge of both physical and biological science. Unless he intends to shun worlds with intelligent natives, as some do, he must add a broad understanding of xenology, and the law requires his ethics meet a minimum standard. This last is seldom enforceable, but few rovers are villains, and in his rough fashion Dunham was a well-intentioned man. He exercised reasonable caution on behalf of others as well as himself. Groundlings are apt to forget that material goods are hardly ever worth seeking among the stars; the real treasure is knowledge.

To be sure, scientific foundations lack funds to purchase word of yet another planetary system, unless there is something extraordinary about it. Dunham's gamble paid off spectacularly. He came upon an Earthlike world of a Sol-like sun. Study from orbit indicated it was without intelligent life, but its biosphere seemed to be sufficiently terrestroid that humans could colonize. If this proved correct, discoverer's commissions would make Dunham so rich that money would cease to have meaning for him.

That might not happen. On certain planets, the death traps are subtle and pervasive. Years of field work would be necessary before this one could be certified. Meanwhile, basic reward would cover Dunham's debts and give him a fair-sized stake.

But circling the globe, he and his instruments found something more down in its cloud-swirled beauty. On one continent in the north tropical zone, several square kilometers had been cleared. Though the forest was coming back, the area remained unmistakable—even without the metallic objects clustered in the middle of it. Yet this world had evolved no thinking, fabricating animal; he felt sure of that. Somebody had visited here before him.

When? Thirty years ago, fifty, a hundred? It depended on how fast regrowth went, which he didn't know.

Who? The databases had nothing about it. And those things didn't much resemble artifacts of any spacefaring race with which humanity was acquainted.

Most men would have brought the news home immediately. The prize for such a clue to a whole new civilization should keep a person comfortably, if not lavishly, for a lifetime. Being what he was, Dunham landed his vessel in a meadow not far from the site.

All communications bands were mute. Having already established that the atmosphere was breathable, he ran biochemical tests and found with glee that nothing could possibly infect him; the proteins were too different from his. His survey in orbit had revealed no sign of animals large enough that they might menace him anyway.

Therefore he left weapons behind when he struck off afoot. If anybody or anything watched over the foreign camp, he'd be outgunned regardless. A show of pacifism was his best bet.

Through hot and leafy reaches he made his way, fighting underbrush, to arrive panting and with heart athunder. He found total desertion. Poking around in bluish-green shrubbery, he came upon crumbling traces of occupation, here what he guessed had been a basement, there a mound low and flat and squared-off, yonder a patch where energy had fused the soil to brick. Several meters tall, smoothly and enigmatically curved, half a dozen distinct structures encompassed a large right-angled parallelepiped which he thought of as a box, since it should reasonably contain something else. Weather had not touched the shiny blankness of the metal casings.

Had the aliens abandoned equipment they no longer needed? That seemed wasteful. Well, they might have a technology so advanced that this apparatus was as easily produced and readily discarded as a plastic wrapper. Dunham scuttled around, dizzy with excitement. He *had* to learn more.

He could climb up the tiers of one machine (?) to the top of the box (?). He did, though the sun-heated steel (?) came near scorching his palms. Above, set flush, was a door he could not resist trying to open. Him and Bluebeard's wife.

Whereupon he found himself inside the box—surely that was it—and another himself to keep him company.

The Dunhams stepped back, never shifting eyes from each other. Lips opened and closed again. Talk was useless. Instead, he'd better start thinking.

What kind of devil's pitfall have I stumbled into? What is this thing that looks and acts just like me?

A robot? No, unless the definition included flesh and blood; and besides, how and why would such a duplicate of him be instantly made?

Duplicate!

The Dunhams cried out before they clamped their jaws against the clattering of their teeth. The truth, what had to be the truth, was upon them.

Matter duplication. The Holy Grail of human engineers for the past

two or three centuries. The wave equations existed; Dunham had seen
them once, without much comprehension. Generate a beam to scan
an object atom by atom. Have the scanner signal direct a forcefield
that builds up a perfect copy out of a gasified matter bank. Of course,
you must complete the whole process in nanoseconds, before quantum
fluctuations make garbage out of the coalescing material. A pretty
problem. Some physicists held it to be inherently unsolvable.

The aliens had solved it. They'd gone on to develop a system that
could assemble the copy in thin air, with no visible apparatus around.
Presumably transmission had been through these walls—

Was the original Dunham still outside?

Two men spun about and beat on steel till their fists were bloody
and screamed till their throats were raw.

When they sagged back in defeat, the silence around their
breathing was a stranglehold. Upon drawing the door partly open, he,
they, had seen the metal of the box was rather thin; it had rung faintly
under boots. A Dunham One would have heard them and
investigated. Since he had not, he did not exist. Nothing lived but they
inside, two men alone. The device must have dissolved Dunham One,
perhaps converted him to energy and projected it into this space to
become part of the matter making up Two and Three.

So he was dead? The twin bodies shuddered.

Countenances hardened. Dunham was a pragmatist. Semantic
games had never interested him. The ego, the continuity of memory
and personality, which was his essential self, lived on. He was
experiencing it the same as always. The reproduction of the pattern
had been perfect. He was not dead, any more than he died because
metabolism gradually replaced the atoms in his body with other
atoms.

Rather, he now lived twice. The duplicator had created two
Dunhams, simultaneously, at equal distances from their respective
corners of the symmetrical room. Which was the real one?
Meaningless question. They both were. Given identical configurations
in identical environments, naturally all their actions would be identical
and simultaneous, if cause-and-effect operated as usual. Right down to
the last molecular stirrings within their cells—

He saw his own grin twist its way across the face that was his.
"HHeelllloo tthheerree, oolldd bbuuddddyy."

A scowl chased it away. The knowledge had not liberated them. The box was growing hotter by the minute. Tongues lay like blocks of wood above parched gullets. At this rate, they'd soon be dead of dehydration, unless the air got too foul and depleted first.

Ridiculous! Here they were, two strong men, with nothing to do to save themselves except reach up and twist a doorknob. Dunham groped in a pocket and drew forth a coin, his lucky piece. His double did also. He opened his mouth to speak and realized he needn't. *Heads I go, tails you go. . . . No, don't you toss. . . . Oh, all right, we'll match for it. . . . No, that won't work either. . . . Let's throw, and agree that heads wins. To the floor.*

Two coins spun. They landed together at the feet of their owners. Both men squatted down to see. Tails. Dunham retrieved his and waited for his double to open the door.

So did the other Dunham.

They tried again. Two heads. Both stood up, stepped forward, and stopped.

Of course. Even the fall of a coin is determined, by a million tiny factors of balance and force which are the same for both of us.

Dunham stared from side to side. There must be some way to break the deadlock. He tautened and leaped for the door.

The bodies crashed together just beneath the sleeve.

"CCoossmmooss wwrreecckk yyoouu,, ssttaanndd cclleeaarr!!"

Dunham shoved. The same push sent him lurching back. He snarled and came in swinging. The other man's fist lanced toward him. Both rolled with a punch that grazed the two left temples.

Then they were on the floor, kicking and slugging and yelling.

The fight ended after a minute or two. They sat and looked dully at the damage wrought. A left eye swollen, miscellaneous abrasions and bruises that would soon blossom in many colors, a trickle of blood from the lower lip, coverall ripped half open, and Dunham abused precisely likewise.

They had not moved from beneath the knob of their desiring. Every force tending to one man's right had been countered by an equal force tending toward the other man's right.

They sketched a smile and clambered to their feet. Maybe they could tear the sleeve loose. The effort led to naught. Each tug was nullified by its opposite. When they finally hit on the idea of applying torque by creating a couple, nothing happened. The cylinder and its attachment were too sturdy.

Horror stared at horror. If only one of them could do just one thing differently from the other, they ought to rouse from the nightmare. They began moving about, retreating to various corners, dancing a wild rigadoon, anything that might break the symmetry. All failed.

Eventually they sat down and regarded each other across the width of their prison. Hatred had died. They were caught together. Each wanted to release his mate nearly as much as he wanted to free himself. Only how?

Dunham leaned against the wall. Sweat-soaked, his garment seemed almost to sizzle from the heat that now dwelt in the metal. His smell filled his nostrils; he stank like a corpse.

Why had the builders made this thing? A torture chamber? What a revenge, killing your enemy twice. No, that seemed unlikely. Could it have been an intelligence test, maybe for officer candidates? Or for any spacefarers who blundered into territory claimed by the aliens?

Dunham knotted his fists and mumbled obscenities. He was dying just when he had won to his dream.

Two of him posed no problem. The prizes for this discovery and the commissions to follow would make them both rich beyond imagination. True, they'd share feelings about a certain fellow explorer, but she would doubtless remain unattainable, friendly enough, mildly regretful that she herself was too purely a scientist to settle down with a man of his sort. Never mind, he'd suffer no dearth of women. Meanwhile, he'd have a crewmate, the best possible, to help him steer home.

If they escaped. Otherwise they'd die in identical pain at the same moment. And the moment was not distant.

Curse it, we can't be helpless! We're free human beings, we've got free will, if only we can figure out how to make use of it. They peered at each other, aware of what went on behind the haggard faces. *Are we mutually telepathic? No, probably not. But it'll be impossible to find out unless we get loose from here.* Two rather gristly laughs rattled forth.

Dunham rubbed his eyes. Hot, hot, his brain was frying in his skull just when he must think. Thought offered his last slight hope.

The identity could not be perfect. Any machine had some limit, however narrow, to its accuracy; and the uncertainty principle was always operative. These two Dunhams were simply possessed of (by?) an extraordinarily high degree of similarity. If they waited sufficiently long, the small accumulated errors would add up, till at last one could do something the other didn't. But that might well take days, and they had mere hours.

The moment they broke the spell, it would stay broken: for their experiences would no longer be the same. As soon as they got out of this symmetrical hell, into the blessed disorder of wind and trees, pebbles underfoot and stars overhead, the inputs they got and their own reactions would diverge more and more. Doubtless they'd have awkward moments, but nothing they couldn't resolve. After a few years of separate living, they'd truly be two different persons. The similarity would last through their lives, but matter no more than it did between natural twins.

All they need do now was establish some order of precedence. "*I* will open the door." At the moment, though, what did "*I*" mean? It was completely immaterial through whose eyes you looked, from whose side you told the story. It was the same story for both.

Never mind philosophy. Work on getting out.

Assume this arrangement isn't meant to be lethal. Maybe it was for conducting certain scientific tests, and we fell into our situation by sheer accident. Something ought to exist here that is not symmetrical, that we can use to tap one of us and say, "You're it." Otherwise we're dead.

If the builders had had the decency to install a coinflipping machine—But no, each Dunham would have picked heads, unless he picked tails.

Beneath the fever-flush of heat, both faces turned a little darker. *He knows me so well, my sins and stupidities, vices and weaknesses. . . . No, what of it? I needn't be any more ashamed than he is. In fact, I can't be.*

They tried to break the simmering stillness. "SSaayy, hhooww aabboouutt—" They stopped. It was worse than not talking at all.

They rose and paced, hands behind backs. There must be a way out, there must, there must must must mustmustmust—*Stop that!*

Could any kind of game or contest have a winner? Tic-tac-toe, matched fingers, which fist holds the coin? No. Their grin was weary. Dunham felt shocked. Did he look that bad?

Up and down, up and down, up and down, prowling the furnace.

Where was the selective element, the random factor? How to find it before you died, when you were dying already?

Hot, hot, hot, the air was withering him, sucking him dry, while its molecules made a tom-tom of his skull. This is the way the world ends, not in chaos but in symmetry, frozen yet blazing hot.

Hot!

The double whoop rang off the walls.

Gas dynamics is an exact science employing deterministic principles. Nevertheless, it bases itself on randomness. Here physics deals with phenomena so complex that, even in principle, it can only analyze them statistically. Given a fair-sized volume of air, the molecules are smoothly dispersed throughout it. However, if you consider very small cells, a fractional millimeter on a side, the odds are that no two of them will have identical distributions at any given instant. A coin is big and heavy. It would take a strong breeze to affect the way it falls. An extremely light object presents a different case.

Twin men stood in a room of steel. Each pulled a hair from his head (the same hair?) and dropped it. Each puffed hard to stir the heat-roiled air still more. The strands drifted lazily, borne on tiny convection currents. *The one whose hair lands first will open the door.*

"All right, friend."

Dunham—no matter which one—crossed to the middle of the room, reached up the sleeve, and turned the knob. When he pushed, the metal discus swung on hidden hinges and he saw the sky.

Empires rose and fell among the stars. Disturbing one unique example of symmetry saved lives in one particular place. It was not a lesson for any other situation, even at the symbolic level. By the thirty-second century, the Stellar Union came under increasing stress as leaders struggled to comprehend—much less coordinate—developments across the known galaxy. Unable to sustain complex harmonies among individuals and societies, the Union flew apart like an overwound spring.

But as Trevelyan had foreseen decades earlier, the self-sufficient, enterprising Nomads bore seeds of knowledge safely through the Third Dark Ages. The antecedents of our own civilization were among those who reaped what the wandering Nomad ships had sown.

By the uncertain dawn of the fifth millennium, Earth's far-flung children had all but forgotten her. The cradle-world had become "less a planet and a population than a dream." But even dreams must have an ending.

The Chapter Ends

"NO," said the old man.

"But you don't realize what it means," said Jorun. "You don't know what you're saying."

The old man, Kormt of Huerdar, Gerlaug's son, and Speaker for Solis Township, shook his head till the long, grizzled locks swirled around his wide shoulders. "I have thought it through," he said. His voice was deep and slow and implacable. "You gave me five years to think about it. And my answer is no."

Jorun felt a weariness rise within him. It had been like this for days now, weeks, and it was like trying to knock down a mountain. You beat on its rocky flanks till your hands were bloody, and still the mountain stood there, sunlight on its high snow fields and in the forests that rustled up its slopes, and it did not really notice you. You were a brief thin buzz between two long nights, but the mountain was forever.

"You haven't thought at all," he said with a rudeness born of exhaustion. "You've only reacted unthinkingly to a dead symbol. It's not a human reaction, even, it's a verbal reflex."

Kormt's eyes, meshed in crow's-feet, were serene and steady under the thick gray brows. He smiled a little in his long beard, but made no other reply. Had he simply let the insult glide off him, or had he not understood it at all? There was no real talking to these peasants; too many millennia lay between, and you couldn't shout across that gulf.

"Well," said Jorun, "the ships will be here tomorrow or the next day, and it'll take another day or so to get all your people aboard. You have

195

that long to decide, but after that it'll be too late. Think about it, I beg of you. As for me, I'll be too busy to argue further."

"You are a good man," said Kormt, "and a wise one in your fashion. But you are blind. There is something dead inside you."

He waved one huge gnarled hand. "Look around you, Jorun of Fulkhis. This is *Earth*. This is the old home of all humankind. You cannot go off and forget it. Man cannot do so. It is in him, in his blood and bones and soul; he will carry Earth within him forever."

Jorun's eyes traveled along the arc of the hand. He stood on the edge of the town. Behind him were its houses—low, white, half-timbered, roofed with thatch or red tile, smoke rising from the chimneys; carved galleries overhung the narrow, cobbled, crazily twisting streets; he heard the noise of wheels and wooden clogs, the shouts of children at play. Beyond that were trees and the incredible ruined walls of Sol City. In front of him, the wooded hills were cleared and a gentle landscape of neat fields and orchards rolled down toward the distant glitter of the sea; scattered farm buildings, drowsy cattle, winding gravel roads, fence walls of ancient marble and granite, all dreaming under the sun.

He drew a deep breath. It was pungent in his nostrils. It smelled of leaf mold, plowed earth baking in the warmth, summery trees and gardens, a remote ocean odor of salt and kelp and fish. He thought that no two planets ever had quite the same smell, and that none was as rich as Terra's.

"This is a fair world," he said slowly.

"It is the only one," said Kormt. "Man came from here; and to this, in the end, he must return."

"I wonder—" Jorun sighed. "Take me; not one atom of my body was from this soil before I landed. My people lived on Fulkhis for ages, and changed to meet its conditions. They would not be happy on Terra."

"The atoms are nothing," said Kormt. "It is the form which matters, and that was given to you by Earth."

Jorun studied him for a moment. Kormt was like most of this planet's ten million or so people—a dark, stocky folk, though there were more blond and red-haired throwbacks here than in the rest of the Galaxy. He was old for a primitive untreated by medical science—he must be almost two hundred years old—but his back was straight, and his stride firm. The coarse, jut-nosed face held an odd strength. Jorun was nearing his thousandth birthday, but couldn't help feeling like a child in Kormt's presence.

That didn't make sense. These few dwellers on Terra were a backward and impoverished race of peasants and handicraftsmen; they were ignorant and unadventurous; they had been static for more thousands of years than anyone knew. What could they have to say to the ancient and mighty civilization which had almost forgotten their little planet?

Kormt looked at the declining sun. "I must go now," he said. "There are the evening chores to do. I will be in town tonight if you should wish to see me."

"I probably will," said Jorun. "There's a lot to do, readying the evacuation, and you're a big help."

The old man bowed with grave courtesy, turned, and walked off down the road. He wore the common costume of Terran men, as archaic in style as in its woven-fabric material: hat, jacket, loose trousers, a long staff in his hand. Contrasting the drab blue of Kormt's dress, Jorun's vivid tunic of shifting rainbow hues was like a flame.

The psychotechnician sighed again, watching him go. He liked the old fellow. It would be criminal to leave him here alone, but the law forbade force—physical or mental—and the Integrator on Corazuno wasn't going to care whether or not one aged man stayed behind. The job was to get the *race* off Terra.

A lovely world. Jorun's thin mobile features, pale-skinned and large-eyed, turned around the horizon. *A fair world we came from.*

There were more beautiful planets in the Galaxy's swarming myriads—the indigo world-ocean of Loa, jeweled with islands; the heaven-defying mountains of Sharang; the sky of Jareb, that seemed to drip light—oh, many and many, but there was only one Earth.

Jorun remembered his first sight of this world, hanging free in space to watch it after the grueling ten-day run, thirty thousand light-years, from Corazuno. It was blue as it turned before his eyes, a burnished turquoise shield blazoned with the living green and brown of its lands, and the poles were crowned with a glimmering haze of aurora. The belts that streaked its face and blurred the continents were cloud, wind and water and the gray rush of rain, like a benediction from heaven. Beyond the planet hung its moon, a scarred golden crescent, and he had wondered how many generations of men had looked up to it, or watched its light like a broken bridge across moving waters. Against the enormous cold of the sky—utter black out to the distant coils of the nebulae, thronging with a million frosty points of diamond-hard blaze that were the stars—Earth had stood as a sign of heaven. To Jorun, who came from Galactic center and its uncountable hosts of suns, heaven was bare, this was the outer fringe where the stars thinned away toward hideous immensity. He had shivered a little, drawn the envelope of air and warmth closer about him, with a convulsive movement. The silence drummed in his head. Then he streaked for the north-pole rendezvous of his group.

Well, he thought now, *we have a pretty routine job. The first expedition here, five years ago, prepared the natives for the fact they'd have to go. Our party simply has to organize these docile peasants in time for the ships.* But it had meant a lot of hard work, and he was tired. It would be good to finish the job and get back home.

Or would it?

He thought of flying with Zarek, his teammate, from the rendezvous to this area assigned as theirs. Plains like oceans of grass, wind-rippled, darkened with the herds of wild cattle whose hoofbeats were a thunder in the earth; forests, hundreds of kilometers of old and mighty trees, rivers piercing them in a long steel gleam; lakes where fish leaped; spilling sunshine like warm rain, radiance so bright it hurt his eyes, cloud-shadows swift across the land. It had all been empty of man, but still there was a vitality here which was almost frightening to Jorun. His own grim world of moors and crags and spindrift seas was a niggard beside this; here life covered the earth, filled the oceans, and made the heavens clangorous around him. He wondered if the driving energy within man, the force which had raised him to the stars, made him half-god and half-demon, if that was a legacy of Terra.

Well—man had changed; over the thousands of years, natural and controlled adaptation had fitted him to the worlds he had colonized, and most of his many races could not now feel at home here. Jorun thought of his own party: round, amber-skinned Chuli from a tropic world, complaining bitterly about the cold and dryness; gay young Cluthe, gangling and bulge-chested; sophisticated Taliuvenna of the flowing dark hair and the lustrous eyes—no, to them Earth was only one more planet, out of thousands they had seen in their long lives.

And I'm a sentimental fool.

He could have willed the vague regret out of his trained nervous system, but he didn't want to. This was the last time human eyes would ever look on Earth, and somehow Jorun felt that it should be more to him than just another psychotechnic job.

"Hello, good sir."

He turned at the voice and forced his tired lips into a friendly smile. "Hello, Julith," he said. It was a wise policy to learn the names of the townspeople, at least, and she was a great-great-granddaughter of the Speaker.

She was some thirteen or fourteen years old, a freckle-faced child with a shy smile, and steady green eyes. There was a certain awkward grace about her, and she seemed more imaginative than most of her stolid race. She curtsied quaintly for him, her bare foot reaching out under the long smock which was daily female dress here.

"Are you busy, good sir?" she asked.

"Well, not too much," said Jorun. He was glad of a chance to talk; it silenced his thoughts. "What can I do for you?"

"I wondered—" She hesitated, then, breathlessly: "I wonder if you could give me a lift down to the beach? Only for an hour or two. It's too far to walk there before I have to be home, and I can't borrow a car, or even a horse. If it won't be any trouble, sir."

"Mmmmm—shouldn't you be at home now? Isn't there milking and so on to do?"

"Oh, I don't live on a farm, good sir. My father is a baker."

"Yes, yes, so he is. I should have remembered." Jorun considered for an instant. There was enough to do in town, and it wasn't fair for him to play hooky while Zarek worked alone. "Why do you want to go to the beach, Julith?"

"We'll be busy packing up," she said. "Starting tomorrow, I guess. This is my last chance to see it."

Jorun's mouth twisted a little. "All right," he said; "I'll take you."

"You are very kind, good sir," she said gravely.

He didn't reply, but held out his arm, and she clasped it with one hand while her other arm gripped his waist. The generator inside his skull responded to his will, reaching out and clawing itself to the fabric of forces and energies which was physical space. They rose quietly, and went so slowly seaward that he didn't have to raise a windscreen.

"Will we be able to fly like this when we get to the stars?" she asked.

"I'm afraid not, Julith," he said. "You see, the people of my civilization are born this way. Thousands of years ago, men learned how to control the great basic forces of the cosmos with only a small bit of energy. Finally they used artificial mutation—that is, they changed themselves, slowly, over many generations, until their brains grew a new part that could generate this controlling force. We can now, even, fly between the stars, by this power. But your people don't have that brain, so we had to build space ships to take you away."

"I see," she said.

"Your great-great-grandchildren can be like us, if your people want to be changed thus."

"They didn't want to change before," she answered. "I don't think they'll do it now, even in their new home." Her voice held no bitterness; it was an acceptance.

Privately, Jorun doubted it. The psychic shock of this uprooting would be bound to destroy the old traditions of the Terrans; it would not take many centuries before they were culturally assimilated by Galactic Civilization.

Assimilated—nice euphemism. Why not just say—eaten?

They landed on the beach. It was broad and white, running in dunes from the thin, harsh, salt-streaked grass to the roar and tumble of surf. The sun was low over the watery horizon, filling the damp, blowing air with gold. Jorun could almost look directly at its huge disc.

He sat down. The sand gritted tinily under him, and the wind rumpled this hair and filled his nostrils with its sharp wet smell. He picked up a conch and turned it over in his fingers, wondering at the intricate architecture of it.

"If you hold it to your ear," said Julith, "you can hear the sea." Her childish voice was curiously tender around the rough syllables of Earth's language.

He nodded and obeyed her hint. It was only the small pulse of blood within him—you heard the same thing out in the great hollow silence of space—but it did sing of restless immensities, wind and foam, and the long waves marching under the moon.

"I have two of them myself," said Julith. "I want them so I can always remember this beach. And my children and their children will hold them, too, and hear our sea talking." She folded his fingers around the shell. "You keep this one for yourself."

"Thank you," he said. "I will."

The combers rolled in, booming and spouting against the land. The Terrans called them the horses of God. A thin cloud in the west was turning rose and gold.

"Are there oceans on our new planet?" asked Julith.

"Yes," he said. "It's the most Earthlike world we could find that wasn't already inhabited. You'll be happy there."

But the trees and grasses, the soil and the fruits thereof, the beasts of the field and the birds of the air and the fish of the waters beneath, form and color, smell and sound, taste and texture, everything is different. Is alien. The difference is small, subtle, but it is the abyss of two billion years of separate evolution, and no other world can ever quite be Earth.

Julith looked straight at him with solemn eyes. "Are you folk afraid of Hulduvians?" she asked.

"Why, no," he said. "Of course not."

"Then why are you giving Earth to them?" It was a soft question, but it trembled just a little.

"I thought all your people understood the reason by now," said Jorun. "Civilization—the civilization of man and his non-human allies—has moved inward, toward the great star-clusters of Galactic center. This part of space means nothing to us any more; it's almost a desert. You haven't seen starlight till you've been by Sagittarius. Now the Hulduvians are another civilization. They are not the least bit like us; they live on big, poisonous worlds like Jupiter and Saturn. I think they would seem like pretty nice monsters if they weren't so alien to us that neither side can really understand the other. They use the cosmic energies too, but in a different way—and their way interferes with ours just as ours interferes with theirs. Different brains, you see.

"Anyway, it was decided that the two civilizations would get along best by just staying away from each other. If they divided up the Galaxy between them, there would be no interference; it would be too far from one civilization to the other. The Hulduvians were, really, very nice about it. They're willing to take the outer rim, even if there are fewer stars, and let us have the center.

"So by the agreement, we've got to have all men and manlike beings out of their territory before they come to settle it, just as they'll move out of ours. Their colonists won't be coming to Jupiter and Saturn for centuries yet; but even so, we have to clear the Sirius Sector now, because there'll be a lot of work to do elsewhere. Fortunately, there are only a few people living in this whole part of space. The Sirius Sector has been an isolated, primi—ah—quiet region since the First Empire fell, fifty thousand years ago."

Julith's voice rose a little. "But those people are *us!*"

"And the folk of Alpha Centauri and Procyon and Sirius and—oh, hundreds of other stars. Yet all of you together are only one tiny drop in the quadrillions of the Galaxy. Don't you see, Julith, you have to move for the good of all of us?"

"Yes," she said. "Yes, I know all that."

She got us, shaking herself. "Let's go swimming."

Jorun smiled and shook his head. "No, I'll wait for you if you want to go."

She nodded and ran off down the beach, sheltering behind a dune to put on a bathing-suit. The Terrans had a nudity taboo, in spite of the mild interglacial climate; typical primitive irrationality. Jorun lay back, folding his arms behind his head, and looked up at the darkening sky. The evening star twinkled forth, low and white on the dusk-blue horizon. Venus—or was it Mercury? He wasn't sure. He wished he knew more about the early history of the Solar System, the first men to ride their thunderous rockets out to die on unknown hell-worlds—the first clumsy steps toward the stars. He could look it up in the archives of Corazuno, but he knew he never would. Too much else to do, too much to remember. Probably less than one per cent of mankind's throngs even knew where Earth was, today—though, for a while, it had been quite a tourist center. But that was perhaps thirty thousand years ago.

Because this world, out of all the billions, has certain physical characteristics, he thought, *my race has made them into standards. Our basic units of length and time and acceleration, our comparisons by which we classify the swarming planets of the Galaxy, they all go back ultimately to Earth. We bear that unspoken memorial to our birthplace within our whole civilization, and will bear it forever. But has she given us more than that? Are our own selves, bodies and minds and dreams, are they also the children of Earth?*

Now he was thinking like Kormt, stubborn old Kormt who clung with such a blind strength to this land simply because it was his. When you considered all the races of this wanderfooted species—how many of them there were, how many kinds of man between the stars! And yet they all walked upright; they all had two eyes and a nose between and a mouth below; they were all cells of that great and ancient culture which had begun here, eons past, with the first hairy half-man who kindled a fire against night. If Earth had not had darkness and cold and prowling beasts, oxygen and cellulose and flint, that culture might never had gestated.

I'm getting illogical. Too tired, nerves worn too thin, psychosomatic control slipping. Now Earth is becoming some obscure mother-symbol for me.

Or has she always been one, for the whole race of us?

A sea gull cried harshly overhead and soared from view.

The sunset was smoldering away and dusk rose like fog out of the ground. Julith came running back to him, her face indistinct in the gloom. She was breathing hard, and he couldn't tell if the catch in her voice was laughter or weeping.

"I'd better be getting home," she said.

They flew slowly back. The town was a yellow twinkle of lights, warmth gleaming from windows across many empty kilometers. Jorun set the girl down outside her home.

"Thank you, good sir," she said, curtseying. "Won't you come in to dinner?"

"Well—"

The door opened, etching the girl black against the ruddiness inside. Jorun's luminous tunic made him like a torch in the dark. "Why, it's the starman," said a woman's voice.

"I took your daughter for a swim," he explained. "I hope you don't mind."

"And if we did, what would it matter?" grumbled a bass tone. Jorun recognized Kormt; the old man must have come as a guest from his farm on the outskirts. "What could we do about it?"

"Now, Granther, that's no way to talk to the gentleman," said the woman. "He's been very kind. Won't you come eat with us, good sir?"

Jorun refused twice, in case they were only being polite, then accepted gladly enough. He was tired of cookery at the inn where he and Zarek boarded. "Thank you."

He entered, ducking under the low door. A single long, smoky-raftered room was kitchen, dining room, and parlor; doors led off to the sleeping quarters. It was furnished with a clumsy elegance, skin rugs, oak wainscoting, carved pillars, glowing ornaments of hammered copper. A radium clock, which must be incredibly old, stood on the stone mantel, above a snapping fire; a chemical-powered gun, obviously of local manufacture, hung over it. Julith's parents, a plain, quiet peasant couple, conducted him to the end of the wooden table, while half a dozen children watched him with large eyes. The younger children were the only Terrans who seemed to find this removal an adventure.

The meal was good and plentiful: meat, vegetables, bread, beer, milk, ice cream, coffee, all of it from the farms hereabouts. There wasn't much trade between the few thousand communities of Earth; they were practically self-sufficient. The company ate in silence, as was the custom here. When they were finished, Jorun wanted to go, but it would have been rude to leave immediately. He went over to a chair by the fireplace, across from one in which Kormt sprawled.

The old man took out a big-bowled pipe and began stuffing it. Shadows wove across his seamed brown face, his eyes were a gleam out of darkness. "I'll go down to City Hall with you soon," he said. "I imagine that's where the work is going on."

"Yes," said Jorun. "I can relieve Zarek at it. I'd appreciate it if you did come, good sir. Your influence is very steadying on these people."

"It should be," said Kormt. "I've been their Speaker for almost a hundred years. And my father Gerlaug was before me, and his father Kormt was before him." He took a brand from the fire and held it over his pipe, puffing hard, looking up at Jorun through tangled brows. "Who was your great-grandfather?"

"Why—I don't know. I imagine he's still alive somewhere, but—"

"I thought so. No marriage. No family. No home. No tradition." Kormt shook his massive head, slowly. "I pity you Galactics!"

"Now please, good sir—" Damn it all, the old clodhopper could get as irritating as a faulty computer. "We have records that go back to before man left this planet. Records of everything. It is you who have forgotten."

Kormt smiled and puffed blue clouds at him. "That's not what I meant."

"Do you mean you think it is good for men to live a life that is unchanging, that is just the same from century to century—no new dreams, no new triumphs, always the same grubbing rounds of days? I cannot agree."

Jorun's mind flickered over history, trying to evaluate the basic motivations of his opponent. Partly cultural, partly biological, that must be it. Once Terra had been the center of the civilized universe. But the long migration starward, especially after the fall of the First Empire, drained off the most venturesome elements of the population. That drain went on for thousands of years.

You couldn't call them stagnant. Their life was too healthy, their civilization too rich in its own way—folk art, folk music, ceremony, religion, the intimacy of family life which the Galactics had lost—for that term. But to one who flew between the streaming suns, it was a small existence.

Kormt's voice broke in on his reverie. "Dreams, triumphs, work, deeds, love and life and finally death and the long sleep in the earth," he said. "Why should we want to change them? They never grow old; they are new for each child that is born."

"Well," said Jorun, and stopped. You couldn't really answer that kind of logic. It wasn't logic at all, but something deeper.

"Well," he started over, after a while, "as you know, this evacuation was forced on us, too. We don't want to move you, but we must."

"Oh, yes," said Kormt. "You have been very nice about it. It would have been easier, in a way, if you'd come with fire and gun and chains for us, like the barbarians did long ago. We could have understood you better then."

"At best, it will be hard for your people," said Jorun. "It will be a shock, and they'll need leaders to guide them through it. You have a duty to help them out there, good sir."

"Maybe." Kormt blew a series of smoke rings at his youngest descendant, three years old, who crowed with laughter and climbed up on his knee. "But they'll manage."

"You can't seem to realize," said Jorun, "that you are the *last man on Earth* who refuses to go. You will be *alone*. For the rest of your life! We couldn't come back for you later under any circumstances, because there'll be Hulduvian colonies between Sol and Sagittarius which we would disturb in passage. You'll be alone, I say!"

Kormt shrugged. "I'm too old to change my ways; there can't be many years left me, anyway. I can live well, just off the food-stores that'll be left here." He ruffled the child's hair, but his face drew into a scowl. "Now, no more of that, good sir, if you please; I'm tired of this argument."

Jorun nodded and fell into the silence that held the rest. Terrans would sometimes sit for hours without talking, content to be in each other's nearness. He thought of Kormt, Gerlaug's son, last man on Earth, altogether alone, living alone and dying alone; and yet, he reflected, was that solitude any greater than the one in which all men dwelt all their days?

Presently the Speaker set the child down, knocked out his pipe and rose. "Come, good sir," he said, reaching for his staff. "Let us go."

They walked side by side down the street, under the dim lamps and past the yellow windows. The cobbles gave back their footfalls in a dull clatter. Once in a while they passed someone else, a vague figure which bowed to Kormt. Only one did not notice them, an old woman who walked crying between the high walls.

"They say it is never night on your worlds," said Kormt.

Jorun threw him a sidelong glance. His face was a strong jutting of highlights from sliding shadow. "Some planets have been given luminous skies," said the technician, "and a few still have cities, too, where it is always light. But when every man can control the cosmic energies, there is no real reason for us to live together; most of us dwell far apart. There are very dark nights on my own world, and I cannot see any other home from my own—just the moors."

"It must be a strange life," said Kormt. "Belonging to no one."

They came out on the market-square, a broad paved space walled in by houses. There was a fountain in its middle, and a statue dug out of the ruins had been placed there. It was broken, one arm gone—but still the white slim figure of the dancing girl stood with youth and laughter, forever under the sky of Earth. Jorun knew that lovers were wont to meet here, and briefly, irrationally, he wondered how lonely the girl would be in all the millions of years to come.

The City Hall lay at the farther end of the square, big and dark, its eaves carved with dragons, and the gables topped with wing-spreading birds. It was an old building; nobody knew how many generations of men had gathered here. A long, patient line of folk stood outside it, shuffling in one by one to the registry desk; emerging, they went off quietly into the darkness, toward the temporary shelters erected for them.

Walking by the line, Jorun picked faces out of the shadows. There was a young mother holding a crying child, her head bent over it in a timeless pose, murmuring to soothe it. There was a mechanic, still sooty from his work, smiling wearily at some tired joke of the man behind him. There was a scowling, black-browed peasant who muttered a curse as Jorun went by; the rest seemed to accept their fate meekly enough. There was a priest, his head bowed, alone with his God. There was a younger man, his hands clenching and unclenching, big helpless hands, and Jorun heard him saying to someone else: "—if they could have waited till after harvest. I hate to let good grain stand in the field."

Jorun went into the main room, toward the desk at the head of the line. Hulking hairless Zarek was patiently questioning each of the hundreds who came, hat in hand, before him: name, age, sex, occupation, dependents, special needs or desires. He punched the answers out on the recorder machine, half a million lives were held in its electronic memory.

"Oh, there you are," his bass rumbled. "Where have you been?"

"I had to do some concy work," said Jorun. That was a private code term, among others: concy, conciliation, anything to make the evacuation go smoothly. "Sorry to be so late. I'll take over now."

"All right. I think we can wind the whole thing up by midnight." Zarek smiled and clapped him on the back to go out for supper and sleep. Jorun beckoned to the next Terran and settled down to the long, almost mindless routine of registration. He was interrupted once by Kormt, who yawned mightily and bade him good night; otherwise it was a steady, half-conscious interval in which one anonymous face after another passed by. He was dimly surprised when the last one came up. This was a plump, cheerful, middle-aged fellow with small shrewd eyes, a little more colorfully dressed than the others. He gave his occupation as merchant—a minor tradesman, he explained, dealing in the little things it was more convenient for the peasants to buy than to manufacture themselves.

"I hope you haven't been waiting too long," said Jorun. Concy statement.

"Oh, no." The merchant grinned. "I knew those dumb farmers would be here for hours, so I just went to bed and got up half an hour ago, when it was about over."

"Clever," Jorun rose, sighed, and stretched. The big room was cavernously empty, its lights a harsh glare. It was very quiet here.

"Well, sir, I'm a middling smart chap, if I say it as shouldn't. And you know, I'd like to express my appreciation for all you're doing for us."

"Can't say we're doing much." Jorun locked the machine.

"Oh, the apple-knockers may not like it, but really, good sir, this hasn't been any place for a man of enterprise. It's dead. I'd have got out long ago if there'd been any transportation. Now, when we're getting back into civilization, there'll be some real opportunities. I'll make my pile inside of five years, you bet."

Jorun smiled, but there was a bleakness in him. What chance would this barbarian have even to get near the gigantic work of civilization— let alone comprehend it or take part in it. He hoped the little fellow wouldn't break his heart trying.

"Well," he said "good night, and good luck to you."

"Good night, sir. We'll meet again, I trust."

Jorun switched off the lights and went out into the square. It was completely deserted. The moon was up now, almost full, and its cold radiance dimmed the lamps. He heard a dog howling far off. The dogs of Earth—such as weren't taken along—would be lonely, too.

Well, he thought, *the job's over. Tomorrow, or the next day, the ships come.*

He felt very tired, but didn't want to sleep, and willed himself back to alertness. There hadn't been much chance to inspect the ruins, and he felt it would be appropriate to see them by moonlight.

Rising into the air, he ghosted above roofs and trees until he came to the dead city. For a while he hovered in a sky like dark velvet, a faint breeze murmured around him, and he heard the remote noise of crickets and the sea. But stillness enveloped it all, there was no real sound.

Sol City, capital of the legendary First Empire, had been enormous. It must have sprawled over forty or fifty thousand square kilometers when it was in its prime, when it was the gay and wicked heart of human civilization and swollen with the lifeblood of the stars. And yet those who built it had been men of taste, they had sought out genius to create for them. The city was not a collection of buildings; it was a balanced whole, radiating from the mighty peaks of the central palace, through colonnades and parks and leaping skyways, out to the temple-like villas of the rulers. For all its monstrous size, it had been a fairy sight, a woven lace of polished metal and white, black, red stone, colored plastic, music and light—everywhere light.

Bombarded from space; sacked again and again by the barbarian hordes who swarmed maggotlike through the bones of the slain Empire; weathered, shaken by the slow sliding of Earth's crust; pried apart by patient, delicate roots; dug over by hundreds of generations of archeologists, treasure-seekers, the idly curious; made a quarry of metal and stone for the ignorant peasants who finally huddled about it—still its empty walls and blind windows, crumbling arches and toppled pillars held a ghost of beauty and magnificence which was like a half-remembered dream. A dream the whole race had once had.

And now we're waking up.

Jorun moved silently over the ruins. Trees growing between tumbled blocks dappled them with moonlight and shadow; the marble was very white and fair against darkness. He hovered by a broken caryatid, marveling at its exquisite leaping litheness; that girl had borne tons of stone like a flower in her hair. Further on, across a street that was a lane of woods, beyond a park that was thick with forest, lay the nearly complete outline of a house. Only its rain-blurred walls stood. But he could trace the separate rooms; here a noble had entertained his friends, robes that were fluid rainbows, jewels dripping fire, swift cynical interplay of wits like sharpened swords rising above music and the clear sweet laughter of dancing girls; here people whose flesh was now dust had slept and made love and lain side-by-side in darkness to watch the moving pageant of the city; here the slaves had lived and worked and sometimes wept; here the children had played their ageless games under willows, between banks of roses. Oh, it had been a hard a cruel time; it was well gone but it had lived. It had embodied man, all that was noble and splendid and evil and merely wistful in the race, and now its late children had forgotten.

A cat sprang up on one of the walls and flowed noiselessly along it, hunting. Jorun shook himself and flew toward the center of the city, the imperial palace. An owl hooted somewhere, and a bat fluttered out of his way like a small damned soul blackened by hellfire. He didn't raise a windscreen, but let the air blow around him, the air of Earth.

The palace was almost completely wrecked, a mountain of heaped rocks, bare bones of "eternal" metal gnawed thin by steady ages of wind and rain and frost, but once it must have been gigantic. Men rarely built that big nowadays, they didn't need to; and the whole human spirit had changed, become ever more abstract, finding its treasures within itself. But there had been an elemental magnificence about early man and the works he raised to challenge the sky.

One tower still stood—a gutted shell, white under the stars, rising in a filigree of columns and arches which seemed impossibly airy, as if it were built of moonlight. Jorun settled on its broken upper balcony, dizzily high above the black-and-white fantasy of the ruins. A hawk flew shrieking from its nest, then there was silence.

No—wait—another yell, ringing down the star ways, a dark streak across the moon's face. "Hai-ah!" Jorun recognized the joyful shout of young Cluthe, rushing through heaven like a demon on a broomstick, and scowled in annoyance. He didn't want to be bothered now. Jorun was little older than Cluthe—a few centuries at most—but he came of a melancholy folk; he had been born old.

Another form pursued the first. As they neared, Jorun recognized Taliuvenna's supple outline. Those two had been teamed up for one of the African districts, but—

They sensed him and came wildly out of the sky to perch on the balcony railing and swing their legs above the heights. "How're you?" asked Cluthe. His lean face laughed in the moonlight. "Whoo-oo, what a flight!"

"I'm all right," said Jorun. "You through in your sector?"

"Uh-huh. So we thought we'd just duck over and look in here. Last chance anyone'll ever have to do some sightseeing on Earth."

Taliuvenna's full lips drooped a bit as she looked over the ruins. She came from Yunith, one of the few planets where they still kept cities, and was as much a child of their soaring arrogance as Jorun of his hills and tundras and great empty seas. "I thought it would be bigger," she said.

"Well, they were building this fifty or sixty thousand years ago," said Cluthe. "Can't expect too much."

"There is good art left here," said Jorun. "Pieces which for one reason or another weren't carried off. But you have to look around for it."

"I've seen a lot of it already, in museums," said Taliuvenna. "Not bad."

"C'mon, Tally," cried Cluthe. He touched her shoulder and sprang into the air. "Tag! You're it!"

She screamed with laughter and shot off after him. They rushed across the wilderness, weaving in and out of empty windows, and broken colonnades, and their shouts woke a clamor of echoes.

Jorun sighed. *I'd better go to bed*, he thought. *It's late.*

The spaceship was a steely pillar against a low gray sky. Now and then a fine rain would drizzle down, blurring it from sight; then that would end, and the ship's flanks would glisten as if they were polished. Clouds scudded overhead like flying smoke, and the wind was loud in the trees.

The line of Terrans moving slowly into the vessel seemed to go on forever. A couple of the ship's crew flew above them, throwing out a shield against the rain. They shuffled without much talk or expression, pushing carts filled with their little possessions. Jorun stood to one side, watching them go by, one face after another—scored and darkened by the sun of Earth, the winds of Earth, hands still grimy with the soil of Earth.

Well, he thought, *there they go. They aren't being as emotional about it as I thought they would. I wonder if they really do care.*

Julith went past with her parents. She saw him and darted from the line and curtsied before him.

"Good-bye, good sir," she said. Looking up, she showed him a small and serious face. "Will I ever see you again?"

"Well," he lied, "I might look in on you sometime."

"Please do! In a few years, maybe, when you can."

It takes many generations to raise a people like this to our standard. In a few years—to me—she'll be in her grave.

"I'm sure you'll be very happy," he said.

She gulped. "Yes," she said, so low he could hardly hear her. "Yes, I know I will." She turned and ran back to her mother. The raindrops glistened in her hair.

Zarek came up behind Jorun. "I made a last-minute sweep of the whole area," he said. "Detected no sign of human life. So it's all taken care of, except your old man."

"Good," said Jorun tonelessly.

"I wish you could do something about him."

"So do I."

Zarek strolled off again.

A young man and woman, walking hand in hand, turned out of the line not far away and stood for a little while. A spaceman zoomed over to them. "Better get back," he warned. "You'll get rained on."

"That's what we wanted," said the young man.

The spaceman shrugged and resumed his hovering. Presently the couple re-entered the line.

The tail of the procession went by Jorun and the ship swallowed it fast. The rain fell harder, bouncing off his force-shield like silver spears. Lightning winked in the west, and he heard the distant exuberance of thunder.

Kormt came walking slowly toward him. Rain streamed off his clothes and matted his long gray hair and beard. His wooden shoes made a wet sound in the mud. Jorun extended the force-shield to cover him. "I hope you've changed your mind," said the Fulkhisian.

"No, I haven't," said Kormt. "I just stayed away till everybody was aboard. Don't like good-byes."

"You don't know what you're doing," said Jorun for the—thousandth?—time. "It's plain madness to stay here alone."

"I told you I don't like good-byes," said Kormt harshly.

"I have to go advise the captain of the ship," said Jorun. "You have maybe half an hour before she lifts. Nobody will laugh at you for changing your mind."

"I won't." Kormt smiled without warmth. "You people are the future, I guess. Why can't you leave the past alone? I'm the past." He looked toward the far hills, hidden by the noisy rain. "I like it here, Galactic. That should be enough for you."

"Well, then—" Jorun held out his hand in the archaic gesture of Earth. "Good-bye."

"Good-bye." Kormt took the hand with a brief, indifferent clasp. Then he turned and walked off toward the village. Jorun watched him till he was out of sight.

The technician paused in the air-lock door, looking over the gray landscape and the village from whose chimneys no smoke rose. *Farewell, my mother,* he thought. And then, surprising himself: *Maybe Kormt is doing the right thing after all.*

He entered the ship and the door closed behind him.

Toward evening, the clouds lifted and the sky showed a clear pale blue—as if it had been washed clean—and the grass and leaves glistened. Kormt came out of the house to watch the sunset. It was a good one, all flame and gold. A pity little Julith wasn't here to see it; she'd always liked sunsets. But Julith was so far away now that if she sent a call to him, calling with the speed of light, it would not come before he was dead.

Nothing would come to him. Not ever again.

He tamped his pipe with a horny thumb and lit it and drew a deep cloud into his lungs. Hands in pockets, he strolled down the wet streets. The sound of his clogs was unexpectedly loud.

Well, son, he thought, *now you've got a whole world all to yourself, to do with just as you like. You're the richest man who ever lived.*

There was no problem in keeping alive. Enough food of all kinds was stored in the town's freeze-vault to support a hundred men for the ten or twenty years remaining to him. But he'd want to stay busy. He could maybe keep three farms from going to seed—watch over fields and orchards and livestock, repair the buildings, dust and wash and light up in the evening. A man ought to keep busy.

He came to the end of the street, where it turned into a graveled road winding up toward a high hill, and followed that. Dusk was creeping over the fields, the sea was a metal streak very far away and a few early stars blinked forth. A wind was springing up, a soft murmurous wind that talked in the trees. But how quiet things were!

On top of the hill stood the chapel, a small steepled building of ancient stone. He let himself in the gate and walked around to the graveyard behind. There were many of the demure white tombstones—thousands of years of Solis Township, men and women who had lived and worked and begotten, laughed and wept and died. Someone had put a wreath on one grave only this morning; it brushed against his leg as he went by. Tomorrow it would be withered, and weeds would start to grow. He'd have to tend the chapel yard, too. Only fitting.

He found his family plot and stood with feet spread apart, fists on hips, smoking and looking down at the markers, Gerlaug Kormt's son, Tarna Huwan's daughter; these hundred years had they lain in the earth. Hello, Dad, hello, Mother. His fingers reached out and stroked the headstone of his wife. And so many of his children were here, too; sometimes he found it hard to believe that tall Gerlaug and laughing Stamm and shy, gentle Huwan were gone. He'd outlived too many people.

I had to stay, he thought. *This is my land, I am of it and I couldn't go. Someone had to stay and keep the land, if only for a little while. I can give it ten more years before the forest comes and takes it.*

Darkness grew around him. The woods beyond the hill loomed like a wall. Once he started violently; he thought he heard a child crying. No, only a bird. He cursed himself for the senseless pounding of his heart.

Gloomy place here, he thought. *Better get back to the house.*

He groped slowly out of the yard, toward the road. The stars were out now. Kormt looked up and thought he had never seen them so bright. Too bright; he didn't like it.

Go away, stars, he thought. *You took my people, but I'm staying here. This is my land.* He reached down to touch it, but the grass was cold and wet under his palm.

The gravel scrunched loudly as he walked, and the wind mumbled in the hedges, but there was no other sound. Not a voice called; not an engine turned; not a dog barked. No, he hadn't thought it would be so quiet.

And dark. No lights. Have to tend the street lamps himself—it was no fun, not being able to see the town from here, not being able to see anything except the stars. Should have remembered to bring a flashlight, but he was old and absent-minded, and there was no one to remind him. When he died, there would be no one to hold his hands; no one to close his eyes and lay him in the earth—and the forests would grow in over the land and wild beasts would nuzzle his bones.

But I knew that. What of it? I'm tough enough to take it.

The stars flashed and flashed above him. Looking up, against his own will, Kormt saw how bright they were, how bright and quiet. And how very far away! He was seeing light that had left its home before he was born.

He stopped, sucking in his breath between his teeth. "No," he whispered.

This was his land. This was Earth, the home of man; it was his and he was its. This was the *land,* and not a single dustmote, crazily reeling and spinning through an endlessness of dark and silence, cold and immensity. Earth could not be so alone!

The last man alive. The last man in all the world!

He screamed, then, and began to run. His feet clattered loud on the road; the small sound was quickly swallowed by silence, and he covered his face against the relentless blaze of the stars. But there was no place to run to, no place at all.

To Earth there's no returning. She vanished with the childhood of our race. Yet as a poet once said, "No matter how far we range, the salt and rhythm of her tides will always be in our blood." One chapter has ended. Humankind's saga flows on.

Chronology of Future

The Complete Psychotechnic League, Volume 1	
Date	**Event/Story**
1958	*World War III*
1964	*"Marius"*
1965	*First Council of Rio establishes U.N. world government*
1975	*Psychotechnic Institute founded*
late 1900s	*Expeditions to Mars and Venus followed by colonization*
2004	*"The Un-Man"*
2009	*"The Sensitive Man"* *Second Industrial Revolution*
2035	*Second Council of Rio and Venusian break with U.N.*
2051	*"The Big Rain"*

The Complete Psychotechnic League, Volume 2	
Date	**Event/Story**
2055	*Planetary Engineering Corps founded*
2070	*The New Enlightenment*
2080	*Corps becomes the Order of Planetary Engineers*
2105	*Solar Union founded*
2125	*Humanist Manifesto published*
2126	*First STL (slower than lightspeed) starship launched*
2130	*Beginnings of Cosmic Religion*
2140	*"Holmgang"*
2170	*Humanist Revolt, Psychotechnic Institute outlawed*
2180	*"Cold Victory"*

Chronology of Future

2200	"What Shall It Profit?"
2206	"The Troublemakers"
2220	"The Snows of Ganymede"
2270	"Brake"
2300	*The Second Dark Ages*
2784	*Hyperdrive (faster than lightspeed) invented*
2815	"Gypsy" *Nomad culture develops*
2875	"Star Ship"

The Complete Psychotechnic League, Volume 3

Date	Event/Story
2900	*Stellar Union and its Coordination Service founded*
3000	"The Acolytes" "The Green Thumb"
3100	"Virgin Planet"
3110	"Teucan"
3115	"The Pirate"
3120	"The Peregrine" [novel not collected here]
3100s	"Entity" "Symmetry"
3200	*The Third Dark Ages*
after 4000	"The Chapter Ends"

This chart was prepared by Sandra Miesel, based in part on Poul Anderson's chronology published in *Startling Stories* (Winter, 1955). Many dates are approximate. Ms. Miesel is responsible for any errors.